Nathan nodded, rubbing at the ache in his chest.

"I can't screw up," he said.

"You'll figure everything out." Pop slapped him on the back. "Just like we did."

He couldn't do this alone. He wasn't prepared.

There had to be someone else he could tap to take care of Isabella.

He thought back to the women he'd dated in Savannah. There was Tracie, but she could barely take care of herself. Gabby—aptly named since she talked everyone's ear off—was kind of an airhead. A nice airhead, but still not right.

He'd never been attracted to the motherly types.

The only mother he knew was...Cheryl. And they lived next door to each other.

He released a deep breath. Cheryl.

Dear Reader,

Welcome back to Fitzgerald House. Cheryl is finally getting her happily-ever-after.

I found the perfect man for Cheryl, but she didn't agree. Nathan's too big, too nonchalant and drinks too much. He's a terrible role model for Josh, her six-year-old son.

Dyslexic Nathan believes he's flawed. What's worse, his twin brother is perfect. Nathan doesn't let people get close, because then they will find out he's stupid (he's not). Nathan avoids kids, because second graders can read better than he can. So when he finds out he's the father of four-year-old Isabella, he begs Cheryl for help.

On a flight last January, I sat next to a man who discovered he was dyslexic in sixth grade. Before that, *he* felt stupid. He willingly answered my questions. Do you forget names of lifetime friends? Yes. Do you have trouble with driving directions? Absolutely. He also told me his brain visualizes in 3-D. Amazing. I hope I captured what life as a dyslexic person is like.

I love hearing from readers. Contact me through my website, www.nandixon.com, where you can sign up for my newsletter. You can find me on Facebook at www.Facebook.com/nandixonauthor. If you'd like to see the pictures that inspire me, check out my Pinterest page, www.Pinterest.com/nandixonauthor. The princess castle Nathan paints for his daughter is there.

Enjoy Savannah!

Nan Dixon

NAN DIXON

The Other Twin

HARLEQUIN® SUPERROMANCE®

Recycling programs
for this product may
not exist in your area.

ISBN-13: 978-0-373-64010-2

The Other Twin

Copyright © 2017 by Nan Dixon

Printed in U.S.A.

Nan Dixon spent her formative years as an actress, singer, dancer and competitive golfer. But the need to eat had her studying accounting in college. Unfortunately, being a successful financial executive didn't feed her passion to perform. When the pharmaceutical company she worked for was purchased, Nan got the chance of a lifetime—the opportunity to pursue a writing career. She's a five-time Golden Heart® finalist, lives in the Midwest and is active in her local RWA chapter and on the board of a dance company. She has five children, three sons-in-law, two grandchildren, one grandchild on the way and one neurotic cat.

Books by Nan Dixon

HARLEQUIN SUPERROMANCE

Fitzgerald House

Southern Comforts
A Savannah Christmas Wish
Through a Magnolia Filter

Visit the Author Profile page at Harlequin.com for more titles.

To Mom and Dad always.

To my wonderful, fabulous family, thank you for supporting my writing. I'm dedicating this one to my guys: Nicholas, Matthew and my three incredible sons-in-law, Dan, Joe and John. I know you make my daughters happy. And of course the bright lights—Lily and Harper and grandchild #3!

Thank you to my Harlequin team: Megan Long, Victoria Curran, Piya Campana, Deirdre McCluskey and the wonderful group who help bring my books into reality. And of course, my fabulous agent, Laura Bradford. I appreciate your guidance, wisdom, humor and tweets!

My critique group challenges me to dig deeper. Thank you, Ann Hinnenkamp, Leanne Farella, Neroli Lacey and Kathryn Kohorst. And my Golden Heart sisters keep me sane—Dreamcatchers, Lucky 13s, Starcatchers and the Unsinkables. And my writing community—MFW, you're the best.

And last—this book is for the group that started it all—my sisters. Mo, Sue and Trish.

CHAPTER ONE

"WE LIVE IN an apartment," Cheryl said. "We can't have a puppy."

"Mom, I'd take care of it." Josh's pleading brown eyes were hard to deny. "I promise."

She shook her head. "No."

"We can move." He tugged on her shorts. "*All* my friends live in houses. They *all* have dogs."

"Not *all* your friends have dogs."

Dogs were expensive. Where would she find the money to feed one?

Josh's chin jutted out, reminding her of his father. When Brad had died in Afghanistan their lives had imploded. Now she and Josh lived in Savannah barely making it.

She wanted a better life for her son. That meant finding a better job, which meant training. Culinary school cost money.

Waiting to cross Bay Street, Cheryl switched the box she carried to her other hand and caught Josh's arm. Mid-May and the temperature, along with tourist traffic, had soared. At Fitzgerald House, where she worked, all the rooms were full. She'd been lucky the day she'd found their ad for maid service. Now she cooked more than cleaned at the B and B.

Once she and Josh crossed Bay Street, he pulled away and ran to the River Street steps.

"Slow down! Hang on to the railing." She sped up, not wanting to lose sight of his blond hair. "Josh!"

As she descended, the brackish scent of the river mingled with the aroma of onions and hot oil from nearby restaurants. Tourists clogged River Street checking out the shops and pubs.

Josh disappeared.

Her heart pounded. Six months ago he'd rarely left her side. Her life had been easier when he'd still been afraid.

Up ahead, she spotted a flash of blond hair as Josh stumbled on River Street's flagstones. When they got to the apartment, they would have a long talk about safety.

She broke into a run, jostling a man as he exited a bar. The scent of bourbon washed over her. "Excuse me."

"Hey, pretty lady," he called. "Slow down. I'll buy you a drink."

She shuddered. Not in this lifetime.

She caught Josh as he stared into the candy shop.

"Don't run off." She grabbed his hand, panting from her rush. "I couldn't see you."

"I'm not a baby."

"You're six." And next week Josh would finish kindergarten. How had he grown so fast? "You know better than to run in this crowd."

He pointed. "Can I get candy?"

"Not today." Not after this behavior.

Scowling, Josh held her hand until they got to their warehouse apartment building.

She dug in her purse for her keys, longing to get inside. Her feet ached from standing and decorating two hundred cupcakes for this weekend's wedding.

"How was school?" she asked.

"Okay. Tommy threw up."

She winced. *Don't let Josh get sick.*

Juggling a bag, her purse and the box, she unlocked the door. "Can you take the bag?"

They headed down the hallway to their apartment.

"What's in the box?" he asked.

"Cupcakes."

"Can I have one now?"

She shook out the apartment key. "Once you finish your chores."

"Let me help with that." The bourbon man from the street snatched the bakery box away.

How did he get into the building? She grabbed for the box. "We're fine."

He held it above his head. "I'm just being neighborly."

Josh glared. "You don't live here."

The guy laughed, his alcoholic stench washing over her.

She jammed her key into the lock, pushed open the door and held out her hand for the box. "Thank you."

He leaned close. Too close. He was big. Almost as big as her brother-in-law, Levi.

She shuddered. When Brad had died two years ago,

Levi had invited her and Josh to live with him. Moving in with Levi had been a big mistake.

"How 'bout I come in?" His words were slurred.

The odor of cigarettes and booze threw her back to her childhood. The lead weight of memories pinned her in place. She was afraid to move. Afraid to push past him for fear he'd hit her like Mama used to.

"Mom!" Josh yanked on her hand.

"Kid, go inside," the guy said. "I wanna talk to your mom."

She inched back, bumping into the wall. No escape. She wanted to duck and curl into a ball. Then when the blows came, they wouldn't hurt as much as a punch in the belly.

"What's your name?" He caged her to the wall with his arms.

"Leave." Her voice was a whisper.

Josh kicked the man's shin. "Get away from my mom."

"Cut it out." The guy pushed Josh into the door.

"Don't touch my son." She tried to shout, but the words were as weak as her knees.

"What'ssss your name?" His slur grew.

"Move." She couldn't get past him to the apartment. He sniffed her neck. "You smell like cookies."

Her skin crawled. Why couldn't she move? Shout? Save her son?

A door at the end of the hallway opened with a metallic clang.

"Go away," she said a little more loudly.

"I jus' want your name." The man thrust out a finger. "Ya don't hafta be a bitch about it."

Josh came at him with a flurry of tiny fists. "Don't call my mom names."

"What's going on?" a deep voice called.

"Help." She shoved at the drunk's chest but he was too big for her to move. "Help."

He shoved her shoulder. Hard.

She smacked into the wall, crumpling to her knees.

Josh kicked and punched. "Leave her alone!"

"Hey!" Boots thumped on the tile floor.

The drunk stumbled away.

Josh's arms wrapped around her neck and she clung to him. "Mommy."

"Are you okay?" her rescuer asked.

She stared at work boots and then up a pair of long legs.

Nathan Forester gazed down at her. He was the twin brother of Bess Fitzgerald's fiancé and Bess was one of her bosses. Nathan had worked in this building off and on since last fall. Cheryl tried to avoid him as much as possible. He was so…large. But since they were connected through the Fitzgeralds, avoidance was impossible.

"We're…fine." A lie. Both she and Josh shook like they were standing in a walk-in freezer.

"Who was he?" Nathan peered down the hall.

"Some drunk." Her voice squeaked.

Nathan held out his hand. His usual cocky grin was missing. A dirty white T-shirt tightened against the muscles in his chest and arms. Sheetrock dust covered his jeans. His ball cap was on backward, but thick blond hair curled on his neck. He was a modern-day James Dean without the cigarette. "Does that guy live here?"

"I don't think so." She put her hand in his and let him pull her to her feet. "He followed me."

Nathan's eyebrows arched. "You shouldn't let strangers into the building."

Had she? "Oh, God. I forgot to pull the door closed."

A door clanged again and Gray Smythe, the building owner, came down the hall. "Something wrong?"

"Some creep hassled Cheryl. I yelled and he hatted."

Gray studied Cheryl. "You okay?"

She nodded, afraid any words she spoke would come out a muddled mess.

"Mr. Gray." Josh threw himself at Gray. "I kicked the guy and he ran away."

Cheryl backed into the apartment. She'd almost mastered not cowering around Gray. She shouldn't be afraid of him. He was very kind and married to her boss, Abby Fitzgerald.

"I don't like this." Gray carried Josh into the apartment and set him down. Nathan followed and shut the door. With two men filling the entryway, she couldn't breathe.

"He was mean. He pushed me." Josh hung his backpack on the hook. "Can I have a cupcake?"

She looked around. "I dropped the box in the hall."

"I'll get it." Gray headed for the door.

"What if the man's still in the building?" Cheryl wrapped her arms around her waist as she headed to her small kitchen.

"He left," Nathan said. "But I suppose another idiot could let him back in."

"Idiot?" she gasped.

"Sorry." But he didn't look sorry. "With all the bars and pubs on River Street, you need to pay attention."

"I do," she protested.

Nathan raised an eyebrow as Gray handed her the smashed box.

With shaking hands, she pulled a plate from the cupboard. Only this time her hands shook because of Nathan. Idiot? She would do anything to protect Josh.

But, just like in her childhood, she'd frozen. Why couldn't she be brave?

In the box, the bright pink and blue cupcakes had smashed together. "Have a cupcake?" she asked.

Josh grinned. "The colors mixed together and made purple."

She grabbed glasses and filled them with milk. "Gray, I meant to tell you, the latch on the entry door isn't catching."

"This is the third time this month someone got in." Gray took a cupcake and paced the small room. "I'll replace the door."

"How about adding a security camera?" Nathan selected a mostly blue cupcake.

"Maybe." Gray nodded.

The two men discussed options and Cheryl backed into the corner, wishing they would leave.

"How often do you work late?" Nathan asked.

She frowned.

"How often do you come in late at night?" he clarified.

She rubbed her arms. "Once or twice a week."

"Too often." Nathan shook his head.

Gray's blue gaze sharpened. "No one's living in the B and B carriage house apartment right now."

Nathan tipped his head. "I start the restaurant renovations next week."

Ever since Cheryl had started working for the Fitzgeralds, a sister had always lived in the second-floor carriage house apartment. But just a few months ago, Dolley, the youngest sister, had moved out to live with her boyfriend.

"Will your crews work at night?" Gray asked.

"No." Nathan pushed off his ball cap and rubbed his hair. "But it'll be busy during the day and I don't want to work around a woman and a kid."

"Cheryl and Josh lived in this building during the renovation and I was glad for the extra security," Gray said.

Nathan grimaced. "I guess."

Gray turned to her. "What do you think about living in another work zone?"

Men working below her apartment? She looked at Nathan and chewed her thumbnail. Having him around most days might bother her, but she couldn't explain that to Gray. She sank into a chair, not able to take this in. "Savannah's safe."

Nathan snorted. "Don't be a fool."

First he called her an idiot and now a fool.

"My mom's no fool." Josh glared.

Nathan held up his hands but didn't apologize.

Nathan knew nothing. This place was a huge improvement from the apartment she and Josh had rented after escaping Levi. Drug deals had happened daily in the nearby Laundromat.

Living in a brand-new apartment had lulled her into a false sense of security. And she'd had to be saved—again. The story of her life.

Her son crawled onto her lap. "He's a butthead," he whispered.

"Josh," she warned. Unfortunately she agreed.

But if Nathan hadn't come along, her son might have been hurt. She shuddered and held him close. Josh had to be safe. That was her job as a mother. Living across the courtyard from work might be the perfect solution.

She swallowed. "I would love to rent the carriage house apartment."

A BUMP ECHOED above Nathan's head. The bare bulbs hanging from the ceiling swayed and dust drifted to the dirt floor of the Fitzgerald carriage house.

What were Cheryl and the kid doing, dropping loaded boxes from the top of the bunk bed?

They'd moved into the carriage house this afternoon, barely a week after she'd let the drunk into a secured apartment building. He'd helped unload the truck.

At least she'd be safer here than walking on River Street when the bars closed.

He checked the time on his phone, but the numbers didn't make sense—6:08 p.m.? It was after dinner. The sun had set. It had to be after eight—8:06 p.m.?

The kid thought he was a butthead. Hell, maybe he was. He planned to keep his distance from the pair. Kids made him uncomfortable. They guessed they were smarter than him.

Everyone was smarter than him. First-graders could read better than he did. Nathan inhaled and choked on the dust.

He unrolled the architect's plans and anchored them on his toolbox. Since he'd remodeled restaurants in Atlanta, he was in charge of this project.

Studying the blueprint, he willed his eyes and brain to work together for once. He planned to lay out the footings tonight. No way would he let the crew see him struggle.

His twin brother, Daniel, might think Mom and Pop had scraped the bottom of the barrel asking Nathan to return to Forester Construction, but he would prove his brother wrong. He'd grown up in the five years since he'd been kicked out of the family company. Nathan wanted back in, permanently, not just while Pop went through chemo in Texas.

For a week every month, Pop and Mom traveled

from Savannah to Houston. Pop was enrolled in a clinical trial to help him beat back the monster Myelodysplastic syndromes. MDS. Cancer.

The thought of not being good enough for the family business still stung. All his life, Nathan had wanted to be normal. Was that too much to hope for? To read without getting confused? To remember the names of people he'd known all his life? Hell, just reading street signs would be nice.

He shook it off. He'd done okay in Atlanta. He'd coped.

Locating the back door on the plans, he calculated where the first wall support would be and recited the numbers into his phone. Then he grabbed a tape measure and a roll of flagging ribbon. Time to translate the plan into the actual space.

He moved to the kitchen area and tucked the end of the tape measure into a crack between the floor and the wall. Checking his phone, he walked straight back. He needed thirty feet. He looked at the numbers on his phone and the ones on the tape measure. The numbers swam and twisted. He closed his eyes and looked again, but it didn't help.

He ripped off a piece of flagging tape and placed it on the floor, not willing to commit. Then he worked his way through the plan.

After he'd taken a half dozen measurements, he stepped away, comparing the markings with the drawing. The architect's plan was a rectangle. His mess of orange tags looked more like a star.

"Damn it!"

He kicked one of the pillars supporting the second story. Why couldn't he do this? He kicked the pillar again and dust rained down.

He'd be here all night and even then he might not get it right. The crew would show up at seven thirty tomorrow and he'd still be doing effing measurements a ten-year-old could do.

He headed to his toolbox, yanked open the bottom drawer and pulled out a flask.

The door to the courtyard creaked open. He tucked the flask in his back pocket and spun to see who was spying on his stupidity.

"Ooh." Cheryl filled the narrow doorway. "What are you doing?"

"Working," he snapped.

She crossed her arms over her chest. Her plain gray T-shirt strained against the swell of her small breasts. Her faded cutoff jeans cupped her ass like a man's hands would.

He fought to keep his eyes on her face. Her blond hair was pulled into a ponytail. He'd only seen it brushing her shoulders a few times. It was straight and fine and would feel like silk in his fingers. Not that he would ever touch Cheryl's hair.

"Abby told me the work wouldn't start until tomorrow. It's almost ten o'clock." She hesitated before stepping inside. "Did you kick something?"

He swallowed. "The post."

Her brown eyes grew as large as dinner plates. She stepped back. *Yeah. Be afraid.*

"What is that?" She moved into the room, pointing at the orange tape.

"A fucking mess."

Her shoulders straightened. "I know you're supervising this project. I'd appreciate you warning the crew that a six-year-old boy lives here. I don't want him learning words like that."

"Sure." He ran a hand through his hair, pushing off his cap. The same kid who called him *butthead.*

It landed at Cheryl's feet. She picked it up, batted it against her leg to dust off the dirt and then handed it to him. "What are the orange tags supposed to be?"

He jammed his cap back on his head. "I was marking off the kitchen. We're pouring footings tomorrow."

Now he'd have to ask one of the crew to help. Apparently, he couldn't measure and mark. The other option was to have his twin help. Perfect Daniel would give him *the look.* The one that said Nathan was an idiot. Besides, he'd lied and told Pop and Daniel he could do this.

Cheryl stared at the mess on the floor, frowned and then moved to the plans he hadn't rolled up. She carried them to where he'd been measuring. "This is close."

"Does it look like a rectangle to you?"

Her head snapped up at the snarl in his voice. Her brown eyes flashed. "Do you want help or not?"

She was willing to help him? Relief ran through

him like a warm shower, easing the strain in his shoulders. "Yeah, I do." Then he remembered her son. What the hell was his name? "What about your…kid?"

"Josh sleeps like a rock." She turned. Clipped to her back pocket was some sort of monitor. "If he wakes, I'll hear him."

His eyes lingered on her lovely rounded butt. He wouldn't mind wrapping his hands around those cheeks.

Too bad she had the kid. Josh. Josh always glared at him. Kids were a deal breaker.

"Let's start over," she said. "What's the scale?"

He knew this. "It's…" The words slipped away. His fingers formed fists.

She stared at the drawings. "Is it an eighth of an inch equals a foot?"

He nodded, afraid the words would tangle. The story of his life. His fingers flexed against his thighs.

"Wait. They already have the feet marked here. That's what this means, right?"

She moved close, showing him the blueprint. She smelled like—apples. His mouth watered. When her head turned, her hair brushed against his arm, a silky, soft brush.

He'd known it would be.

She shook the blueprint. Using her thumb, she pointed to a number. "Is that the measurement from one wall to another?"

"Yes." He choked out the word, hoping he'd answered correctly. Sometimes, as much as he concentrated, everything came out twisted.

"Let's see where you went wrong." She set down the plans. "Can you hold the other end of the tape measure?"

He headed to the wall to be a friggin' anchor.

"This one's right." She tapped the first piece of tape he'd placed.

They slid along the wall.

"This one needs to be here." She moved the orange tape. And kept checking and rechecking each measurement. He'd gotten half of them right. What had taken him thirty minutes took her five.

"That looks right, doesn't it?" She held the blueprint and compared it with the tape they'd run and anchored.

He stood behind her, inhaling another whiff of apples. "Yeah."

He could see the space now. There were the doors into the kitchen and more doors into Abby's large storage area.

Cheryl helped him mark off the walk-in freezer, too.

"Now I can finish running the tape for the footings." Relief eased out of him like a curl of wood from a plane. "Thank you."

"You're welcome." She dusted off her hands. "Anything else you want to get done tonight?"

"I'll mark the wall and doors." That way, if the crew moved the tape when they did demolition, he'd know where everything was supposed to go. He'd developed tricks over the years to convince people that he was in control.

"Then I'll head home."

"Thank you." Too bad Cheryl had a kid. Otherwise he would ask her out.

She moved to the door, stopped and turned back. "Do you...have trouble reading?"

Reality slapped him in the face. "I can read," he growled. *Sometimes*.

"I could help." She gave him a small smile. "At the army school, I worked with kids who had trouble reading."

His face heated with shame. *Kids*. She'd helped *kids*. "I don't need help."

She jerked back a step at the snap in his voice. The woman was scared of her shadow. "It's just..."

"Thanks for the help." He pulled the flask out of his pocket. He wouldn't admit his flaws.

Her face paled and she crept backward again. "I'd appreciate if you didn't drink in front of my son."

"I'll bet you would." He took a big swig. Not wanting her to see she'd hurt him.

She dashed outside. Her footsteps pounded the stairs to the carriage house apartment.

He twirled the cap back on. He'd been a jerk. But he didn't need any help from a do-gooder like Cheryl Henshaw. His flaws couldn't be fixed.

Thump!

Cheryl jolted out of a deep sleep.

Josh? Had he fallen out of bed?

She raced into his bedroom. When she didn't find him on the floor, she scrambled up the ladder. He was still asleep, his hand tucked under his pillow.

She rubbed her forehead as she headed back to bed. Maybe she'd been dreaming.

Her alarm clock flipped to six thirty. Her first morning to sleep in for five days and she was already awake?

Thump!

The noise came from the second floor.

It had been a week since she'd helped Nathan measure. Since then, the work crews always arrived at seven thirty and they only worked on the first floor. This noise was next door. A chill raced over her skin.

Cheryl threw on yesterday's shorts, tucked in the T-shirt she'd worn to bed and grabbed her phone. Slipping her feet into her Keds, she hurried to the kitchen.

The carriage house apartment had two doors. The main door led to the outside steps and down to the Fitzgerald House courtyard. The kitchen door opened into the interior of the carriage house's second floor.

Holding her breath, she put her ear to the kitchen door.

Bang. Bang. Bang.

She dug out the dead bolt key from the kitchen drawer and paused in front of the door. The key jangled in her shaking hand. Who was back there? Thieves? A homeless person?

Forcing herself to breathe, she shoved the key into the lock. For Josh and the Fitzgeralds she had to be brave. The Fitzgeralds had done so much for her—saved her. It was her turn to stand up for them.

Before turning the key, she punched in 9-1-1 on her cell phone, but didn't hit Dial.

Inhaling, she unlocked the door and twisted the knob. Nothing.

She pulled and tugged, then put her foot on the door frame and yanked. The door gave way with a soft *whoomp*. She stumbled, clutching the knob to stay upright.

In the dark hall, she waited for her eyes to adjust and her heart to stop pounding.

A screech of wood on wood came from around the corner. So did a sliver of light.

Cheryl tiptoed silently toward the light. Her childhood had taught her well. She touched the scar next to her ear. Mama had been a mean drunk.

Before she rounded the corner, she heard a deep voice swear. Her phone clattered to the floor. As much as she wanted to escape to the apartment and throw the bolt, she didn't. She snatched up her phone and held her thumb over the dial button.

"Who's here?" she called.

Silence.

She turned the corner. The door was ajar, weak light leaking out. "I've called the police."

"Now, why would you do that?" A man moved into the hallway, blocking the light.

All she could see was *big*. Big man. Big shoulders. Big hands fisted on his hips.

"Get out before they arrive," she whispered through chattering teeth.

"Cheryl." The man moved closer.

The man knew her name. He rushed toward her.

She turned to run, pressing the dial button on her phone.

"Wait," he said.

She knew that voice. "Nathan?"

"Did you really call the cops?" he asked.

She looked at her phone. The call had already connected.

She pulled it to her ear. "I'm sorry. I didn't…"

Nathan's hands slapped against his thighs.

"Nine-one-one, what is your emergency?" a woman asked.

"I…I don't have one. I dialed accidently." She forced the words out.

"Are you sure?" the woman asked.

"Yes."

There was silence on the line. Then the operator asked, "Do you need help?"

"I heard a noise, but it's nothing." At least she hoped it was nothing. What was Nathan doing here?

After the woman checked one more time, she hung up. What if they sent a patrol car anyway? The Fitzgeralds might decide she wasn't worth all the trouble she always caused. She shivered. Only last year, Gray and Abby had saved her and Josh from her brother-in-law, Levi.

"You didn't convince *me* nothing was wrong. And I know everything's all right." Nathan smacked the wall. "I'll be lucky if I'm not in jail within the hour."

She jumped. "Why are you here? You worked until almost nine."

And not just last night, but for the entire week since she'd helped him measure. Not that she was checking on him. While tucking Josh in bed, she'd glanced out the window and Nathan's truck had still been in the lot.

"I'm… I just…" Nathan shrugged. "I want to live here while working on this project."

"Here?" she squeaked. *No way.*

"Yeah. In the carriage house."

She hated the idea of Nathan living next door. Even in the dim light she caught his blush. "Why?"

"You saw how slow I am." He paced into the room and then back. "This is the first major project I've handled for the company."

"I don't understand," she said.

"Story of my life." His fingers rattled against his jeans. "If I'm living here, I can work more hours."

"But no one's lived here in years," she said.

He waved her over. "What do you think?"

She nodded, wanting him to walk in front of her. No way was she letting him get between her and the door.

He rolled his eyes and held up his hands like he was harmless.

He wasn't harmless, but she followed.

A trouble light hung off a fixture, the orange cord dissecting the room. The apartment was a mirror image of hers. The kitchens backed up to each other and the closed door was probably one of the two bedrooms. Sitting in the middle of the living room was a canopy bed that used to be in her apartment.

"What was the thumping?" she asked.

"I moved the bed to access the water valve." He indicated an open panel in the living room wall.

"That's a strange place to put water valves."

"It's probably here because the carriage house didn't have running water when it was built." He crouched next to a wrench.

A wrench could do a lot of damage. Cheryl made herself smaller, less of target. And hated her actions. Her hands formed ineffective fists. All the good years with Brad and she was back to her childhood. Because of Levi.

"You're shivering." Nathan's gaze dropped to the thin T-shirt she'd slept in. His nostrils flared. "Are you cold?"

"I'm fine." But the heat in his eyes made her shake harder. She wished she'd thrown on a bra.

"I think this apartment will work for me." His gaze snapped back to her face. "I'll talk to Abby."

"Sure." She backed out of the room. "I'd better check on Josh."

She dragged her kitchen door closed, turned the lock and sank to the floor. Her nipples had pebbled from Nathan's hot look. Only Brad had made her feel like she was desirable.

She didn't want to feel that way about Nathan. He was trouble. With his swearing and drinking, he'd be a terrible role model for Josh.

She couldn't let him live next door.

CHAPTER TWO

THIS COULD WORK. Nathan shut off the water and unplugged the trouble light.

He moved into the hallway just as Cheryl's lock clicked.

She'd been shaking earlier. Fear? He'd heard some of what had happened last year. Her brother-in-law had been stealing her military survivor checks. Instead of stopping him, she'd run away but the asshole had found her at Fitzgerald House. Gray and Abby had protected Cheryl and her kid. He couldn't imagine such a frightened woman standing up for herself.

But she'd checked on the noises he'd been making. Shoot, this morning she'd actually called the police. That was something.

Once Jed, his site supervisor, showed up, they mapped out the day's tasks. Then he headed over to the B and B to catch Abby. He might even snag breakfast. Food was a perk of working at Fitzgerald House. Usually Pop or Daniel reaped those benefits.

The Fitzgerald sisters, Abby, Bess and Dolley, were like his sisters. The Foresters and the Fitzgeralds even spent holidays together, so he wanted to make sure Abby's restaurant was perfect.

Cheryl also spent holidays with the Fitzgeralds, but he couldn't think of her like a sister. This morning her T-shirt had been worn and nearly transparent. Her nipples had tightened as he'd stared.

He shifted, his jeans growing snug. He had to keep remembering—she had a kid.

But Cheryl's body rocked.

He peeked in through the kitchen window and spotted Cheryl's kid sitting on a small sofa, drawing.

The door was open; the scent of sugar and spices had his mouth watering. He grabbed the door handle.

"Did you ever hear noises in the carriage house?" Cheryl asked Abby.

Noises? He paused. Nathan should let them know he was listening, but he didn't. What was Cheryl up to?

"Lots of creaking," Abby replied. "Why? Has great-aunt Persephone been trying to scare you?"

Persephone was the mansion's ghost. Pop had worked on Fitzgerald House for years. When Nathan and Daniel were small, they would come to work with him and try to find the ghost who haunted the old mansion.

"I hope not," Cheryl replied. "Does she visit the carriage house?"

"No." Abby laughed. "Are you worried?"

"I…" There was a pause. "The drunk getting into the River Street apartment shook me more than I thought."

"Gray and I are right next door," Abby said.

"I guess…it's nice knowing there's only Josh and me in the building." Cheryl's words gushed out.

What the hell? She was sabotaging his request before he'd even made it. *No way!* He pushed through the door.

The screen slapped shut and Abby turned. "Hey, Nathan."

He moved to the counter, narrowing his eyes at Cheryl.

Cheryl's mouth formed a little O. She slid away from him. "Josh, breakfast."

The kid tucked his stuff into his backpack and headed to the table, snaking a wide path around Nathan.

"What's up?" Abby asked him.

"I wanted to ask you something." He raised his eyebrows at Cheryl.

"Sure." Abby pulled a pan from the oven. "Can I get you breakfast?"

"I wouldn't say no." He leaned against the wall as she cut into the egg casserole. "Smells great in here."

After dishing him a generous helping, Abby sliced the rest into squares.

Cheryl took the pan and put it on a cart along with other dishes and baskets of muffins. As she backed out the door, she shot Nathan a guilty look. "Josh, eat up. The bus will be here soon."

Nathan took a bite of the egg dish and moaned. It was a Mexican fiesta in his mouth. "How come Gray isn't fifty pounds overweight?"

Abby laughed and handed him a cup of coffee. "I won't let him."

He took a sip. Time to get down to business before

Cheryl returned. Staying on-site was the perfect way for him to work long hours without anyone knowing. "I checked out the other carriage house apartment."

Abby's glance shot to Josh as he plowed through his breakfast. "Did Cheryl hear you this morning?"

"Maybe." *Yes.* "I want your restaurant to shine. I'd like to be on-site, keeping everything on track. What do you think about me renting the apartment?" The words tumbled out of his mouth. He didn't even worry that they might not be the right words or in proper order. "I'd be on top of everything."

That might be a first.

"No one's stayed there in years."

"I checked the water. It works." A little rusty, but that was from lack of use. "I could patch and paint the place for you."

"You want to live and work on-site?" She picked up a wicked knife and cut melon slices. "In a place that's been empty for a decade?"

"You live next door in the Carleton carriage house." He nodded to Josh. "Now Cheryl's in the Fitzgerald carriage house."

Josh looked up at the mention of his mother's name, daggers in his eyes. Or maybe they were lasers. Who knew what weapons kids used nowadays?

"I like the idea." Abby hacked off the top of a pineapple. "I'll talk to Dolley and have her work on a lease. Maybe with you next door, Cheryl won't worry."

Nathan doubted that. Maybe he should have talked directly to Dolley. She was the sister in charge of contracts. But Cheryl might have sabotaged his request if he'd waited.

A timer dinged. Abby patted his back and moved to the ovens. "Can I interest you in a muffin?"

"Sure." He checked his watch. "I'll take it with me."

Cheryl hustled back into the kitchen. "Almost done?" she asked her son.

"Yup." Josh scooted off the chair and took his dishes to the dishwasher without anyone reminding him. "Thank you, Miss Abby."

Abby ruffled his hair. "You're welcome."

Cheryl handed him his backpack. As they headed out of the kitchen, Nathan followed. "Got a minute?"

Her back stiffened. "Josh needs to catch his bus."

"One minute." He wanted to see her reaction when she heard the news.

"Josh, wait on the porch. I'll be right there."

The kid stepped between Nathan and Cheryl. "It's my first day of summer camp. I don't want to miss my bus 'cause it's only for two weeks."

"You won't." Cheryl guided Josh down the hall. Then she turned and crossed her arms. "What can I do for you?"

He almost smiled at her belligerent tone. "I wanted you to be the first to know. I'm your new neighbor."

Her face went pale. "I…I…"

"You'd hoped your conversation with Abby would keep me from moving in?" He pointed a finger at her. "She thinks you'll feel more secure with me living there."

"It wasn't that." Her gaze swung away from him. She was lying.

"Nice." He shook his head. "Guess I won't be expecting a 'welcome to the neighborhood' from you. I don't know what I did to rile you up and I don't care. I'll stay out of your way. You and the kid stay out of mine."

"THE BUTTHEAD'S MOVING IN," Josh said under his breath, climbing into his chair.

Cheryl's eyes went wide. "What did you say?"

Josh looked at her through thick blond eyelashes. "Nothin'."

"Don't you use that kind of language. Ever." She slid a grilled-cheese sandwich on his plate and added celery and carrot sticks. It wasn't the most creative meal, but now that it was June, the temperatures had skyrocketed.

"I can't help what he is." Josh squirted ketchup on his plate.

"Are you looking to lose television privileges?" Again.

What had happened to her compliant boy? She didn't want him to be afraid anymore, but she didn't want disrespect, either. Rubbing her temples didn't stop the headache brewing.

"How was camp?" she asked.

He shrugged.

This wasn't normal. "What's wrong?"

"Nothin'." He swirled a carrot stick in his ketchup.

Yuck. She cut his grilled cheese into four triangles. "Something's bothering you."

He slammed his hand on the table. "Zach's *my* friend. But he and Dustin ran off together. I didn't have nobody help me find bugs."

"Anybody." She sighed. "Did you ask them both to work with you?"

He shrugged. "Zach didn't keep his word. He's a bu—"

"Don't," she interrupted. At least she knew why he was in a bad mood.

"Zach and Dustin get to play together after camp 'cause they live next to each other. Why can't we live in a house?" He smashed his sandwich into the ketchup. "Why do I have to live here? I never play with nobody. I want a dog."

She took a deep breath, trying for calm. They'd had this conversation. "You can invite a friend over on my next day off."

"You never get days off. Other guys have moms *and* dads. They do stuff all the time." He jabbed his carrot into his sandwich. "I'm stuck here."

"That's not true." Her teeth ground together. "I'm off Monday. You can have a friend come over Sunday night and we'll do something fun." Something that didn't cost money.

"I can?" Josh looked her in the eye.

"Yes." Was she bribing her son into a good mood? "I'll call Zach after dinner."

The rest of the meal was normal. At least, Josh was happier.

After they cleaned the dishes, Josh took her cell phone into the living room.

She pulled out a basket and added fruit, cheese and some sausage. It already held cookies and banana bread. Tying on a big yellow bow, she smirked. He didn't expect a "welcome to the neighborhood." Wouldn't Nathan Forester be surprised?

Josh was still on the phone with his friend, a big smile on his face.

"I'm taking this next door," she said.

He nodded, his hands waving as he talked to Zach.

She unlocked the door and hoisted the basket. Time to greet—or irritate—her neighbor.

The banging had stopped. Maybe Nathan was gone and she could leave the basket at his door.

She rounded the corner and found his door wide open. Luck was never with her.

The only time she'd been lucky had been when she'd met Brad. Being with him had made her forget Mama's drinking. And Josh was her lucky charm. He made her count her blessings every day.

She knocked on the door frame.

"Come on in," Nathan called.

Boxes filled the hall. In the living room, Nathan sprawled in a recliner, a bottle at his lips. Empty beer bottles, along with a six-pack and a pizza carton, sat on a stack of boxes.

He'd stripped off his T-shirt. Good lord, the man was ripped. A trickle of sweat ran between her breasts.

She lifted the basket. It blocked the view of the six-pack. Both six-packs. "Welcome."

Nathan grinned. Then shook his head as if he'd gotten water in his ears. "You brought me a basket? With a big bow?"

Since she didn't see any table space, she set it on the floor. "Enjoy."

She turned to leave.

Before she could go, he was out of the chair and had grabbed her hand. "Thanks."

She wrenched herself out of his grasp.

"Sorry. Sorry." He held up his hands. "I forgot. You don't like to be touched."

She scooted back and hit the living room wall.

"Or crowded." He shoved his hand through his hair. The blond mass looked like he'd been doing that all night. "I'm sorry I snapped at you the other day."

"It's…fine." She straightened, pretending his closeness didn't bother her. But her chest was so tight she could barely draw a breath.

"It's not fine. My mom would have my head." He sighed. "I thought you were trying to get Abby not to rent to me."

"Oh." He was right. "I brought a peace offering."

He pointed at the basket, a grin lighting his face. "What did you bring me?"

"Healthy snacks," she said primly.

"Healthy?" His smile faded. "Um, thanks."

She laughed. "And maybe cookies."

"Cookies." He crouched at her feet and dug through the contents. "Sausage. Cheese. I can deal with fruit."

"Like I said, enjoy." She shuffled sideways but there was nowhere to go. Nathan and the basket had her caged next to the wall.

He looked up. "Do you want a beer?"

She couldn't hold back a shudder. "I don't drink."

"Ever?"

"Maybe once a year." She'd sipped champagne at Abby's wedding.

He frowned. "Are you an alcoholic?"

"No!" But based on all the empty bottles, he might be.

This was a bad idea. She'd wanted to show him she was the better person. And, to be truthful, she was feeling guilty. She'd hoped Abby would turn him down. *So sue me.*

He dug out a cookie and took a bite. His eyes closed and he gave a little moan. "What are these?" he asked, his mouth full.

"Snickerdoodles." Josh's favorite.

"Thanks for this." He stood and his gaze caught hers.

She'd never been this close to him. Golden sparks flickered in his coffee-colored eyes. Her fingers ached to push his unruly sun-kissed hair away from his forehead.

Had to be a mother's instinct and not the desire to stare into his eyes.

She hadn't been this close to a man since…since Levi attacked her. Now that she looked closer, his eyes were bloodshot. She inhaled and caught a whiff of the beer.

Just like Levi.

"I've got to go." She pushed past him, brushing against his chest even though she made herself as small as possible.

She hurried down the short hall between their doors and flipped the lock behind her. She and Josh didn't need the kind of trouble Nathan could bring.

NATHAN PRESSED THE trowel against the concrete they'd poured a couple of hours ago. "It's setting up," he called to Jed.

Jed wiped his arm across his face. "Amazing in this humidity."

While the crew built the next forms, Nathan moved to the floor next to the exterior wall. In the still-drying concrete, he sketched a steaming cup of coffee and a piece of pie. Then he added his initials below. If anyone spotted it when the job was over, they wouldn't have a clue who NEF was, but drawing in the concrete had become a tradition on all his jobs.

Maybe the Fitzgeralds would want to do the same thing?

Nathan moved over to Jed. "You got this?" he asked the supervisor.

Jed watched the chute as the concrete spilled into the next section of floor. "Yup."

"I'll be right back." Nathan headed across the courtyard.

He knocked and stepped into the kitchen. "Anyone here?"

"Me." Abby moved into sight. "What's up?"

"We're pouring the restaurant floor. I wondered…" Now the idea sounded stupid, like most everything that came out of his mouth.

She wiped her hands on a towel hanging off her apron. "Wondered what?"

"Do you want to…write something in the concrete?" He let loose a breath. "Your initials?"

She grinned. "I'd love to!"

Maybe his instincts had been right. "Are Bess and Dolley around?"

"I'll find them." She nodded. "When do you want us?"

"In about two hours."

"We'll be there." She touched his arm. "I'm glad you asked." Then she frowned. "How come Daniel didn't ask me to do the same thing when they poured the floor in *my* house?"

"Because I'm the nice twin," he lied. But the tension in his body eased.

"That you are." She grinned. "You just earned the crew afternoon cookies. What kind do you like?"

He'd devoured the cookies Cheryl had given him a couple of days ago.

The cookie name wouldn't come. Something about laughing? No. He inhaled. Sometimes a deep breath helped his brain to sort out words. Sneaky? That described him, not a cookie.

"Whatever you bring over would be great." Because his stupid brain couldn't remember the name of the best cookie he'd tasted in months.

Tension slammed back into him. "So. Come over in…" He'd just told her how long it took to cure. Now no words would come.

"Two hours?" She checked her watch.

"Yeah. Yeah. Two."

"See you then."

In the courtyard he wanted to kick something. Anything. He needed an interpreter between his brain and his mouth.

Thankfully, between pouring the floors and checking the forms, he didn't have to say much to the crew. Two hours passed more quickly than he expected.

"We're here." Abby carried a tray, Bess a thermos and Dolley her camera. Cheryl and Josh carried in a table.

"We brought cookies. Snickerdoodles," Josh said. "My favorite."

Snickerdoodles. Nathan shook his head. That was the name he couldn't dig out of the spaghetti that was his brain.

"We'll set up," Abby said.

"There's lemonade," added Bess.

The crew honed in on the table like wasps on a Coke can. That was okay. They'd worked hard today.

"Hey, guys, look over here." Dolley snapped pictures of the crew and space. "Okay if you end up on the website?"

"Sure," they agreed.

Abby tapped Dolley's arm. "Let's get our initials in the concrete before it sets."

"Follow me." Nathan led the Fitzgerald sisters back to the kitchen area. "I thought you could do your thing at the service entrance. There won't be tile here."

"Come on." Abby waved to Josh and Cheryl. "You're part of this, too."

"Really?" Josh ran over. As he rushed by, he stubbed his toe and went flying.

Nathan lunged and caught the kid before he face-planted in the cement. "Hang on there."

"Nice catch, Nathan," Jed called.

Josh squirmed in his arms like an eel. "Let me go."

Nathan moved away from the concrete and set Josh on his feet. "You can't run in a construction site."

"Miss Abby needed me." There was a stubborn set to the kid's chin.

"No running. We talked about that two minutes ago." Cheryl took Josh's hand, smiling at Nathan.

That was a first. Usually she looked scared.

"No harm done." He handed out carpenter pencils. "Here."

"Thanks." The kid started to run.

Cheryl called, "Slow down."

Josh huffed out a sigh. "I want to draw a picture."

"Only if you follow the rules." Cheryl and the kid knelt, blond heads together.

"I wish Zach had slept over last night instead of Sunday." Josh grinned up at his mother. "This is cool."

The sisters knelt on the second drop cloth he'd laid down. Their fiery red Fitzgerald hair gleamed in the harsh work lights.

This was a bigger production than he'd expected. The sisters debated wording, Josh had his tongue tucked in between his teeth as he drew and Cheryl watched.

Might as well get a cookie. Snickerdoodle. Snickerdoodle. Laughing drawing? He'd never remember.

The crew hovered next to the treat table.

"Hope you left me some crumbs," Nathan joked.

"These are good," Jed said. "But I wouldn't let these savages eat them all."

Jasper, one of the crew members, elbowed Jed in the ribs. "I told you to leave some for Nathan."

Nathan grabbed the last two cookies and took a bite. As good as he remembered.

"Nathan?" A woman's voice called from behind him.

He turned, searching for the source.

"Nathan Forester!" A blonde wearing a tight T-shirt waved from the doorway.

He knew her. But the name wouldn't surface. Was she a high school friend? Acquaintance? From some bar?

"Hey," he said.

The crew watched with undisguised interest.

He moved to cut the woman off before she entered the work site. "How are you?" *Who are you?*

Her lips formed a straight line. "I'm Heather."

"Sorry." *Heather. Right.* He shook his head. Wait. They'd dated years ago, when he'd first moved to Atlanta. "How did you find me?"

"I heard you were working for your family. Some lady told me what job site you were at." This wasn't the pretty blonde he remembered. Her skin was ashen, her hair lank. She'd loved to party—hard. So had he. It looked like partying had taken its toll.

When they'd been together, her long nails had been her pride and joy. She'd jabbed them into his skin more times than he cared to remember. Now her fingernails were chewed to the quick.

He took Heather's arm and moved out to the courtyard.

"How long has it been? Three years? Four?" he asked. And why was she here?

"Closer to five." She shifted on her feet.

"What are you doing here?" he asked.

"Looking for you."

He raised an eyebrow. "Why?"

She paced the path, the action jerky—nervous. "I'm sorry. Sorry."

He sniffed. She didn't smell like she'd been drinking, but he'd always suspected she might have done drugs. "Sorry?"

"I never told you." She bit her thumb, her gaze dart-

ing around. "I didn't know when I moved and then—"
She shook her head.

He rubbed his neck. He needed to get back to work.
"What are you—?"

"You're a father," she interrupted.

"What?" The word whispered out. His heart stopped.
Then started pounding.

"You're a daddy."

His knees gave out. He collapsed on a nearby bench.
Daddy? He could barely remember being with her.
"We used protection. Always."

"There was that one night." Tears streaked her
cheeks.

Crap. "The condom broke," he whispered.

"Yeah." She hiccupped. "Surprise."

"This isn't funny," he snapped. "No way am I a
father."

"You are." She wiped her face with her hand. "I
should have told you, but I'd moved. By the time I
knew, I was living with Thad."

"What do you want? Money?" He pushed off the
bench and shifted away.

She laughed, a watery, snotty sound. "No."

He let his head sink to his chest. "What?"

"I…I have to get away. I mean go away." She
scanned the courtyard. Again. "Um…to treatment."

He pushed his hand through his hair.

She clutched his hand. "You have to take Bella."

"Are you crazy?" A kid? This had to be a nightmare. *Wake up.*

"There's no one else. You have to." She squeezed his fingers. "I've had her for four years. It's your turn now."

He shook her hand away. "I don't do kids."

Heather's eyes narrowed. "Until she came along, neither did I."

"Why can't—" words and names jumbled in his head "—whoever the guy you're living with take care of…her?"

"Her name is Isabella." Tears streamed down her cheeks. "Thad's gone."

Nathan swore. "I should just take your word this is my kid?"

Her eyes filled with fire. She jabbed him in the chest. "I know who my daughter's father is."

"I don't. I need a…a paternity test." The words exploded out of him.

Heather waved her hand in a come-here motion.

No. Fucking. Way. She'd brought the kid here? Each breath he took seared his lungs like a welding torch.

"Nathan, turn around," Heather said.

If he turned around, it would be real. This child would be real. "I can't."

"You have to." Heather tugged on his hand. "Bella has no one else."

He took in a deep breath, turned and looked down.

The kid had ratty blond hair. Her shirt was streaked with stains and was too small, showing a thin belly. Her shorts were grayish white. Wrapped around her shoulders was a blanket that might once have been pink.

Brown eyes looked into his. Brown eyes just like his. Like Daniel's. *Shit.* It was like looking at a picture of himself as a child.

Heather knelt. "Bella, this is Nathan."

The kid didn't say a word.

He swore. "I can't…" He waved his hand, words tangling and looping in his head. "Don't…"

"You have to." A metal chair screeched across the stone over by the fountain and Heather jumped. "A little on-the-job training won't hurt." She rattled the words out like a nail gun.

It might hurt the kid. What was her name? It wouldn't work its way through the maze in his mind.

Heather stroked the kid's hair. "You'll stay with Nathan. He's your daddy."

Tears trickled down the kid's face.

Heather grabbed two grocery bags and shoved them at him. "Here's her stuff."

"You can't do this."

"I don't have a choice," she hissed.

"But…" Nothing came out past the lump in his throat. Nothing.

"Remember what I told you." Heather knelt in front of the crying girl, pressed a finger to her lips and kissed her forehead. "Be good for your daddy."

This couldn't be happening. His life couldn't be… this screwed up. "Don't."

She pointed at the bags in his arms. "Her birth certificate is in there."

He shook his head. "I can't." He turned to set the bags on the bench.

Scuffling noises sounded behind him. When he spun around, Heather was sprinting to the side gate.

"Stop!" He started to move, almost knocking the kid down. Setting her on the bench next to the bags, he stuck a finger in her face. "Stay."

Nathan dashed along the courtyard paths. Where was Heather?

Tires squealed on the street. He headed for the noise. She couldn't leave…the kid with him. No way. Hell, he couldn't even remember her name.

A truck with blackened windows raced past him. He caught a glimpse of Heather through the cracked windshield just before she turned the corner.

"Wait! Stop! How do I reach you? What's your phone number?"

His boots pounded on the sidewalk, echoing the hammering of his heart. His lungs burned, his legs ached. She couldn't do this.

She turned the corner. By the time he got there, she'd vanished.

He swore. If words could form clouds, they'd have been black and thundering above his head.

He trudged back to the courtyard. Each foot weighed a ton. What the hell was he supposed to do with a kid?

The girl sat where he'd left her, staring at him with

eerily familiar brown eyes. Tears washed her cheeks, but she didn't make a sound.

"Kid." Damn it. What was her name? He dug through the first bag and pulled out a packet of papers. Flipping through them, he found what he assumed was a birth certificate.

His name was in the middle of the page, next to what looked like the word *father*. What the hell?

He scanned the jumble of letters. Belisala. No. He exhaled and tried again. Isabella. That rang a bell.

He looked at the girl. He couldn't take care of a kid. Kids were smarter than he was. He shoved his hat off his head. What about work? He needed every hour to make sure he didn't screw up Abby's restaurant.

He was too stupid to be a dad.

Mom. Mom would know what to do. Mom could take care of…Isabella.

CHAPTER THREE

CHERYL SMILED AS Josh laughed at something one of the workers said. His belly laugh warmed everything inside her. The Fitzgerald sisters joined in.

She inhaled. With Nathan gone, she could take full breaths again. She didn't like being near big men. But the other crew members were almost as large and didn't make her belly quiver like Nathan did.

"Time to let the crew get back to work," she called to Josh.

"Mom." Exasperation laced his words.

"Miss Abby wants her restaurant built," she said.

Abby nodded. "But thanks for drawing that wonderful picture in the cement."

"I'll grab the table," Cheryl said.

"Thanks." Abby picked up the tray and the three sisters headed out.

"Come on, Josh," Cheryl said.

"Mr. Jed said I could pour concrete."

She looked at Jed. "I don't know."

"Couple of minutes?" Jed asked.

"I guess." She folded up the table.

Nathan entered the carriage house and she swore the temperature shot up. Where was the woman who'd come looking for him?

The men started to pour, letting Josh push the cement down the chute. Nathan headed to Jed and they talked in hushed voices.

"I need to get back to work," Cheryl called to Josh after a few minutes.

"They need my help," Josh insisted. "It's summer vacation, Mom."

She tipped her head. "Now."

Josh kicked the floor but joined her. She could almost hear the pout in his footsteps. Nearing the door, she spotted a little girl with tears hanging from her eyelashes. "Are you lost?"

The child looked around. A tear plopped onto her T-shirt.

"Are you a guest?" Cheryl knelt next to her. "Where are your parents?"

A silent sob racked the little girl's chest.

Looking at the men, Cheryl asked, "Is your daddy here?"

The girl pointed at Jed and Nathan. Jed's daughter? Why would she be at a dangerous work site?

Josh inched back to the men near the concrete mixer.

"Josh."

"One more minute."

"One." Cheryl held out her hand. "Let's see your father."

It took a few seconds but the girl put her hand in Cheryl's and they walked over to Jed and Nathan.

"Jed?" she asked.

Both men looked up.

"I wasn't sure where you wanted your daughter to stay," she said.

Jed's eyes went wide. "She's not mine."

Cheryl's mouth dropped open. She shifted her gaze. "Nathan?"

"I...I..." His face paled. "I guess."

"You guess?" No one had hinted Nathan had a child. How could he be so indifferent to Josh if he was a father?

"Is-Isabella. She's m-mine." Nathan looked miserable. "Her mother...left her."

She herded the child next to Nathan, but the girl clutched her hand, forcing her to peel the girl's fingers out of her grasp.

"Josh." She backed away. "Time to go."

Her son smoothed wet cement. "Just a little longer."

"Now," she insisted.

For once Josh didn't talk back. The man he was helping gave him a high-five.

"Call if you need me," Nathan said to Jed.

She hurried to get out the door ahead of Nathan and his daughter. But Josh said goodbye to every man in the carriage house. Everyone except Nathan.

At least Nathan and the girl were heading to the parking lot. She watched their body language. The little girl dragged her feet. Nathan's shoulders were stiff as granite.

Not her business. She had wine-tasting appetizers to prep.

Nathan opened his truck door and lifted the girl into the front seat.

"What are you doing?" Even though she should

mind her own business, she rushed over. "Where's her car seat?"

Nathan rubbed his forehead. "Car seat?"

"You can't put her in the front seat. The airbag could...hurt her." She grabbed Nathan's arm. "And she needs to be in a car seat, otherwise the seat belt could injure her, too."

"Sh—" Nathan pressed his temples. "I mean shoot."

Josh moved beside her. "Every dummy knows you need a car seat."

Nathan glared so hard at her son, Cheryl put her arms around Josh's shoulders.

"I don't have one." Nathan paced a few steps away. "I just..."

The man was pale. This didn't look like a clueless father—he was too panicked for that. He looked lost.

"Josh's booster seat is in my car," she volunteered.

Relief softened his face. "Could I borrow it?"

"It's hard to get the clips undone. Just...take my car." She dug in her pocket for her keys. "She might not weigh enough for that booster seat. You need to get the right seat for her right away. What's her name again?"

He dug through a bag and pulled out a piece of paper. "Isabella. Isabella," he repeated, as if memorizing the name.

What was going on?

Nathan picked up the girl and carried her like a Ming vase. He set her next to the car.

Cheryl hurried over and unlocked the door.

Josh touched the little girl's hand. "You have to climb into the seat."

The girl nodded.

"Let me show you how to buckle her in."

Cheryl demonstrated, then unbuckled her and let Nathan try.

"Thank you." His eyes were glazed.

"Why didn't he know her name?" Josh asked as they watched the car drive away. "Is he stupid?"

"Don't call people names."

He kicked at the pavement. "But he's dumb."

"I'm sure there's an explanation."

The little girl hadn't said a word. She wasn't much younger than Josh. Something was wrong.

Cheryl chewed on her thumb. Poor thing. But Isabella wasn't her problem.

"I'M TAKING YOU to your grandma and grandpop." Nathan couldn't believe the words came out of his mouth. A kid. *Isabella.*

She didn't speak. Just looked at him with her deer-in-headlights eyes.

Hell. How old was she?

"Can you talk?" He turned so he could see her.

She nodded, tucking the dirty blanket next to her face. That was something.

At his parents' house, he pulled out the birth certificate. And stared. Father—Nathan Forester. He checked the birth date then counted on his fingers.

He didn't trust his brain. Four. He thought the kid was four.

That made sense. It had been five years or so since he and Heather had been together. But his memory was as holey as a pegboard, especially under stress.

He clicked open the booster seat latches. Isabella ignored his outstretched arms and scrambled out of the car. It was freaky the way she never said a word.

"Anyone home?" he called, leading her into his parent's house.

The scent of lemons greeted them. "You're in luck. Mom must be baking pie."

Isabella popped her thumb in her mouth and stared.

His mom stuck her head out of the kitchen. "What are you doing here?"

He swallowed. How did he introduce Isabella to his parents? New evidence he was a screw-up.

"I...I brought someone to meet you."

Mom's gaze dropped to the girl standing next to him. "Who is this?"

"Mom, meet Isabella." His voice cracked.

His mom looked between the girl and him. Her mouth dropped open. "Nathan?" she whispered.

"Can you say hi?" Nathan touched the kid's shoulder. Isabella shook her head.

Mom knelt and brushed back the dirty hair covering her eyes. "Hey there, Isabella. Are you hungry? Would you like something to eat?"

Isabella nodded.

Mom took her hand. "Let's wash up and I'll fix you a sandwich."

Nathan headed into the kitchen and went straight for the fridge. He pulled out a beer and popped the cap. Swearing under his breath, he took a big gulp, then another.

"Put that down." His mother's voice was drill sergeant worthy.

"What? Why?"

"Because you drove a little girl here." Mom helped the kid onto a chair.

Isabella's hair was brushed and her face and hands were cleaner now. Thank God.

"Talk to me." Mom pulled out bread, butter and leftover ham. She made a quick sandwich and cut it into four triangles.

The girl watched Mom with brown eyes that dominated her tiny face.

Nathan waved a hand. "Go ahead and eat."

Mom poured a glass of sweet tea and stood next to him. "Who is she?"

"She's…" God, he wanted that beer. And maybe another six. "She's my daughter." The words flew out of his mouth.

His mother's face paled. She grabbed a chair, sinking in it. "Daughter?" Her voice barely carried over the hum of the fridge.

He nodded. "I thought about doing a test."

Mom shook her head. "Look at her. She's the spitting image of you and Daniel."

He stared as Isabella devoured her food.

"When did you find out?" Mom stroked a hand down Isabella's hair.

"About twenty minutes ago."

"Today?"

He nodded.

"I have a granddaughter." Her voice filled with wonder.

Good. He needed Mom's enthusiasm.

Mom touched Isabella's shoulder. "How old are you, honey?"

She held up her hand and pulled her thumb down.

"Four?" Nathan hoped the numbers weren't jumbling in his head.

The girl nodded and took another sandwich triangle.

Mom hustled over to the cupboard, found a small glass and poured milk. Then she diced pieces of ham and slid them onto the plate.

"Where has she been?" Mom asked.

"I…" Nathan ran a hand through his hair. "Heather dropped her off and left. She said something about going into treatment."

Mom hugged his shoulders. "You get to take care of this precious girl."

"I can't." He was panicking just thinking about it. "I don't know anything about kids."

"No parent does at first." Mom squeezed his hand. "You'll learn. There are plenty of books that can help."

All his muscles tensed. "I can't read."

"It takes you longer, but you *can* read." She frowned. "You could try books on tape, too."

"I don't have that kind of time." He had a restaurant to build.

Mom raised her eyebrows. "For children, you make the time."

"I was h-hoping you'd help," he sputtered.

"Of course I will." She grinned. "I have a granddaughter."

"I mean…" He waved his hand around. "Have her live here. With someone who knows about kids."

"She's *your* daughter." The smile slipped off his mom's face. "You need to get to know her."

"I will." He paced.

Her chair squeaked as she stood. She headed to the fridge and brought back the milk carton. "She'll live with you."

He ripped at his hair. "I don't know what to do."

"You'll learn."

"Learn?" His voice grew louder. "Me? Impossible."

Isabella stopped eating. Her gaze bounced between Nathan and his mom.

Pop came down the back stairs, rubbing his neck like he'd just taken a nap. He probably had. His chemo treatments were brutal. He stopped, looking between Nathan and his mom as they faced off.

Then Pop spotted the kid. "Who do we have here?"

Mom took Pop's hand. "Samuel, meet Isabella, our granddaughter."

"Our…" Pop's gaze shot to Nathan. Disapproval tightened the lines around his mouth. "Our granddaughter?"

Nathan swallowed. Not able to find the words, he nodded.

"Nathan just found out," Mom added.

Pop crouched in front of the girl, his knees popping. "What's your name again?"

"Isabella," Nathan and his mom said together. Nathan set a hand on the kid's trembling shoulder. "She doesn't say much."

"Debbie, do I smell pie?" Pop asked.

Mom nodded.

"Well, why don't we try some of that?" Pop asked Isabella.

The kid nodded. She'd already finished the sandwich and extra ham. Hadn't Heather fed her?

While Mom pulled out plates and the pie, Nathan whispered, "I don't know how to care for a kid. How about you and Mom handle that for me?"

Pop raised a bushy white eyebrow. "I've raised my kids."

Nathan rubbed at the ache in his chest. "I can't screw up."

"You'll figure everything out." Pop slapped him on the back. "Just like we did."

He couldn't do this alone. He wasn't prepared.

Mom set a piece of pie in front of him.

Nathan stabbed at the slice, bringing a forkful to his lips. The tart lemon made his mouth water.

There had to be someone he could tap to take care of the kid.

He thought through the women he'd dated in Savannah. There was Tracie, but she could barely take care of herself. Gabby—aptly named since she talked everyone's ear off—was kind of an airhead. A nice airhead, but still not right.

He'd never been attracted to the motherly types.

The only mother he knew was…Cheryl. They lived next door to each other.

Hope had him releasing a deep exhale. Cheryl.

CHERYL COULDN'T AFFORD to pay for her next culinary class. She swallowed back a sour taste. She would have to apply for grants and financial aid.

She stared at the paperwork scattered over her kitchen table. Well, not *her* kitchen table—the Fitzgeralds'. She'd left all her furniture behind when she'd run from Levi.

What a sorry life. The only things she and Josh owned were their clothes and a car. And the bank owned most of the car. A car Nathan still had.

It was after seven. What was he doing? She'd planned to go grocery shopping after work. She needed her car.

"Bath time, Josh," she called.

"I took one last night," he yelled from the living room.

"And today you poured concrete and moved dirt for Miss Bess."

Josh came into the kitchen. "Can I take a shower?"

"If you promise to scrub. Everywhere."

He looked offended. "Promise."

She turned on the shower taps while he stripped. "In the hamper, please."

Back in the kitchen, she straightened her papers. She had to apply for loans online, but didn't have a computer. Luckily, the Fitzgeralds didn't mind her using the business center. She'd head over in the morning.

There was a knock at the kitchen door and Cheryl jumped. Couldn't help it. No one knocked on that door. Even though it had to be Nathan with her car keys, her belly did a little flip.

She was safe. Levi was in prison. "Who is it?"

"Nathan."

Unlocking the dead bolt, she pulled on the swollen door to find Nathan and Isabella on the other side. Nathan's face was drawn and solemn.

"I could fix that for you." He examined the sides of the door.

"I don't use this door."

His gaze snapped over to hers. "Can we come in?"

She wanted her keys. Stepping back, she let them into the kitchen. Isabella swayed on her feet. "Shouldn't she be in bed?" Cheryl whispered.

Nathan shook his head. "I...I don't have a bed for her."

He helped Isabella up onto a kitchen chair. She

crossed her arms on the table, put her head down and closed her eyes.

Cheryl gnawed her lower lip. "She's old enough not to fall out of bed if she sleeps with you."

"I don't know what to do with a kid." He paced to the table and stared at the papers. "I need help." He held her gaze with those deep brown eyes.

"What?" She wanted to sweep up the loan paperwork so he wouldn't see her financial state.

"You have a bunk bed." He stepped closer. "Can she sleep here?"

"Here?" Her voice squeaked.

"Could you help me out?" His body slumped. "Please?"

His issues weren't hers. She had problems of her own.

Isabella whimpered. Nathan didn't comfort her.

Cheryl's resolve cracked. The child shouldn't suffer because Nathan didn't know what he was doing. "Just for tonight."

A smile broke over his face like a sunrise. She hated the gooey feeling it gave her.

"When Josh is done in the bathroom, you need to give her a bath," she warned.

His smile evaporated. "But she's a girl."

"Yes." She shook her head. "Does she have pajamas?"

"I don't know." Nathan sighed. "I'll check." He escaped to his apartment.

Cheryl stroked Isabella's back. The girl blinked, but didn't say anything. That was…different.

"Are you ready for a bath?" Cheryl asked.

Isabella nodded, her eyes heavy. Cheryl held out her arms and the girl reached up. Josh was so sturdy, but Isabella felt like she would float away.

The shower was off. Cheryl knocked, then bumped the bathroom door open with her hip, still holding the sleepy girl.

Josh was brushing his teeth. "What's she doing here?" he asked, his mouth full of foam.

She should have asked Nathan to look for a toothbrush for Isabella. "She's sleeping in the bunk bed tonight."

"A girl?" He shook his head. "That's for my friends."

Maybe Cheryl needed to set more play dates with both boys and girls. The few kids Josh had asked to sleep over were all boys. That was fine but she didn't like his attitude. "She'll sleep there tonight."

Josh finished with his teeth and started to leave.

"Hang up your towel." She turned on the faucet and filled the tub. "And please bring Isabella a towel and washcloth from the closet."

He grumbled but came back with a towel set she'd used when he was a baby. The memory was bittersweet. That had been such a wonderful time. Brad had been in-country and they'd been happy.

"Thank you." She stripped the dirty T-shirt off Isabella. "You can read until I bring Isabella in."

Josh grumbled but, as she undressed Isabella, she heard the ladder creak as he climbed to the top bunk.

Cheryl could count Isabella's ribs. Even at their worst, she'd always made sure Josh had enough to eat.

"Climb in, honey." She helped the little girl sit in the tub.

The pop of the swollen kitchen door announced Nathan's return. She turned, hating that her back was to the door.

He came in with a grocery bag. "I couldn't find any PJs, but there's shorts and T-shirts." The clothes he held up were obviously dirty.

"We're not putting her in those. I'll…find something of Josh's."

"Thanks." He backed out the door.

"Where are you going?" Cheryl kept her tone mild because Isabella watched them.

"I thought I'd…" He pointed down the hall.

"You need to give her a bath."

His eyes widened.

"She needs a toothbrush, too." She poured soap on the washcloth. "Here."

"You want me to scrub?" Nathan's eyes were huge now.

She handed him the washcloth. "She's your daughter."

Squeezing past him, she inhaled his scent. He smelled good. Citrus and woodsy.

"Mom, what's this word?" Josh asked as she came into his room.

She stood on the edge of the bottom bunk to see. *"Kayak."*

"Kayak." He giggled. "It's a funny word. Shouldn't it be pronounced like 'kay' in *okay*?"

"I guess it didn't want to be plain." She kissed his cheek. "I love you."

"I love you to the moon and back." He hugged her.

This was her little boy. The one who gave hugs and told her he loved her. *Why can't he always be this way?*

She dug in the box of his outgrown clothes and found a pair of PJs with ducks all over them.

"Those are mine." Josh quacked.

Brad had always quacked when Josh wore those PJs. Cheryl couldn't believe he remembered. "Isabella's going to borrow them," she choked out.

"Yuck. They'll have girl cooties." Josh wrinkled his nose.

She shook her head and moved back to the bathroom.

Nathan knelt next to the tub, filling the space.

"I guess we need to wash this hair." Nathan grabbed the plastic cup she used for Josh and dipped it into the tub. "Ready?"

Isabella covered her eyes with her hands.

Nathan didn't tip the girl back, just dumped the water over her head. And she didn't complain. He picked up Cheryl's shampoo.

"Not that one. It'll sting." She reached over his head and grabbed the baby shampoo from the corner rack. Her breast brushed the top of his head.

He took in a breath. She scrambled back.

"Here." She held out the bottle, her face hot.

He had to stretch to get the shampoo. Squirting a little in his hand, he held it up for her inspection. "Enough?"

She nodded.

Nathan bit his lip and rubbed the shampoo through Isabella's wet hair. His actions were so slow and gentle it was possible nothing was getting clean. Isabella kept her hands over her eyes.

Another time she would suggest he make shapes with Isabella's soapy hair. Josh used to like being a dragon or a lion. He'd spend his bath time roaring.

Her son was only six and Cheryl was already reminiscing about his childhood.

She got closer, making sure she didn't bump into Nathan. Hard when he took up so much space. "Why don't I help you rinse?"

"Thanks." He let out a deep breath.

"Lean back." She tipped Isabella down. Nathan filled the cup and carefully worked the soap out of Isabella's hair.

After sitting her up, Cheryl found a comb and ran it through the girl's wet hair. "Is everything clean?"

"Yup," Nathan said.

"I brought some PJs." She handed Nathan the towel. "Let me find a toothbrush."

By the time she came back, Nathan was struggling to pull the top over Isabella's head.

Cheryl checked on Josh. "Time to call it a night, sport."

"But they're on the lake and they've lost their paddle." His voice was thick with sleep.

"You'll save them tomorrow." She climbed up and kissed him. "Love you."

"Love you." His eyes closed. "Don't tell my friends a girl slept here."

"Humph." She set the book on the nightstand and clicked off the light.

Enough light spilled from the hallway to guide Nathan to the bunk bed. Cheryl pulled back the sheets on the lower bunk and Nathan set Isabella in the bed. She brushed a kiss on Isabella's forehead. "Good night, angel."

Isabella whimpered and thrashed, as if searching for something.

"Does she have a blanket or a toy that she sleeps with?" Cheryl asked.

"God. How would I know?" He stumbled out the door. There was rustle of paper. He rushed back into the room. "I found the blanket she was carrying, but it's filthy."

Isabella grabbed it, hugging it to her cheek. Nathan winced.

"It'll be okay." Cheryl started to pat his shoulder, but that was too intimate in the darkened room. "You can wash it tomorrow."

Nathan knelt and touched his daughter's shoulder. "Night, Isabella."

Cheryl didn't stay to see if he hugged or kissed the girl. Heading back to the kitchen, she filled the kettle for her evening cup of tea.

Without turning, she knew from the way the air changed in the room that Nathan stood in the doorway. She asked, "All tucked in?"

"Yeah." He paused. "How much would I have to pay you to keep her?"

"Your daughter?" Horror raced through her like a wildfire.

"How much would you charge to take care of her for the next couple of months?"

CHAPTER FOUR

MAYBE THIS WAS a mistake, but Nathan was desperate.

"You'd pay me to take care of *your* daughter?" Cheryl's face filled with shock.

"You're an expert." He held up his hands.

"I can't—"

"Can you think about it?" he interrupted.

"No." Cheryl looked at him like he was sludge from a sewer line. "She's *your* daughter."

"I don't know how to take care of her. It's dangerous leaving a child with someone like me. Just…think about it. Please." He yanked open the door. "Thanks for helping today."

She slammed the door in his face and snapped the lock shut.

Nathan threw open his apartment door and headed straight to the fridge. His beer opened with a hiss. Now what? If Cheryl refused, who else could he turn to—Daniel? They weren't that close. His brother would tell him to clean up his own damn mess. Besides, Daniel and Bess were getting married this summer. He wasn't stupid enough to suggest they take on a kid.

Tipping his head, he slammed back half the beer. How long would Cheryl let—his brain wouldn't retrieve his kid's name—stay? He finished the beer and pitched the bottle into the open recycling bin.

After four years, why would Heather insist he take care of their kid?

He dug through the bags, but couldn't find anything that looked like Heather's phone number.

He grabbed another beer from the fridge. What the hell should he do now? He kicked back in the lounge chair and drank.

SOMEONE SCREAMED.

Nathan jerked upright. The leg rest on the lounge chair snapped closed. Hell, he'd fallen asleep.

Another muffled scream came from next door. His heart hammered against his ribs.

Rushing down the hall, he tried Cheryl's door. Locked. He pounded on it. "Open up!"

His only answer was another scream.

He raced back to his apartment and grabbed his keys, searching for the carriage house master key. No wonder his brother labeled everything, not that letters would have made any sense right now.

He shoved key after key into the lock. Finally one turned. He pushed on the stubborn door, promising he would fix it if everyone was okay.

Another cry broke out. He honed in on the sound and sprinted down the hall.

"You're safe. You're all right," he heard Cheryl murmuring. He burst into the kids' bedroom.

Cheryl jumped, his daughter in her arms. "What?"

"I heard screaming." He searched the room for an intruder.

Fear filled Cheryl's eyes. Josh stared at him like he was the burglar. His daughter shrieked again.

Nathan drew in a breath. "I thought someone had broken in."

"*You* did." Cheryl glared at him, handing him the girl.

"What? No!" He held up his hands and stumbled back.

"Take her," Cheryl whispered. "Comfort her."

"Shush now." He took the kid and ran his hand hesitantly down her back She trembled like a bird cornered by a cat. What had made her scream? "Hush."

Jesus. Now what?

Cheryl tucked Josh back into bed. "Go back to sleep, honey."

Nathan bounced Isabella a little. Didn't people do that with babies? But his daughter was four.

Her arms wrapped around his neck and her muscles softened. How could she trust him? He was a screw-up.

"I think she's asleep." He tried to hand her to Cheryl.

She shifted away. "Put her in bed."

The sheets were pulled back, so he set her in the middle of her pillow. Isabella curled into a ball and whimpered.

"Rub her back." Irritation filled Cheryl's voice.

He did and Isabella relaxed under his hand. His tension eased with each stroke. Pulling up the covers, he tucked the sheets into the edge of the bed. His mom had done that. As kids, he and Daniel pretended they were caterpillars, tucked in a cocoon.

After joining Cheryl in the hall, he whispered, "What the hell was that?"

"Night terrors." Cheryl put her fists on her hips. "How did you get into my apartment?"

"I heard screaming. You didn't answer the door," he shot back. "I used the master key."

Her lip trembled. "Don't you ever—*ever*—use that key again."

He backed away. "Got it."

There went his idea that they could work together, that she'd take on the role of nanny. That idea had come with his third beer.

Cheryl sniffed. "You've been drinking." She said it like he was a serial killer.

"A couple of beers." No big deal.

"Get your act together. You have a daughter depending on you." She stalked down the hall to the kitchen and then pointed at the open door. "You didn't even close the door!"

"I was worried." How could he have known about night terrors?

"Out. Pick up Isabella by eight."

Damn. Who would watch the kid tomorrow?

CHERYL TAPPED ON the top bunk. "Last call for breakfast."

Both kids were exhausted from Isabella's nightmare. Cheryl was tired, too. But the day wouldn't wait.

She pulled back Isabella's bedding and caught a whiff of urine. *Great.* "Time to get up, Isabella."

She tugged off the little girl's wet bottoms and led her to the bathroom.

Last night she'd washed Isabella's meager laundry. When the girl was finished in the bathroom, Cheryl helped her put on the least stained clothes she'd found.

"Josh." She shook his shoulder. "Unless you want to miss the camp bus, you need to move."

He pushed off the covers, hung over the railing and dropped to the floor. "What's that smell?" He pretended to choke, then headed for the bathroom, still gagging.

"Come on, Isabella." She headed to the kitchen and the silent girl followed. She would deal with the sheets later.

She set her in Josh's old booster chair and poured a bowl of cereal. By the time she was buttering toast, Josh joined them.

"That's my chair," he complained.

"And you're too big for it."

He took his toast to the table and started eating.

Cheryl quickly pulled his lunch together. Sandwich, apple, carrot sticks and a cookie.

"Can I have three cookies?" He turned those big brown eyes at her.

"Three? That's too many," she said.

"My friends like your cookies."

"You're giving them away?"

"I share."

Great. Did the other parents know the kids were trading food? It was only for another week, so she tucked two more cookies into the bag.

Sipping her tea, she watched the kids finish their breakfasts. Josh had forgotten his resentment and chatted on and on. He even gave Isabella the last piece of toast.

The girl didn't speak but she nodded every now and then. What would Nathan do with Isabella today? Not Cheryl's concern.

At exactly seven thirty, the construction crew arrived. They were better than an alarm clock. Low voices murmured on the ground floor. She could measure the restaurant's progress with each hammer strike and screech of the saw.

She wanted to work in Abby's new restaurant, but she hadn't gathered the courage to ask her boss. She'd hoped to take more classes, but that would bury her in debt.

"Brush your teeth," she told the kids. Nathan should be here soon.

Right on time, she heard someone climbing the outside steps followed by a knock on the door.

She threw the dead bolt.

Nathan hadn't shaved. His eyes were bloodshot. Had he been drinking all night?

Crossing her arms, she stepped back as far as she could to let him in.

"Did she have any more problems sleeping?" he asked.

"She wet the bed. You should buy Pull-Ups."

He shoved his hand through his hair. "What the hell is a Pull-Up?"

"They're a nighttime diaper," she explained with a sigh. "Maybe Isabella wasn't used to the bed." *Or to her father.*

"Crap. I don't have a clue what I'm doing." He held out a hand. "Did you think about taking care of her?"

"I can't." She wasn't taking on his responsibilities when she had so many of her own. "You'll learn."

His shoulders slumped.

"Josh," she called, "we have to go."

Nathan caught her hand. At his touch, an unwanted zing went through her body. She tried to pull away, but he hung on.

"I need help. I need... I don't even know." He squeezed her fingers. "Can you at least help me shop? Please?"

His brown eyes were darker than her son's. Darker than Brad's. At the memory of Brad's laughing eyes, she yanked her hand away. "Josh, hurry."

The kids came to the door. Isabella wrapped her arm around Cheryl's leg, hiding from Nathan. He reached down, but the girl scuttled back.

"It's okay." Cheryl picked her up and handed her to Nathan.

"Please help me shop for her. I'll...pay you. Twenty bucks an hour. For..." His voice trailed off.

He couldn't remember his own daughter's name?

"Isabella." She didn't have time to get involved, but her heart ached for the frightened girl.

"Fine. You don't have to pay me," she said. "Just… buy me and Josh dinner."

NATHAN PULLED CHERYL'S car in front of his parents' house. Begging to use her car again hadn't been fun.

Mom had agreed to watch Isabella during the day. At least until he found day care or his parents left for Pop's monthly cancer treatments in Texas. He wanted to turn the whole mess over to someone more capable than him, but no one volunteered.

"We're at grandma's." He unbuckled Isabella. She held up her arms and latched onto him like a monkey. His heart stuttered. He stroked her hair. "You'll have fun."

He wasn't sure if he believed his lies. *Fake it until you make it, right?* That had been his motto in school. That or "Screw it. I don't understand, so why bother?"

This time not bothering wasn't an option.

"Come on, kid." He hoisted her higher onto his hip. "You remember grandma from yesterday?"

She nodded.

Mom met them at the door. "Here you are. We're going to have fun today."

Isabella clung to his neck. "I've got to work, kiddo." He'd already checked in with Jed, but he needed to get back to the site.

"Come on, honey." Mom pried Isabella off his shoulders and hugged her.

"You sure you won't reconsider having her live here?" he asked.

Mom shot him a look. "What time will you be back?"

"Five thirty." He took in a deep breath. "Cheryl's helping me shop."

Mom set Isabella down. "We'll see you then."

He ruffled the kid's hair. "See you later."

Isabella's face crumpled.

He knelt down to her level. "Tonight we'll shop for your bed."

She nodded but didn't smile. Hell, he couldn't remember ever seeing her smile. Josh was always grinning or laughing. How did Cheryl do it? Could Cheryl get the little girl to smile?

He pushed his daughter out of his head as he drove back to Fitzgerald House. He needed to concentrate on Abby's restaurant. He arrived in time to check the lumber order. The numbers didn't dance and it looked like the right amount of wood. He signed off, then he and Jed carried it to the staging area. "Let's build a staircase. My brother should be here soon."

He could visualize the gorgeous, curved wood staircase winding up to the old hayloft.

"Are we ready?" Daniel walked in, strapping on his tool belt.

"Yeah." He and Daniel tended to fight on job sites, but since they were building something this technical, he wanted his brother's expertise.

"Why do women always want curved staircases?" Jed asked as they shaped the semicircular walls.

"To make us crazy." Daniel hammered in another two-by-six.

"I told Abby it would cost more," Nathan said.

"That's never stops a Fitzgerald," Jed drawled.

It was tough, exacting work. Nathan made the first calculation. Jed verified and Daniel would agree or disagree. There wasn't much talk, just the screech of the saw, the pounding of a hammer and the creak of the wood. The morning flew by.

"I love the smell of freshly cut wood," Cheryl announced from the doorway.

Nathan's gaze snapped over to her.

"Abby was pulled away by a guest." She held up a tray. "She wanted me to bring over lunch."

She avoided Nathan's gaze but a blush dusted her cheeks. A streak of flour decorated her shirt, just under her breast. Nathan wouldn't mind tidying her up.

He froze. That wasn't the way to think about the woman who was helping him with his daughter. He couldn't screw this up.

"What is that?" Cheryl stopped next to the staircase framing.

"We're building the beam that will anchor the risers." She frowned, so Nathan added, "The staircase steps."

"We'll add the inner core and build in slots for each riser." For once his words flowed smoothly. "But first we have layers of laminate to glue to ensure the stairs are stable."

"That's fascinating." She reached out to touch the curved plywood.

He shook his head. "Don't."

"I can't wait to see everything come together." Green sparks gleamed in her brown eyes. She tapped her lip. "We never settled on a time for tonight."

"Yeah." He pushed his hat off and scratched his head.

Daniel watched them, glaring.

Nathan hadn't figured out how to tell his brother about Isabella. It was embarrassing to find out he had a four-year-old kid. His perfect brother would never be in this situation.

Lowering his voice, Nathan asked, "What time are you off?"

"Five thirty." Cheryl leaned in. She smelled of apples and…cookies.

"Around six then?" He didn't want to shout that they were making plans.

"That works." She chewed on her lip. "I'll see you then."

Cheryl waved to Daniel and Jed as she left. Daniel stalked up to him. "Got a date?"

Nathan shook his head. "She's helping me…shop."

Jed looked at him. "For your kid? Where is she?"

Daniel choked on the drink he'd just taken from his water bottle. "Kid?"

"Yeah." Nathan rolled his shoulders.

"When did this happen?" Daniel's voice cracked.

"Apparently four years ago."

"Who's the mom?" his brother asked. "Anyone I know?"

"A woman from Atlanta."

"A kid?" Daniel shook his head. "Boy? Girl?"

"Isabella." The words were running today. "Mom has her right now."

"I'm an uncle?" Daniel punched Nathan's arm. "Why didn't you tell me?"

"Because I just found out." He smacked his hat against his thigh. "The kid's four and I just found out."

"That's screwed up."

"Yeah." Appropriate since Nathan was the family screw-up.

"What's Cheryl helping you with?"

"Everything. Furniture, clothes, stuff." He grabbed a sandwich and sat on an overturned bucket. "I'm not even sure what I need."

"Just don't mess with Cheryl." Daniel crossed his arms, his muscles bulging. "She's had a rough life."

"I'm won't." Nathan's teeth ground together. Of course Daniel would think the worst of him. "I don't know squat about kids. That's why she's helping me."

Daniel pointed with his sandwich. "Make sure you keep it that way."

As if he didn't have enough problems, now his brother was threatening him. He planned to keep his hands to himself.

Once Heather was out of treatment, Isabella would leave. His life would be normal again. Or as normal as his life could be.

"I'M HUNGRY," JOSH SAID.

Cheryl checked the time. Just after five thirty. She peeled and sliced an apple, setting it in front of Josh. "This should tide you over."

"I don't want to go with *him*."

"We offered to help."

Shopping with Nathan wasn't a good idea. She had to stop letting people take advantage of her.

But poor Isabella shouldn't suffer because her dad was a rookie.

Cheryl took a deep breath. She would help Nathan make a home for his little girl. Then she and Nathan could stay away from each other.

Except that he lived next door.

She nibbled on an apple slice and worked on Nathan's list. Maybe she could hand him the list and send him on his way.

Her thoughts were mean. When she'd arrived in Savannah, so many people had helped her. It was time to pay it forward.

"Why do we have to go with Mr. Nathan and Isabella?" Josh finished off the last apple slice and took the plate to the dishwasher.

"Because Mr. Nathan doesn't know much about kids. He asked for our help." She needed to remember this herself.

"But she's four. How come he needs help?"

"I don't know." What mother wouldn't tell the father of her child that she was pregnant? Maybe Nathan had done something that had stopped her from telling him? He drank a lot, like Levi.

There was a knock. Josh had the door open before she could ask him to wait.

Nathan held Isabella in his arms. His muscles were rigid. Isabella's shoulders were stiff, too.

She picked up her purse. "Josh, let's go."

"Why do I have to come?" Her son pouted. "I'm not getting anything."

"You're getting dinner," she reminded him.

They headed to her car. Josh climbed into his booster seat.

"Oh, shoot." There was only one seat.

Nathan ran a hand through his hair. "I didn't think."

Based on the gossip about Nathan around the B and B, that wasn't unusual. He'd sold drugs in high school; always in trouble but not enough to end up in juvie. He'd even been kicked out of the family business. Dolley, the youngest Fitzgerald sister, laughed about the number of women he'd dated.

"I can ride without a booster." Josh puffed out his chest. "I don't use a booster on the bus."

"This isn't a bus." But her son had a point.

They weren't going far. She chewed her lip. "This is the only time."

She held out her hand for the keys. "If my son isn't in a booster, I'll drive."

Nathan handed the keys over without arguing. They were warm from his pocket.

She buckled Josh in and moved to the driver's seat. Nathan fought with Isabella's buckles.

"You have to snap here." Josh pulled on the seat belt and locked Isabella into the seat.

"Yeah." Nathan sat in the front seat. "Where to first?"

Cheryl handed him the list she'd created.

He glanced at it then shoved it into his pocket. "Thanks."

He hadn't bothered to read the list. Maybe he was illiterate.

"There's a secondhand store nearby."

"I don't mind buying new." Nathan rolled down the window.

"Let's try this store first."

She triple-checked that every intersection was clear before turning. Nathan tapped his fingers on the outside of the car, but she wasn't going to rush.

"Did you finish the staircase?" she asked, tired of the silence.

"We have a couple more layers to go." Nathan described how distressed oak would be glued as the last layer. "We ordered iron spindles. They'll match the hinges still in the space."

Josh asked questions. And he and Nathan had a real conversation. Isabella didn't say a word, just cuddled her ratty blanket.

At the strip mall, Cheryl pulled up in front of the store. "Everyone out."

Josh didn't need help with his buckle and he unlocked Isabella's chair, too. "Come on."

The little girl crawled out Josh's side of the car and took his hand. Nathan stood with the car door open, confusion filling his face.

Cheryl stopped on the sidewalk. "Has she said anything?"

"No." He rubbed his neck. "Is that normal?"

"I don't know." After Levi, Josh had been pretty quiet, too. "Maybe."

"What should I do?"

He looked so lost, she patted his arm. "Give her stability. Give her love."

"I guess." He wiped a hand over his face. "Where do we start?"

"Where's the list?"

He pulled it out of his pocket and handed it to her. He pointed down two doors from the store. "I've been to that bar and never knew there were stores here."

"I've been in this store and never knew there was a bar here." And didn't that highlight their differences?

"Let's go." She wanted this evening over, but the two kids were kneeling next to a shrub.

"I found a really cool bug." Josh pointed at a branch.

"Wow." Nathan crouched next to the kids. "It's a praying mantis."

Josh reached out to pick up the bug.

"You should leave it alone." Nathan told him. "They eat the bad insects."

"How come we haven't seen any at my camp?" Josh's eyebrows were pinched together.

"They aren't that common," Nathan said. "They're cool-looking, aren't they?"

"I guess." Josh shrugged.

"I haven't seen a praying mantis in years." Nathan smiled.

Something loosened in Cheryl's chest as she ushered them into the store. She'd been around Nathan's identical twin a lot. She should be used to looking at his handsome face. But there was something different about Nathan. His face was…weathered. Like he'd seen too much, done too much, felt too much.

She straightened her shoulders. It was a mistake to romanticize Nathan. He'd lived a tough life—on purpose.

Nathan set a hand on her shoulder. "I forgot to thank you for helping me."

She slipped away from his disturbing touch. "No problem."

She headed for the booster seats while Josh zeroed in on the play equipment. She kept an eye on him as Nathan settled Isabella into each booster seat, testing the size.

Cheryl read the weight restrictions. "Do you know how much she weighs?"

He shook his head. Picking the girl up, he threw her over his head. She gave a bright chirp of a giggle. "Can't be more than thirty pounds."

"This one should last you a while." Cheryl pointed.

"What do you think?" Nathan crouched next to his daughter, who shrugged.

"I guess that's a yes." He looked around the store. "What else?"

"She's small, so she could use a booster seat at the table."

"I'll need to buy a kitchen table." Nathan picked up two booster seats. "One for my folks' house."

She checked on Josh. He was coloring on an easel. She took in a breath. Her son loved drawing and coloring. How much would an easel cost?

Guiding Nathan to the strollers, she asked, "Do you want a stroller?"

Panic flared in his eyes. "Do I need one?"

"Not necessarily, but it's nice when they're tired and you don't have enough arms to carry stuff and her."

He stared at the choices, not moving. To speed up the selection process, she guided him to a small umbrella stroller. "This should work."

Isabella sat in the seat, tugged up her blanket and stuck her thumb in her mouth.

"I guess that means we'll take it." Nathan rubbed Isabella's hair.

"We can look at furniture now."

He shook his head. "No used furniture."

Wouldn't that be a nice attitude to have? Cheryl checked through the second-hand clothes instead. "Do you want clothes? This is nice." It was a pretty pink cotton sundress.

"Sure." His lost expression was back.

She grabbed a few outfits and then called to Josh, wanting to pull him away from the art supplies before he could ask for something she couldn't afford. "Can you help us find a stool for Isabella?"

"Over there." Josh pointed to the side of the store, not moving toward her.

"Come test them out."

He rolled his eyes. "I'm too big for this."

"That's because you're taller. Isabella, can you try it out?" The little girl stepped on the stool.

"That looks good. Right?" Nathan asked.

"Yup." Cheryl checked through the rest of the store, but didn't see anything else on the list. "I think that's it. Josh, take Isabella's hand and we'll check out." By helping, maybe her son wouldn't be upset he hadn't gotten anything.

"Hang on." Nathan headed to the back of the store.

Cheryl didn't have a chance to wonder what he'd spotted. She pulled the clothes out of the stroller and set them on top of the booster chairs on the counter.

"Your daughter will look precious in that dress." The cashier smiled as she rang up the charges.

"Thanks, but she's not my daughter. That's my son."

The clerk blinked. "Wow. The kids look alike."

Cheryl looked between Josh and Isabella. They both had blond hair and brown eyes. "I never noticed."

Nathan joined them at the counter.

"Are they cousins?" The clerk's smile changed, a little more flirtatious.

"They aren't related." Nathan carried the easel Josh had been admiring. "This, too."

Josh's face turned into a thundercloud.

Nathan set his hand on Josh's shoulder. "Thanks for helping out tonight."

Josh's frown deepened. "Is that for Isabella?"

"It's for you." Nathan grinned.

Cheryl saw the price. "It's too much."

"Mom," Josh pleaded.

"He had to share his bedroom last night. I think it's okay." Nathan stroked the easel. "I had one like this when I was a kid."

Cheryl twisted her hands together. She wasn't comfortable with Nathan buying her son a gift, especially such an expensive one.

Josh stared at her. "Please."

She swallowed. "Okay."

He grinned. "I'll carry it."

"What do you say?" she reminded him.

"Thanks."

She looked at him.

Josh took a deep breath. "Thank you, Mr. Nathan."

"You're welcome." Nathan nudged her shoulder. "That's a cool trick," he said under his breath.

"What?"

"Getting him to talk with just a glare." Nathan touched his daughter's hair. "Can you do the same with Isabella?"

Cheryl's heart lurched. "Maybe she just needs more time."

"Maybe." He handed his credit card to the cashier. "Where to next?"

She checked her watch. "We need to eat."

"Okay." He grabbed the booster seats and stroller. The clerk handed her the shopping bag. Josh carried the easel like it was nitroglycerine. Too bad he wasn't always that careful. He'd broken a plate just last week.

While Nathan installed the car seat, she and Josh put the rest of the purchases in the trunk, but kept out the stroller.

"There's a café around the corner that's fast," Cheryl said. "We can walk over."

"I'll follow your lead."

"Get Isabella in her stroller, unless you want to carry her."

He grimaced. "I was hoping you'd do the honors."

"You need to learn." No matter how helpless he looked, she refused to enable him.

"Let's give this a try." He took his daughter's hand and strapped her in the chair. "That wasn't hard."

Four women piled out of a car, laughing as they headed to the bar. Nathan watched as they passed.

"What a cutie." A woman leaned over the stroller, flashing poor Isabella her abundant cleavage.

"Thanks." Nathan grinned.

The woman looked at Nathan and sighed. "All the good ones are taken." She looked at Cheryl. "Lucky you."

The blonde joined her friends and they entered the

bar. The sound of laughter and loud voices drifted out through the open door.

Cheryl shook her head. "I can't believe that."

"Yeah." Nathan looked longingly at the bar. "She didn't even check to see if we were wearing rings."

That's what he'd noticed? Not the woman's flirty tone or too-tight shirt?

"I'm hungry," Josh complained.

"Okay." She took his hand, leaving Nathan behind them to push the stroller.

"The bar has pretty good food," Nathan said.

She turned. "No."

He sighed. "It was just a thought."

At the café, Cheryl asked for a table. "We'll need a booster seat."

Nathan's gaze dropped as the waitress seated them. Cheryl frowned. Had he just checked out the woman's ass?

Once settled at the table, she glanced at the menu. "What do you want?" she asked Josh.

"What do they have?"

She pointed to the kids' menu selections on the placemat and helped him sound out the words.

"Pancakes," he said.

"Sure." At least it came with applesauce.

Nathan hadn't opened the menu. Cheryl nodded at Isabella, prompting him.

Nathan winced. "What do you want?"

The little girl chewed her lip. Nathan pointed at the pictures on the placemat she was coloring. "Chicken fingers. French toast. Hot dog. Grilled cheese. Pancakes." He waited until she stabbed a finger at the French toast.

The waitress came over and Nathan gave her a smile. "I think we're ready to order. The half-pint will have French toast."

"And to drink?" the waitress asked.

Nathan looked at Cheryl.

She sighed. "Milk. And she'll have the applesauce."

"What will you have, ma'am?"

Ma'am? Cheryl wanted to roll her eyes. "Chicken-salad sandwich with the side salad. Milk to drink."

Josh ordered his pancakes.

"And what will you have?" The server looked at Nathan.

"What beer do you have on tap?"

Cheryl stiffened.

The server laughed. "We don't serve alcohol."

"Shucks." Nathan winked. "I'll have a burger."

"Which one?" The server flipped the menu open to the burger choices.

Nathan didn't even look. "What's your spiciest burger, darlin'?"

"The jalapeño burger."

"Then that's what I want."

He'd said he could read. Cheryl didn't believe him.

After the server left, Nathan asked, "What else do we need to pick up?"

She handed him the list.

He looked through it. "We ticked off a lot."

Could he identify the items they'd bought? She handed him one of Josh's crayons. "Go ahead and cross them off."

His eyes narrowed. Looking through the list, he struck a couple of items, folded it and tucked the paper in his shirt pocket.

When their food came, Nathan watched her cut Josh's pancakes, then he cut Isabella's French toast. "Is it good?"

Isabella nodded. She picked up a piece with her fingers and dipped it in the syrup he'd poured.

Cheryl wanted to tell the girl to use her fork, but that was Nathan's responsibility.

They were quiet until Josh said, "We forgot to get paper for my easel."

"Da—" Nathan stopped and then said, "Shoot. We'll fix that."

Josh sighed. "I wanted to draw the bug."

"The praying mantis?" Nathan asked.

"Yeah. That mantis thing."

"We still have to go to another shop," Cheryl warned. "It'll be bedtime when we get home."

Nathan leaned over to Josh. "I used to use stuff my dad had from the construction site."

"That's 'cause you had a dad. Mine died." Josh dragged a pancake through his syrup.

Cheryl swallowed, not looking at Nathan. "Josh…" But she didn't know what to say.

"I'm sorry your dad died." Nathan squirmed in his

chair. "But if we have time, there's paper in the carriage house that might work for now."

"Cool." Josh dug back into his dinner.

Cheryl took a few bites of her sandwich and then pushed it around her plate. She didn't feel like eating anymore.

She wanted this night to end. It should have been her and Brad having dinner with their kids. Not a clueless man she'd rather avoid.

NATHAN TUCKED THE dinner receipt away. Assuming the numbers hadn't twisted, he'd fed four people for his usual bar tab.

Cheryl led the kids back to the car, this time letting Josh push the stroller.

She'd gotten quiet after her son had announced his dad was dead. Nathan was pretty sure her husband had been killed overseas.

He might have hated his own childhood, hated being labeled the *other* twin, the *dumb* twin, but at least their family had been intact.

Since Cheryl was helping him out, the least he could do was get her to smile sometime during the evening. He was pretty good with the ladies.

"Thank you for dinner," Cheryl said, climbing into the driver's seat after the kids were strapped in.

"Thank you for helping me," Nathan said. "I really appreciate it."

"Yeah, thanks for dinner," Josh chimed from the backseat.

As usual, Isabella didn't say a word. He drummed his fingers on his shorts. Should he get her checked out? He leaned over to Cheryl. "How often do kids have to go to the…" He lost the word. Damn. That hadn't happened all evening. "You know, where they get shots and stuff."

"The doctor?"

He nodded.

"By her age, once a year unless they're sick." She backed out of the parking spot. "Did you find vaccination records in the stuff her mother gave you?"

"I don't know."

"I could look through it for you." She kept her eyes on the road.

Crap. She thought he couldn't read. He could figure out if Heather had given him medical records. He hoped. "I'll check."

She didn't say anything. Just focused on the streets. Fine. He knew what he could and couldn't do.

Cheryl pulled into the parking lot of a Babies "R" Us.

"She's not a baby," he said. See, he *could* read.

"They sell more than baby things." She held up a hand. "This is the easiest place to grab what you need."

"Okay." He unbuckled his daughter. "Are we talking about a lot of things?" he asked, lifting the girl out of the car.

"Depends on what 'a lot' means to you." She took Josh's hand.

"Guess it's good I haven't spent much money lately." Hell, he'd been living at his parents' house half the time he'd been back in Savannah.

He took Isabella's hand. She looked up at him silently with those deep brown eyes.

The door whooshed open. Cheryl said something to Josh, who ran ahead and pulled out a cart. She'd made her son feel useful and burned out some of his energy. How would he learn to be that good a parent?

"Bed first." Cheryl led the way. Was she familiar with the store or was she reading the signs he could barely interpret.

"What are you thinking?" she asked.

He looked at the beds. There were cribs and short beds. Bunk beds and a massive white-and-pink princess bed. He turned in a circle. "How do we pick?"

"How much do you want to spend?"

He looked at the price tag. "Is this thousand bucks just for the bed or the whole set?"

She peeked at the tag he was holding. "The whole set."

He rubbed a hand on his face. "And I need a bunch of other crap, too."

"Language," she muttered. "Yes, you need other *things* besides a bed and dresser. But you don't have to spend this much."

She took Isabella's hand. "What bed do you like, sweetheart?"

The little girl pointed at an all-white bedroom set

covered with a pink-and-pale-green comforter. It was a low platform bed.

Cheryl checked the information. "It comes with a railing, so she won't fall out. There's storage and a small bookshelf at the foot of the bed. And storage in the headboard, too."

Isabella hopped on the mattress and wiggled into the pillows. A tiny smile dawned on her face.

Cheryl stroked the finish. Her expression got even sadder. "I wanted a bed like this when I was a girl."

Kid's shopping shouldn't be depressing, should it?

Nathan sat on the bed. "The mattress isn't too bad. You like this?" he asked Isabella.

She nodded.

A clerk came over. "I'm Stephanie. Do you need help?"

"Hi, Stephanie. This is Busy Issy." Nathan nodded at his daughter. "And she'd like this bed."

Stephanie checked the inventory on her iPad. "You're in luck. We have this in the warehouse."

"Mom, this is boring," Josh said. "Can I go over to the toys?"

"Not right now."

"Mom." He drew the word out like it was a six-foot long snake.

"Joshua." She did the same thing. "Why don't you help Isabella pick out her bedding?"

"She's a girl."

Nathan laughed.

"Fine." Josh took Isabella's hand. "What do you like?"

Isabella walked over to the brightest, pinkest, bagged-up comforter.

Josh pretended to gag. "That?"

She nodded.

Nathan winced. "I guess we're taking that, too."

Stephanie pulled the correct size from the shelf and then grabbed sheets and a waterproof mattress pad.

Nathan's dinner churned a little more with each pink selection his daughter made.

The pile in the cart grew and a second cart was retrieved.

"I don't think I had a lamp on the list." Cheryl peeked over his shoulder.

"Come on, Issy." He liked the nickname. Then he held up pink lamps until the little girl pointed at her choice.

"Are we done?" Nathan swung his daughter into his arms, making her giggle.

Cheryl shook her head. "Clothes?"

Josh rolled his eyes. "Can't I check out toys?"

"Tell you what." Nathan set Isabella down. "Could you pick out a dozen outfits for Issy, while Josh and I look around?"

Josh frowned at Nathan.

"Josh?" Cheryl asked.

"I guess." He and Nathan headed to the toys.

"Can you help me choose a couple of toys you liked when you were young?" Nathan asked.

Josh pointed at Legos. "These are fun. And there's even pink." He pretended to gag.

Nathan picked up a Lincoln Logs set he and Daniel had had when they were kids and a few more toys. Josh stopped next to the art supplies. Art had been the only area in which Nathan had excelled.

Josh pointed at a large tablet of paper. "Look what I found!"

"Grab it." Nathan tossed art supplies in the cart for Josh and Issy. Maybe his daughter had gotten some of his creativity.

What if she'd gotten his dyslexia? Nathan swallowed. Could that be why she didn't speak?

They met Cheryl with a sleepy Issy in her arms at the cash register.

"Mom, Mom." Josh tugged on her shorts and held up the tablet. "Look what I got."

Cheryl checked the price and shook her head. "Honey, we're not buying anything today."

"I'm paying for it." Nathan set the art supplies on the counter.

Cheryl shook her head and Josh's bottom lip quivered, his eyes filling with tears. "It's for the easel."

"I understand." Instead of smiling like he'd hoped, Cheryl frowned.

"Please, Mom. My notebooks are too small. They'd be stupid on the easel."

Nathan touched her shoulder and she stiffened.

"It's not much. Come on." Nathan grinned.

She looked at him and then at her son. Heaving out a sigh, she nodded. But she didn't smile.

Cheryl handed Issy to Nathan. The girl whimpered at the trade-off, clinging to Cheryl's neck.

"Go to your daddy," she said.

Nathan peeled off her fingers and took her. Shouldn't this be natural?

"Where do I pick up the bed?" Nathan asked Stephanie as Cheryl unloaded the cart.

"At the warehouse or we deliver."

"You said it was available."

"It is, but it's at the warehouse."

"They'll deliver tonight?"

"The warehouse is closed," Stephanie said. "But they'll call tomorrow when everything is ready."

Where would Issy sleep tonight? Nathan glanced at Cheryl.

Her eyes narrowed.

Nathan paid, gave the store his contact information and he and Cheryl pushed the rest out to her car.

"I'm not sure everything will fit." Cheryl stared at the half-filled trunk.

"We'll figure it out." He pulled and rearranged packages, lamps and Josh's easel. Cheryl packed bags between the two booster seats and on the floor.

It was a quiet ride back to Fitzgerald House. Cheryl carried Issy while Nathan grabbed some of the bags and they headed up the stairs to Cheryl's apartment. Josh carried his easel.

Nathan dropped the bags by the door and headed back to the car. "I'll bring up what's left."

"I can carry my stuff," Josh insisted, going with him.

He balanced the tablet on his head and held his art supplies in his hand.

"Be careful," Nathan warned, pulling the booster seats out of the trunk.

"I know." Josh ran toward the steps.

"Slow down," Nathan warned again.

Halfway up, Josh tripped. The tablet and bag squirted out of his arms. His chin cracked against the steps. Nathan dropped the seats and started for the kid.

Cheryl ran and thrust Isabella into his arms. She turned Josh over. "Are you all right?"

He sat up, shaking his head. "I'm okay."

She ran her hands on his face. "Did you bump your chin?"

Josh winced. "Yeah."

"Stick out your tongue," she said. "No blood." She touched his front teeth. "Nothing loose."

"My stuff." Josh scooted down the steps and dug through the bag. "A brush broke," he wailed.

Nathan scooped up the rest of the things Josh had dropped.

"I need another brush." Josh stomped up the stairs.

"You need to slow down when you're told," Cheryl said.

Josh glared at Nathan and Isabella. "If we'd been alone, I wouldn't have broken the brush."

"If we'd been alone, you wouldn't have any of those things," Cheryl reminded him.

Great. Now both Henshaws were frowning.

Josh pushed into the apartment and threw the broken paintbrush in the corner.

"Pick that up," Cheryl said.

Josh trudged to the corner and jammed the brush on the tray, rattling the easel.

"Go get ready for bed."

The boy shot one more searing glare at Nathan before heading to the bathroom.

"Is he okay?" Nathan asked.

"There's a bump on his chin." She wrapped her arms around her waist.

"I'm sorry," he said. "I did tell him to slow down."

"Mmm-hmm." Cheryl didn't look at him. She stared down the hallway.

Nathan cleared his throat. "Can Issy sleep here again?"

Cheryl jumped. "I guess."

"I'll get her PJs." He handed Isabella to her.

"Don't forget the Pull-Ups."

"Right." Nathan grabbed bags and brought them to his apartment. Then he dug for everything Issy needed.

Back in Cheryl's place, he handed her the pajamas. She shoved them back at him. "I need to check on Josh."

He swallowed. "Sure. I'll get her ready."

Cheryl headed to the bathroom.

He turned back to Issy. "Arms up."

Getting her undressed and dressed was easier with each attempt. But it was unnerving the way she didn't say a word.

After helping Issy in the bathroom, he tucked her into the bottom bunk.

Cheryl stood on the ladder. "I love you to the moon."

"Love you to the moon and back." Even as mad as Josh had been, he gave his mom a hug.

Nathan tucked the blankets around his daughter. "Night, short stuff."

"Night, little one." Cheryl brushed a kiss on Issy's hair. Without a word or a smile for him, Cheryl left.

He stood there, his fists on his hips. Exhaustion hit him like a two-by-four. His feet dragged as he trailed Cheryl to the kitchen. "Thank you for the shopping help and letting Issy stay."

"Let's hope she doesn't have nightmares again." She filled the kettle.

"I could sleep on the sofa. Then you wouldn't have to get up with her." Nathan leaned against the archway separating the kitchen from the living room. Cheryl would never agree to his suggestion.

She turned and gave him a once-over. "Fine."

He straightened. "Really?"

She shrugged. "I need a good night's sleep."

He puffed out a breath. "I'll go change."

The kettle whistled and she added a tea bag to a mug. "All I have is the throw on the sofa. Bring a pillow and a blanket. And don't forget to lock the door."

By the time he returned from his apartment, Cheryl had disappeared. And he'd never gotten her to smile.

CHAPTER FIVE

NATHAN ROCKETED TO his feet and rushed into the kids' bedroom.

Issy was curled in a ball, whimpering. What should he do?

She jerked upright and screamed.

"Hey, hey." He stroked her back. "It's okay. I'm here."

Issy wailed, her cry ripping chunks out of his heart. "It's okay."

She shook so hard the bed rocked. "You're safe. It's okay," he murmured.

"Make her shut up," Cheryl's kid moaned.

Nathan scooped Issy up, bouncing her in his arms. That's what Cheryl had done last night. But she kept sobbing.

Heading to the living room, Nathan glanced at Cheryl's door. No movement.

Settling into the rocking chair, he stroked Issy's hair, hoping she'd stop shuddering.

"Mommy," she sobbed.

It was the only word she'd said, and he couldn't help her. "Sorry, kid, it's Daddy."

Her tears soaked his T-shirt. What the hell was he doing? He didn't know anything about having a kid. Issy had been screwed in the parent lottery.

"Are you hungry?" he whispered. "Need a glass of water?"

Issy whimpered. He rubbed her back. The chair creaked as he rocked.

"Come on. It's not so bad." He patted, bounced, rocked. Nothing he did calmed her. She sobbed nonstop.

He stared at Cheryl's bedroom door, willing it to open. She'd know what to do. He strained, hoping to hear her moving, anything to indicate she would rescue his daughter.

The only sounds were Issy's cries and the whir of the air conditioner.

Sighing, he hummed the cheery song Mom used to sing. The tune reminded him of better times. A time when he and his brother were on equal footing. Before they'd been compared and he'd come up lacking.

Issy's back eventually relaxed.

He searched for another tune. The only song that came to mind was "American Pie." He hummed and hummed, sometimes breaking into the words.

Halfway through the song her body molded to his shoulder. He slowed his rocking. This was only the second night and exhaustion already weighed his muscles like they'd been made of concrete. Would Issy always wake like this? The back of his head clunked the top of the wooden chair.

Cheryl's door opened. "She okay?"

He nodded, wishing she'd emerged twenty minutes ago.

"Good work." She closed the door.

Good work? That's all she had to say? He was dog-tired. But Issy was asleep and that was important.

In Josh's room, he tucked the covers around her chin. Brushing her hair back, Nathan sighed and returned to the sofa. His feet hung over the arm, so he curled into an uncomfortable ball.

Issy needed more help than he could provide. Why couldn't anyone see that? The little girl deserved better. Winging it, handling this crisis hour-by-hour, wasn't doing it. He yawned. Tomorrow he needed a real plan.

"Hey, Bess." Cheryl waved as the middle Fitzgerald sister entered the kitchen.

"Hi." Bess headed to the coffee station. "No Abby this morning?"

"She and Dolley are meeting with the accountant." It was strange that she was telling Bess what her sisters were doing.

"Better them than me." Bess rolled her eyes. "How are you and Josh settling into the carriage house?"

"Good." Sort of.

Having Nathan sleep on her sofa had kept her awake. With his daughter he was…different. When she'd finally fallen asleep, she'd had an erotic dream. Not about Brad, but Nathan. Her face heated and she bent over the dishwasher, hoping Bess wouldn't notice.

When Isabella had screamed, Cheryl had stayed in her room. Nathan had to learn how to calm his daughter. But she hadn't gone back to sleep until she'd checked on the pair.

"I understand Nathan moved in," Bess said.

"About a week ago." Cheryl pulled the last plate off the cart and set it in the dishwasher. Good. Now she could make Welsh cakes. "Did you know he had a daughter?"

"Daniel told me last night. Unbelievable." Bess splashed cream in her coffee. "Have you met her? What's she like? Shoot. I don't even know her name."

"Isabella. She's…quiet."

After she and Josh had run from Levi, Josh had been quiet. But Isabella *never* spoke. "I'm pretty sure she can talk. But she's only screamed 'mommy.' She has night terrors."

"The poor girl." Bess leaned against the sitting-area sofa and pulled her gorgeous red hair into a ponytail. All the Fitzgerald sisters had red or golden-red hair.

The sisters were awesome. They'd built a fabulous B and B out of their family home and then expanded the business to the mansion next door.

Cheryl wouldn't be surprised if her eyes turned green with envy. She envied them. Envied the fact that they had it so together. That they had each other.

But she had Josh. And that was enough. At least it should be. He was the reason she had to find the courage to ask Abby about working in the restaurant.

Between helping Nathan and Isabella, she hadn't figured out what to do about culinary classes. Maybe she wouldn't need them. She straightened her shoulders. It was time to talk to Abby.

"I get to meet Isabella tonight." Bess pushed away from the sofa. "Debbie and Samuel are having the family over for dinner."

Bess was engaged to Nathan's twin brother, Daniel. Another twinge of envy shot through Cheryl. If she had a family or a partner, life would be easier. "Don't be surprised if Isabella doesn't talk."

"If anyone can get her relaxed and talking, it'll be Samuel and Debbie." Bess tugged on a cap. "Time to work in the gardens before it gets too hot." She headed out into the courtyard.

Bess and Daniel had something special. All the Fitzgerald sisters had gotten lucky in love.

Once upon a time, Cheryl had, too. Brad was the love of her life. After he'd died—two years ago last month—she'd been adrift.

Now she wanted more. And that meant showing Abby she was an asset in the kitchen.

She grabbed a food processor and poured sugar in. After pulsing it, she let the swirling sugar dust settle. Voilà. Her first batch of caster sugar.

She carefully gathered the ingredients for the tea cakes, then painstakingly measured, mixed, cut and put a test circle of dough on the griddle.

When the timer went off, she flipped it. The cake was a lovely golden brown. And the other side came out perfectly, too. She split the cake and dusted it with the caster sugar.

She broke off a piece and let the warm spices and dried fruits melt in her mouth. "That's good."

"Those smell great," Abby said, coming into the kitchen and pulling off her coat.

"I think they're right." Cheryl pointed to the sample cake she'd tried. "Can you test one?"

Abby picked up the rest of the cake and bit in. "Delicious," she mumbled. "Why don't I make the filling?"

Cheryl smiled and grilled the cakes. Abby cut them open and dusted them with the sugar and spread the filling. They worked side by side in a nice rhythm.

"The guests will enjoy these." Abby packed the cooled cakes into containers.

"I'm glad." Cheryl bit her lip so she didn't grin too broadly. Growing up, she rarely received compliments. Maybe from her grandmother. Never her mother. This could be the perfect time to ask Abby about a job.

"Do you feel safer with Nathan living next door to you?" Abby asked.

"I guess." And the opportunity disappeared.

She wasn't about to tell her boss Nathan had spent the night in her apartment. Even though it was for his daughter, it didn't sound appropriate. "He was building your stairs yesterday." She changed the subject.

"I stopped by last night and was impressed." Abby bumped her shoulder. "Let's take them some cakes and check on their progress."

A little zing went through Cheryl. She was spending

too much time around Nathan, but she looked forward to seeing him.

Abby grabbed the thermos of lemonade she kept on hand for the construction crews while Cheryl took the cakes.

Male laughter came through the open carriage door. Hammer strikes rang out, the solid thuds echoing through the courtyard.

They stepped out of the sunlight and into the shadowy carriage house. Nathan, Daniel and Jed bent wood around the spiral curve. Cheryl couldn't tear her gaze away from Nathan's straining muscles.

"Clamp," Daniel called to Jed.

Jed handed it up to him like a surgical nurse.

"It's going to be gorgeous," Cheryl said.

Abby sighed. "I can't wait."

"What's going on the second floor?" Cheryl asked.

"Dining or private party space. Between Fitzgerald and Carleton House, we'll have plenty of rental space options."

Now was her chance. Cheryl inhaled. "Will you have full-time chefs working under you?"

Abby nodded, moving closer to where the men worked. "Line and sous chefs."

"What skill sets are you looking for?" Cheryl hung back, not wanting the men to hear her questions.

"I'll look for experienced chefs." Abby kicked a piece of wood out of her way. "I wish my old sous chef hadn't moved to Atlanta."

"Will I have the skills you're looking for by the

time the restaurant opens?" Cheryl's voice squeaked but she pushed the words out.

Abby's bright green stare pierced her. Cheryl forced her gaze not to drop to the floor.

"Are you still taking culinary classes?" Abby asked.

"I'm trying to fit more in next semester." But money was a roadblock.

Abby nodded. "Keep taking classes and we'll reassess in a couple of months."

"Thank you." Cheryl released the breath she'd been holding. She must have spoken more loudly than she'd intended because all three men turned toward her.

"We brought treats," Abby called and then sighed. "My stairs are gorgeous."

"Glad you like them," Nathan said.

The men dusted their hands and moved to the food table.

"What's on the menu today?" Nathan asked Cheryl.

"Welsh cakes."

"Never had them." He walked too close.

"This is the first time I've made them," she confessed, stepping back.

He took a bite and closed his eyes. "Great," he mumbled. "They melt... Ooh." He moaned and grabbed another cake.

His reaction made her stand a little taller.

This was what she wanted to do. Somehow she would find the money for culinary classes. She would prove to Abby that she belonged in her restaurant.

NATHAN PARKED HIS truck in the warehouse lot and Daniel pulled in next to him. Though he'd hated asking his brother for help, he couldn't haul all Issy's furniture in one load and he didn't have the time for two trips. His first lesson as a father—kids worried if you were late.

Daniel met him at the warehouse door. "I can't wrap my head around the fact that you're a dad."

Nathan snorted. "Do you think I can?"

Daniel slapped him on the back. "Maybe this will settle you down."

Nathan tamped his resentment. "Maybe I don't want to settle down."

"It's pretty sweet." Daniel had a goofy grin on his face.

Nathan opened the door. "I don't have a woman waiting for me every night."

Daniel grinned. "I do."

"It's good Bess is making an honest man out of you. You can carry on the Forester name and all that." Nathan wouldn't be having any more kids. Women didn't stick. Or he didn't stick with women. Better to love 'em and leave 'em, than to have them realize he couldn't read something as simple as the washing instructions on their clothes.

At the warehouse desk, Nathan gave his name and the employee handed him an invoice.

He took a deep breath, hoping the words would stay in order.

Monterey. White. Platform. Nightstand. Captain.

Storage. Dresser. Cubby. Mattress. Bench. Headboard.

He blinked, trying to make the phrases come together. He could picture the furniture, but the words didn't make sense. He took a deep breath. He could look at the boxes and visualize the layout.

A man pushed a pallet of boxes and furniture wrapped in packing material to the door.

"Walk me through what's on here," Nathan asked him.

"Platform bed with drawers. The headboard with shelves. The foot-of-the-bed shelves." The man touched each box. "End table."

Nathan closed his eyes. "Mattress? Railings? Dresser?"

The man pointed behind him. "Coming next."

His brother pushed the cart out the door and they filled Daniel's truck. When the worker arrived with the rest, Nathan signed the paperwork and they loaded his truck.

"Looks like we've got a night of assembly ahead of us." Daniel's door creaked as he opened it. "When did mom want us for dinner?"

"Six thirty." He checked his watch. It was already five. "If we put the bed together, I can handle the rest." As much as Nathan would prefer Issy sleeping at Cheryl's, it was clear Cheryl didn't agree. He rolled his shoulders. His sleeping on a short sofa hadn't been easy, either.

"Guess we'd better get back to the apartment." His

home. Nothing like Daniel's place. His brother had bought and gutted his own house five years ago. But then, life had always been easier for Daniel. Nathan had never wanted anything permanent.

Did he want it now? A home, a kid and a woman? No. Because he could only hide the fact that everything garbled in his head for so long. Hell, Cheryl thought he was illiterate.

He headed to the carriage house, his face burning. He hated the pity and questions he'd seen on Cheryl's face. He wanted her to look at him with desire, not sympathy. But he needed her help with Isabella. His daughter didn't deserve a father like him. She didn't deserve a disappearing mother.

This afternoon, he'd called Information, searching for Heather. There was no record of a phone in her name in all of Georgia. What kind of mother up and vanished?

But even with all the stress and the unknowns, having a daughter was pretty amazing.

When he pulled into the Fitzgerald House parking lot, Daniel and Gray were unloading. Nathan propped opened the door and ran up the stairs to unlock the apartment. Gray and Daniel followed with the bed frame.

"Heard you have a daughter." Gray forced the mattress around a tight corner. "Are congratulations in order?"

"Hell if I know." What else could he say?

Gray's eyebrows shot into his hairline. Embarrassed, Nathan headed back to the trucks.

Josh leaned over the stair railing and hollered, "I thought Mr. Gray and Mr. Dan were here."

"They're in my apartment."

Josh tapped his foot, the wooden sound echoing through the courtyard. "Can I help?"

Nathan blinked. Josh wouldn't give him the time of day, but he loved Daniel and Gray. "Can you carry the railings?"

Josh rushed down the stairs and made a muscle. "Yeah!"

Nathan balanced the box on Josh's shoulder. It was the only way the kid could carry it. The boy wobbled, but headed up the stairs.

Nathan grabbed another box. Josh was still making his way up the stairs.

"Can I help?" Nathan asked.

"I've got it," he grunted.

"Josh." Gray came down the stairs. "Let me carry that."

"Thanks," the kid gasped.

Gray could help, not Nathan. His gut twisted. Even after buying Josh art supplies, the kid detested him.

They emptied the trucks and stood in the extra bedroom, three men and Josh. The kid imitated their widespread stance, his arms crossed over his chest. Nathan had to smile. If he told Cheryl, would she be amused?

"I can lend a hand putting things together," Gray

said. "I should learn this stuff for when Abby and I have a child."

Daniel jerked. "Is Abby pregnant?"

"No." Gray's blue eyes gleamed. "She wants to open the restaurant first. But it's sure fun to practice."

"Watch the language." Nathan's gaze shot to Josh. Luckily, the kid didn't look like he understood what Gray was talking about.

Nathan rubbed the back of his neck. He missed sex. With Issy living with him, the chances of him getting lucky had fallen to zip.

The memory of Cheryl in her near-transparent T-shirt zipped through his mind. His body filled with enough heat to warm the carriage house in a Savannah cold snap. Then he sighed. He and Cheryl would never happen.

"What can I do, Mr. Gray?" Josh asked.

Gray looked over at Nathan. "What's first?"

Josh scowled. Of course he expected Gray to be in charge. Nathan pointed. "The bed."

With the three of them working together and Josh hauling cardboard to the hallway, they got the bed and shelving put together. And never looked at the instructions. His kind of assembly.

"I thought this would take longer." Without all the help, it would have. Nathan headed to the kitchen. "Anyone want a beer?"

"I'm good." Daniel shifted the dresser into place.

"None for me." Gray broke down cardboard. "This is a sweet bedroom setup."

It was. But now the walls looked dingy. And they needed pictures or artwork to make the place—warmer.

He heard Josh in the outside hallway. "Mom, Mr. Gray and Mr. Daniel needed my help."

Nathan's teeth snapped together.

Cheryl came in, staring her son. "You're not allowed to wander through the carriage house. We've talked about this. I don't care who you thought you were helping."

"But they needed me," he argued.

"Sorry, Cheryl." Gray gathered cardboard. "I should have made sure he had permission."

"Yes." Cheryl glanced around the room and smiled at Nathan. "The furniture looks great."

Her smile brightened the room. The heat that had dissipated ramped back up. "I need to paint the walls."

She nodded. "Did you wash the bedding?"

"Wash the bedding?" Nathan frowned. His apartment didn't have a washer and dryer. "I…I guess I'll take them to Mom's."

"You're back doing laundry at Mom's?" Daniel laughed.

"Ha, ha," Nathan shot back. Daniel never missed an opportunity to take a jab.

"I think we're finished. See you at Mom and Pop's after you gather your laundry." Daniel chuckled as he left.

"Sure." Nathan pushed on the ache in his temples

that always bloomed when he was with his twin. "Thanks for your help."

Gray also headed out. Josh followed the men. Hero worship was hard to watch.

"Josh, say goodbye and come back here," Cheryl said.

"Yeah, Mom," he replied.

"I could throw a load or two in for you," Cheryl offered.

It would be one less thing to worry about. "Thank you."

"No problem. Isabella's a sweet child." Cheryl picked up the bedding. "Has she said anything more?"

He shook his head. God, what if this was something she'd inherited from him? Dyslexia affected his speech. His chest ached. He didn't want his child to live through the same pain he'd endured in school. "We're having dinner at my parents. I won't be back for a while."

"If you trust me with your key, I'll make the bed."

"Thanks." He was so relieved, he yanked her into a big hug.

The bag of bedding dropped to the floor with a thump. Her arms clutched his waist.

It wasn't a move on his part. He was thankful for her help. But her breasts pressed against his chest. She stared up at him, her eyes going dark.

"Let go of my mom!" Josh stormed into the room. He pummeled Nathan's leg with sharp jabs.

"Hey, slugger." Nathan let go of Cheryl and she staggered back.

"Don't hurt my mom." Josh kicked him.

"Josh, stop." Cheryl caught his hand and pulled him away. "Nathan was thanking me for helping him."

"He touched you!"

"Not in a bad way," she insisted.

Nathan slumped onto Issy's bed. What the hell was happening? Had someone touched Cheryl in a *bad* way?

"Is…is everything okay?" *Are we okay?*

She knelt next to Josh. "Apologize to Mr. Nathan."

"He shouldn't touch you." Josh stuck his chin out.

"It's fine." Nathan ran his hands through his hair. He nodded at Josh. "He was protecting you. That's good."

Josh glared back.

Cheryl looked at Nathan. "It's never okay to hit someone." She squeezed her son's shoulder in silent communication.

"Sorry." The kid spit the word out like it was venom.

"I understand." Nathan nodded. "It's a guy thing. We have to protect our moms, right?"

Josh didn't answer. Thank goodness the kid didn't have superpowers or Nathan would have been incinerated by the fire in his eyes.

"I'll leave the door open when I go," Nathan said as Cheryl and Josh headed into the hallway.

"We'll keep an ear out," she said.

"Thank you."

But Cheryl had turned the corner.

Nathan didn't move. What had happened to Cheryl to make Josh so protective?

CHERYL ADDED THE numbers again. She'd spent the evening pulling financial information together for her school loan application.

Once more she wished she had a computer, but her old one had died six months ago. A new computer was a luxury her budget couldn't afford.

She would use her break tomorrow, and hope the B and B's business center was empty. Abby needed to know she was serious about wanting to work in the restaurant.

A knock sounded on the kitchen door. "It's me," Nathan said from the other side.

Her heart picked up a few extra beats. She'd avoided thinking about how Nathan had hugged her. Just a friendly hug. Then Josh had hit him. And when she'd tried to talk to her son about his behavior, he'd been so full of sass, he'd lost television privileges for the night.

But Nathan's hug had been…nice. More than nice.

Too bad she only had time in her life for one male— the pouting boy who'd been sent to bed early.

She took a deep breath and flipped the locks. Nathan pushed the stubborn door open. "I'll fix that."

"It's fine."

He stared into her eyes. Did he know she'd been thinking about him? About how good she'd felt pressed to his body?

"Where's Issy?" she asked, shaking herself back to the present.

"Asleep." He held his monitor. "Thank you for making the bed. I appreciate it."

He moved into the kitchen and the room shrank. She scuttled back and bumped into the kitchen table, knocking her papers to the floor. She began picking them up and Nathan knelt next to her. His shoulder brushed hers.

"I'll get this mess," she insisted.

"It's my fault." Nathan shook his head. "I know you're nervous around men. I shouldn't get too close."

Her face burned.

He held up a hand. "You may not believe me, but I would never hurt you."

She stopped gathering papers and took in a deep breath. "I know."

Or thought she knew.

He reached out a finger and stopped, like he was waiting for permission to touch her. She looked up and found his deep brown eyes locked on hers. She nodded.

"I won't hurt you." He touched her chin.

She forced herself to hold still. "My head knows. My body wants to run."

"Tell me why you're afraid. Did someone hurt you?"

She nodded, ashamed at her weakness. "Levi." Her mom.

His hand cupped her cheek. "I'm so sorry."

"Me, too." Her voice was a whisper.

It had been so long since a man had touched her gently. She leaned into his hand. His other hand touched her shoulder and he shifted closer.

Too close. She jerked. "I need to pick up this mess."

Nathan's eyes narrowed. Then it was like shutters slamming down. He scooped up the last of the papers from under the table. "What is all this?"

"My school application."

He stared at the papers in his hands as he stood. "But this is all numbers."

"I'm applying for grants." Loans. She held her hand out for the material.

He finally relinquished the papers, but his fingers grazed hers. On purpose? "Wouldn't this be easier to do online?"

She swallowed back a sigh, almost dropping everything again. "My computer died."

He tilted his head. "You can use mine."

"Yours?" She shook her head.

"No big deal." He headed out the door, leaving it open behind him. "I'll be right back."

Using his computer would save her time. But she and Nathan were becoming entrenched in each other's lives. She needed to be an island, focused on Josh, work and school.

That didn't sound like much fun.

Nathan came back into the kitchen. "Here."

He plugged in the laptop and set it in front of her. Leaning over, he opened the lid. With his arms encasing her body, his woodsy scent wrapped around her like a warm blanket.

What was wrong with her? She didn't think about men and their colognes and warmth.

"You can use this anytime," he said, sitting at the table. "You did me a favor. I'd like to do the same for you."

Was he planning to stay while she filled everything out? "I can bring this back when I'm done."

He shook his head. "It's nice to rest for a minute."

She logged in to the website, staring at the screen instead of Nathan. After registering for two classes, she headed to the loan website and entered her financial information.

Nathan pushed away from the table and prowled her kitchen.

Her neck ached, and she hated that he was behind her. Levi had snuck up on her too many times. "I have juice, if you're interested."

"No beer, right?" he joked.

"No." She looked up and the tension in her shoulders eased a little when she found he was across the room.

"I was kidding." He opened cupboard doors, finding a glass. "Do you want anything?"

"I usually have tea."

"Okay." He filled the kettle and turned on the burner.

"You don't have to do that." She rolled her shoulders but the muscles wouldn't relax.

"I'm on it."

She went back to the computer, but watched as he went through her cupboards.

"Do you want this sleepy stuff?" he asked. "My mom drinks that, too."

"Yes, thanks." Even though he looked like his twin, sometimes she forgot he was a Forester.

She focused on the screen, wishing he would finish and leave her apartment. The kettle whistled and he made her tea, setting the mug next to the computer.

Leaning over her head, he looked at the screen. "You're applying for a loan."

Darn it, he could read after all. "Yes."

He rubbed his chin, the rasp of his stubble the only sound in the room. "Hang on. This might be the answer."

What was he talking about?

He took a seat, setting his glass down. "I have an idea."

"What?"

"We could...work together." His eyes gleamed. "I could help with your school expenses. You could help me with Issy. Teach me to be a good father."

"What?"

"I need help. You need money." He caught her hand. "When you go to class, you'll need someone to watch your kid."

"But..."

"We can work together." He scooted his chair closer. "I want to make sure the renovation goes without a hitch and that means putting in long hours. And I don't want to screw up with Issy."

"We'd share child-care duties?"

"Yes!" His fingers tightened on her hands. "We could work together, be a team. Eat together. Take care of each other's kids."

She pulled her hand away and rubbed her head. "This doesn't make sense."

"How much is your tuition?"

She blurted out the number.

"I can pay that." He set his hands on her legs and leaned in. "We can help each other."

She slid her chair back with a screech. What was he assuming she would do for tuition money? "Don't touch me."

His hands shot up and he shifted backward. But he was still too close.

"You want me to trust you with Josh?" The only thing that mattered in her life?

"I trust you with Issy." His gaze was too intense.

"But…" He didn't know anything about kids. About keeping them to a schedule, keeping them safe.

"Help me." He waved a hand at the computer. "And I'll help you. Helping with your education is a better use for my money than just sitting in my checking account."

She swallowed. "You have that much sitting in your checking account?"

"I know I should invest it." He shrugged. "Maybe buy a house."

Nathan's child monitor erupted as Issy whimpered.

"I've got to go. Think about this. Please." He touched her face and headed to the door.

After throwing the locks, Cheryl left her hand on the smooth wood. Could she trust him?

The idea of not incurring debt was tempting. And it might ensure a position for her in Abby's restaurant.

And, to complicate everything, Nathan was the first man she'd been attracted to since Brad. An ache formed behind her eyes.

If she accepted, she would have to trust Nathan to keep Josh safe. A man who'd had a daughter for two days. What kind of mother would that make her?

CHAPTER SIX

NATHAN JAMMED HIS cap on backward and nailed on risers. He was fueled with coffee. Not because of Issy's nightmares. This time he'd lost sleep because he was worried Cheryl would reject his suggestion. He wanted to call, to find out what she was thinking, but he was giving her space. Besides, he didn't have her phone number.

He placed the board, set the nails and banged them into place. Joint parenting would work. Cheryl just had to say yes.

"You're early," Daniel called over the music Nathan had selected. His brother headed to the radio.

"Don't touch." Nathan pointed with his hammer. He'd gotten in early, partly so he wouldn't have to listen to the hard metal crap Daniel loved and partly because Issy had been up since five. She was eating breakfast with her grandma now. And bluegrass played from the battered player. His kind of sound.

"Do I have to listen to this all day?" Daniel complained.

"Yup." He set another riser and nailed it into place. He and Daniel worked together for a couple of hours, setting and pounding in the steps. "Railings come today," Nathan said when they took a short break.

Daniel guzzled from his water bottle. "What time?"

"Noon."

"Good. We can anchor it this afternoon."

Nathan nodded, wiping the sweat from his forehead.

"What are you going to do about your daughter not talking?" Daniel asked.

"I'll give it another week." Or two. Nathan slapped a hand on his thigh and sawdust flew. "Maybe there's been too many changes in her life."

Daniel tilted his head, looking at his twin. "It's... odd."

"I know." He pinched between his eyebrows. "I don't have a clue what kind of life she had before this."

"Maybe you should take her to a doctor."

"As soon as she's added to my insurance." Mom had contacted the health insurance company, and he was waiting on paperwork. "Let's get Abby's steps on."

They finished the risers and released the clamps. "Pretty gorgeous work," Nathan said.

They ate lunch while waiting for the railing. And waited. Had he'd given the supplier the wrong date or time?

Finally the beeping of a backup alarm sounded.

"There's the railing." He exhaled, heading to the door.

The iron railing was a thing of beauty. After he and Daniel anchored it into place, his brother gave him a high-five.

"Just like I imagined." Pride had Nathan standing a little straighter.

Daniel picked up his tools. "I'd better head to the Abercorn site."

"I think I'll see if Abby wants to look at her stairs."

"You're just looking for treats," Daniel said, heading out the door.

"It is pretty great working here." Nathan tucked away the clamps scattered on the floor and swept. Maybe Cheryl would be in the Fitzgerald kitchen and have an answer for him.

He needed her help. This was the perfect solution. What else would convince her? A kiss? Not likely. Cheryl jumped if he got too close.

But he'd touched her cheek and she'd let him. Even settled her face into the cradle of his hand. He'd never dated a woman like her but, damn, he wanted to kiss her.

He knocked on the kitchen screen then walked in. Even though Fitzgerald House was air-conditioned, the heat from the ovens hit him first. At least the sweat on his brow could be blamed on that. But it was really because Cheryl was leaning over to pull out a tray and her ass was…right there. Cupped in shorts.

He wanted his hands on those rounded cheeks. Not the cheeks he'd touched last night.

"Hey, Nathan." Abby blew strands of hair out of her face. "What's up?"

He ripped his gaze away as Cheryl turned. Lord. Her tank top clung to her breasts. Was she trying to kill him?

"I thought you might like to see the finished stairs." He forced the words out through clenched teeth.

"It's done?" Cheryl set the tray on the counter.

He nodded. This was ridiculous. He didn't get

tongue-tied around women. Not from lust. His speech problems were from dyslexia.

"I need to wait for the next batch of madeleines to come out of the oven," Abby said. "Then I'll run over. Cheryl. Go check it out."

"Are you sure?" Cheryl asked.

"Go," Abby insisted. "I'm five minutes behind you."

"I guess." Cheryl avoided his gaze as she pulled off her apron. She brushed past him as he held the door and he inhaled her sweet scent and wished he could take a nibble.

"What?" she asked.

"Hmm?"

"You snorted," she said.

"I was thinking how good you smell. Like a cookie."

"And that disgusts you?" Her eyes were huge.

They stepped into the dimly lit carriage house. "No." He touched her arm. "I was thinking I'd like to take a nibble out of you."

Her hands clasped against her chest. "What?"

He stepped closer. "You heard me."

She stood there, her mouth open enough that he could see her pink tongue. "That's not a good idea."

He inhaled. "I can't help it."

She paced away. "I was thinking of agreeing to your offer."

Everything inside him lightened. "Really?"

"I was." She waved her hand between them. "But I don't want you to think about nibbling. There won't be any nibbling."

A chill rolled down his spine. What did he expect? No one as sweet as Cheryl could be interested in someone as stupid as he was. "I get that."

"We'll work out a schedule." Her hands twisted in front of her belly. A firm, slim belly. Not that he would ever see it in the flesh.

"Yeah, we'll do that."

"Good. Maybe we should talk tonight."

"Dinner?" he asked.

"How about after dinner?"

She didn't want to eat with him. That was fine. But an ache grew in his chest, like she'd stabbed him with a chisel and thrown salt on the open wound.

Cheryl headed toward the stairs like she couldn't escape fast enough. "This is beautiful."

She stroked the railing and the sight of her fingers on the curved metal went right to his groin. Didn't the woman know what her innocent moves did to him?

"I love it!" Abby hustled into the carriage house. She stopped next to Cheryl. "Can I stand on it?"

He nodded. But the pride he'd felt in his work dissipated. At least, Cheryl had agreed to help him with Issy.

What else could a guy like him expect? That Cheryl would be attracted to him?

She wasn't that stupid.

CHERYL GRABBED HER KNIVES, tucking them in her tote. "Are you ready?"

Josh glared. "I don't want *him* to watch me."

"I need to get to school." It was her first class. Nathan had paid her tuition and would be watching Josh tonight for the first time.

They'd helped each other for almost two weeks. Isabella had gotten into Josh's day care and they'd taken turns dropping off and picking up the kids. She took a deep breath. And she'd made it clear there wouldn't be any hanky-panky between them.

Nathan *was* making her life easier. And going to school should help her qualify for a job in Abby's restaurant.

"Grab your stuff." She picked up the list she'd written for Nathan. Bedtimes. Reminders on brushing teeth and taking showers or baths.

"Why do I have to go there?" Josh whined. "Babysitters always come to me."

"This is different," she said.

"I never have any fun." He shoved his sketchbook into his backpack. "You're always gone."

Guilt made her stomach churn. How could she explain she was trying to make a better life for them? "Bet you'll have fun."

"If it was Mr. Gray or Mr. Dan, I would." He trudged to the back door. "But it's the b—"

"Stop." Josh had called Nathan butthead too often. "No name calling."

He shrugged. Then stood on his tiptoes, but couldn't reach the lock.

She leaned over his head and unlocked the dead bolt. Before she opened the door, she knelt and took his shoulders. "This is best behavior time. You need to show Isabella how to be good."

"She's a baby."

"She'll be like a…a little sister." She regretted the words the minute she said them. "You can show her how to be a big kid."

His eyes narrowed. "I guess."

They headed to Nathan and Isabella's apartment. Josh knocked, tapping his foot as they waited by the door. And waited.

Her son looked at her. "Should I knock again?"

She nodded. Had Nathan forgotten?

"Coming," Nathan's muffled voice called out as Josh pounded harder.

The door opened. Nathan's hair stood straight up. Isabella was tucked under his arm like a football. "Sorry. We were cleaning."

Noodles were mushed in Isabella's hair. A streak of tomato sauce was on her cheek. Cheryl pressed her lips together, trying not to laugh.

"Don't you dare," he whispered.

She laughed. Couldn't help it.

Nathan stepped away from the doorway to let them in. A few toys were scattered on the living room floor. As Cheryl walked past the kitchen, she saw dinner dishes still on the counters and table. Tomato sauce decorated the booster chair. A pile of noodles sat on the floor.

"Rough dinner?" she asked.

"I have a new motto. Make Issy use a fork." He

rolled his eyes. "And move the plate away from the table's edge."

"Josh, help pick up, please," she said.

Her son frowned.

"Hey, thanks for the doctor you recommended," Nathan said. "I finally got an appointment for Issy."

"Good. You'll like her." And maybe they would find out why Issy wouldn't talk.

"I made a list." She started to hand it to Nathan, but his hands were full of mucky kid.

"Can you set it down?" Nathan looked around. "On the counter."

"Will do." She walked into the kitchen and wanted to start cleaning, but didn't have the time. "Be good," she warned Josh before she left.

As she walked to school, her thoughts stayed with Nathan and the kids. Had he read her list? Were the kids in the bath? Had he cleaned the kitchen before the sauce and noodles dried?

In class, the students sharpened their knives. Not the time to be daydreaming. Abby had lent her Fitzgerald House's knives, otherwise Cheryl would have incurred more debt. Then the students practiced on onions.

Using carrots, they moved on to julienne cuts and then chiffonade, continuing through the techniques she'd already learned thanks to Abby.

"You've had instruction," the professor noted.

"I work for Abby Fitzgerald," Cheryl explained.

"She's talented. I've tried to get her to teach a class or two."

"She's busy with the B and B." Cheryl smiled. "And just got married."

"I'll get her eventually." The professor walked to the front of the room to dismiss the class.

After cleaning her knives, Cheryl rolled up the case. Wouldn't it be wonderful to have people wanting you to teach their classes?

Stepping out of the air-conditioned building, she stripped off her chef coat, glad she'd worn a tank top.

The streetlights blinked on as she made her way through the square. Laughter and voices carried from hidden corners and people filled the sidewalks. A fountain splashed on the opposite side of the square.

A photographer crouched behind a camera set up on a tripod. From the glint of the streetlight off the red curls, the woman had to be Dolley Fitzgerald. Dolley had started a photography career after apprenticing with Liam, her boyfriend. It gave Cheryl hope that she could learn a new career, too.

Dolley spotted her and waved.

Cheryl waved back, but didn't interrupt Dolley's work. She wanted to get back to Josh. He should be asleep by now.

In her apartment, she put away the knives. Unlocking the kitchen door, she propped it open.

Nathan must have fixed her sticking door because it opened easily. He could really be thoughtful.

His door was open. She rapped softly, not wanting to wake the kids. When there wasn't an answer, she moved into the apartment.

Nathan was sprawled in his lounge chair, a beer in his hand. A baseball game played on the flat screen, the volume low.

Her shoulders tightened. "Were you drinking around the kids?"

His head jerked. "Hello to you, too."

She waved away his sarcasm. "Did you drink around my son?"

"I just sat down. Decided to have a beer." He pushed out of the chair.

She crossed her arms. "Please don't drink around Josh."

"It's *one* beer." Nathan held up a single finger. "But I'll always make sure he's asleep."

Levi had never had just one beer in his life. She chewed her lip. The rumors about Nathan's drinking had made her think he was a heavy drinker. Rumors could be wrong. But this was her son. "I'd rather you not drink at all when you're watching him."

"Fine." He headed down the hall.

"Wait. How did it go?"

Nathan turned, his eyebrow arching over his caramel eyes. "He's as suspicious of me as his mother is."

"What happened?" Her hand clapped over her mouth.

"He told me I wasn't doing anything the way you

would. That he didn't need to go to bed when I told him to, even though I showed him the note." Hurt filled his eyes, leaving them a rocky brown. "He'd rather be with Mr. Gray or Mr. Dan."

"I'm sorry." Was Josh reacting to her apprehension? "I'll talk to him."

"I put him in my bed. He refused to get in Issy's girly bed."

"I didn't even think about where he would sleep." She'd been too worried about Nathan staying on Josh's schedule. What kind of mother didn't think about where her son would sleep?

They walked into Nathan's bedroom. A canopy bed was set against the wall. Not the bed she pictured this large man sleeping in. She pinched her lips together, holding in a laugh.

"Yeah, yeah." Nathan pointed a finger at her, his voice soft. "It was easier to keep the Fitzgeralds' bed."

She went to pick Josh up.

"I've got him." Nathan pushed back the covers and scooped up her son.

"What about Issy?" she whispered, wanting to carry her son.

"I've got the monitor." It was clipped to his waistband.

She followed them into her apartment and couldn't help but admire the way his shorts hugged his butt. Had she ever admired a man's butt before? Even if

Nathan usually looked like he'd just rolled out of bed, he was in shape.

He headed to Josh's bedroom. The night-light made the room intimate.

"Do you want him on the top bunk?" he asked.

It was too dangerous to carry him up the ladder. She flipped back the covers on the lower bunk. "Put him here."

Nathan settled Josh in the bed before pulling up the covers and brushing his hair back. "Sleep tight."

A chill ran through her. That was *her* job. *She* was the one to tuck Josh in and smooth back his hair.

She bent and brushed a kiss on his forehead. "Love you to the moon and back."

Backing up, she bumped into Nathan. He wrapped his arms around her, pulling her against his chest. His body was a furnace. She went from cool to sizzling, like a chicken breast tossed into a fiery pan.

"Careful now." Nathan's breath fluttered around her ear. His voice was low and gravelly and made her insides melt.

She couldn't move. Stepping forward would bang her into the bed. Behind her was a hot wall of man.

His hands rubbed her arms like he was soothing her. "You're shaking."

Shaking? "I…"

No man had touched her this way since Brad had died.

No one except Levi. And he'd mashed his disgusting mouth against hers. She shivered harder, frozen.

Nathan turned her around. She was pinned between his heat and the bed. Her every breath filled with his scent of citrus and fresh-cut wood.

"Are you cold?"

She couldn't speak. Shaking her head, she rubbed her arms, but that only made her think of the way his hands had touched her. Was she getting sick?

There shouldn't be any sparks between her and Nathan. But she couldn't stop staring into his dark eyes.

He tipped her head up with a finger, his concerned gaze locking on hers. "Are you all right?"

"Fine," she croaked.

There was a rustling on the monitor attached to Nathan's shorts. Isabella whimpered.

"Shoot." He stepped back.

She pulled in a deep breath, the air still infused with his scent.

"I have to catch her before she goes into a full meltdown." He backed up, worry furrowing his forehead. "You're okay?"

"Perfect." She followed him to the kitchen. "It's been a long day."

He hurried out the door. "See you tomorrow."

She waved, but he'd already turned the corner. The lock on the kitchen door clicked and she let her forehead thump on the wood. She sure hoped she was getting sick. Because the other option, being attracted to Nathan, was not possible.

No nibbling. She'd made that rule. So why did she want to take a big bite out of someone she barely trusted?

CHAPTER SEVEN

"WE'LL GET ISSY caught up on her immunizations." Dr. Sanders made notes on the chart in her hand.

"Okay." Nathan didn't care about immunization. He wanted to know why Issy wouldn't talk.

The doctor wasn't much older than Nathan, but her hair was already showing strands of salt and pepper. She had an aura that made him trust whatever she said.

The doctor showed Nathan where she was on the height and weight chart. Well, where she should be. She wasn't on the charts.

Why couldn't anything in his life be regular? Was one day of normalcy too much to ask? "She eats well."

"Keep that up. Offer healthy snacks, nothing too salty or sugary."

"Got it." Cheryl always gave Josh and Issy carrots, fruit and those weird rice cakes that looked like anemic hockey pucks. He'd ask her to shop with him. It was better than trying to read the books and parenting magazines. It would take him hours to get through those. This parenting gig wasn't for sissies.

"What about her speech?" He set his hand on Issy's shoulder. "She doesn't talk."

His little girl looked at him, her bottom lip caught between her teeth. She leaned into him and he wrapped an arm around her, rubbing her back.

The doctor sat on the rolling stool face-to-face with Issy. "Can you tell me your name?"

Issy buried her face in Nathan's belly. Something warm wormed its way through his chest. She wanted comfort—from him.

"You can tell the doctor," he encouraged her. "She's nice."

Issy shook her head. Her finger covered her lips.

"I have dyslexia," he choked out. "Is this another form of that…flaw?"

"Dyslexia isn't a flaw." Dr. Sanders touched Issy's nose. "You just interpret the world differently."

Easy for the doctor to say. She didn't have to live with the challenges. And the label of being slow in school.

He didn't want that for Issy. He wanted her life to be normal.

"There have been a lot of changes in her life." Dr. Sanders kept a smile on her face. "Has she said anything?"

He let out a deep breath. "'Mommy' once."

The doctor pulled out an otoscope. "Open your mouth, sweetheart."

Issy always did what she was told. Never talked back. Nathan couldn't relate to a child like that.

The doctor peered at her throat.

"There's nothing physically wrong with this little cutie." Dr. Sanders gave Issy's shoulder one more pat. "We can go down the path of checking out all the options."

"Yeah. I want to know." He wanted a pill, a treatment. Anything that would show he hadn't passed his defects on to his daughter.

He held Issy, wincing every time the nurse stabbed her with a needle and rattled off the vaccine names. The information Heather had left hadn't showed Issy getting any vaccinations in three years, so they were catching up.

"It's okay, Busy Issy." He pressed a kiss to her forehead. "It won't hurt for long."

Dr. Sanders came in as he pulled on his daughter's bright pink shirt. "Do you have any other questions?" the doctor asked.

"Um, bedwetting?"

"At this age, it's not unusual to not have full control. Limit her liquids at night." The doctor made a note on the chart. "Make sure she goes to the bathroom before bed and use a nighttime diaper. I'll get you more information."

He nodded. Cheryl had told him the same thing.

The doctor handed him a pile of pamphlets. Nathan suppressed a groan. It would take him forever to decode the information.

"Come on, Issy."

He needed to get back to work. Hell, he'd been gone for almost two hours. Now that they'd roughed in the walls, the electricians were supposed to start rewiring the entire carriage house. But the electricians hadn't arrived by the time he'd needed to take Issy to her appointment.

On the way to his truck, he turned his phone back
on. Jed had left him a message.

Called the electricians. They had start date wrong.
Daniel pulled us for framing at Abercorn.

Damn. Had he messed up? He checked his clip-
board and the emails he'd sent to the supervisor of
the electricians. The date was the same. For once, this
wasn't his screw-up.

He signed Issy back in to day care and watched as
she joined her class. He'd been lucky to get a spot in
Josh's day care.

The teacher read a book. Issy sat on the floor next
to another little girl. His daughter nodded, never saying a word. The kids stayed quiet, but there were still
rumbles about the story.

If Issy didn't have physical problems with speaking, what was wrong?

Since there wasn't any work happening on the restaurant, he headed to his apartment and caught up on
paperwork. Payroll was due.

When Pop had first gone to Texas for his cancer
treatments, Nathan and Daniel had tried to do all the
bookkeeping Mom usually handled. That had been
such a disaster, they'd finally hired an accountant.

The accountant preferred getting everything by
email, but Nathan didn't trust his brain. Sometimes
what he typed wasn't anything like what he intended.

He double- and triple-checked his crew's hours and

then pulled together the information for the invoicing. His head ached by the time he shoved the paperwork into a folder. He should have enough time to drop off the files and pick up the kids.

Even though he drove to the accountant's every two weeks, when he turned the corner nothing looked familiar. *No.*

He stared at the buildings. Had he ever been here? He slammed his hand on the steering wheel. The street signs were in a foreign language.

He pulled into a small lot. He couldn't tell if this was private property or a public parking lot, but at this point it didn't matter. Pulling out his phone, he called up his GPS app. At least he could use verbal commands.

He didn't have a clue if the address the GPS's female voice rattled off was right. He doubted anything would make sense right now. He pulled out of the lot and waited until the directions caught up with him. Some white-haired guy tooted. Nathan waved. The guy could have been mad or someone he'd known all his life. He was clueless.

Each turn had his heart pounding a little faster. Nothing looked familiar. Hell, what was the bookkeeper's name? Had he already been on this street?

He drove by Sadie's, recognizing the bar by the colors on the sign. He could almost taste the ice-cold beer. Was he close?

Two more turns and the GPS had him pulling into a strip mall. It looked right. He matched the address on the storefront with his phone and headed to what he hoped was the right door.

The receptionist looked up. "Can I help you?"

"I'm dropping this off for…" The name wouldn't come. "Our accountant." God, he hated looking like an idiot.

"Kerrianne Dreyer?"

Kerrianne. That was her name. "Yeah."

She shook her head. "Her office is across the street."

Shit. "Really? Which one?"

She pointed out the window. "Right there."

"Thank you." His cheeks felt hotter than a welding torch. He could make out a *K* and *D* on the sign.

He barely waited for the traffic to clear before crossing the street. The door jingled when he shoved it open.

"Hey, Nathan." Kerrianne emerged from her office, her white hair piled in a bun. She'd babysat him and Daniel as kids, which made forgetting her name even worse.

"Kerrianne." He pushed the panic back. "I've got the payroll and invoice info."

She checked her watch. "You almost missed the deadline. I wish you would use email."

"I like stopping in," he lied. Winking, he asked, "How else could I ask you out?"

"You couldn't keep up with me." Her cheeks turned pink. She looked through the information. "I'll let you know if I have any questions."

Out on the sidewalk, he exhaled a shaky breath,

taking his time crossing the street. At least he couldn't lose his truck. It was in plain sight.

He took a moment to roll his shoulders. It had been years since he'd gotten so turned around. He tugged a water bottle from the backseat and took a big swig, wishing it was something stronger. He checked the time. Cheryl would kill him if he stopped for a drink before picking up the kids.

To be safe, he paired his phone with his truck and requested Fitzgerald House as his destination. He'd probably drive to Tybee Island if he wasn't careful.

He didn't need the prompts from the GPS to get back to the B and B. He pulled in next to Cheryl's car. She was setting up the wine-tasting tonight and he had both kids until she was done. He would pick up Issy and Josh and figure out dinner. He'd just been at their day care center. This shouldn't be a problem.

But it was.

When he got out of the truck and headed to the street, he froze. Should he turn right or left from the B and B? Swearing, he pulled up the map app on his phone. This was ridiculous. He plugged in his earphones, just in case he ran into someone he knew. He didn't want people knowing he couldn't remember how to get his own damn daughter.

Finally, he found the day care. It was quiet. Too quiet. The receptionist was missing.

He signed out Issy and Josh and headed back to their classrooms.

Issy's room was locked and dark. His breath caught. Where was everyone?

Muffled voices came from a door down the hall. He rushed over and pulled it open. Josh talked with a teacher Nathan hadn't met yet. The teacher glared at him as he walked in.

Issy fit together a puzzle. She looked up at the creak of the door and smiled. Josh glanced over and scowled.

Exactly the reactions Nathan had expected.

"You're late." Josh moved over to a locker and pulled out his backpack. "You're supposed be here when the little hand is on the five and the big hand is on the six. The little hand is on the six."

"I had work to finish." He held out his hand for Issy and she put her hand in his. "Let's go."

The teacher walked over. "You're new?"

"Yes. Nathan Forester. I'm picking up Issy and Josh."

She put a protective hand on Isabella's shoulder. "She's…quiet."

Tell him something he didn't know. "There's been a lot of changes in her life."

"Normally, you'd be assessed a penalty because you're here after six, but we'll waive it for today."

"Thanks." He gave Issy's hand a little tug, but she ran to grab a folded paper and handed it to him.

"What do you have?" He knelt and opened the paper. Pink and white exploded on the buff-colored paper. "Wow. It's beautiful. What is it?"

Josh looked over his shoulder and sneered. "Her bed."

"It's wonderful." He folded the paper. "We'll hang it on the fridge."

She nodded. He needed to get magnets like his mom had used. She'd always hung Daniel's papers with A's on the fridge. The only thing she'd hung on the *wall of fame* was his art.

"Let's go," he said.

Josh threw on his backpack. Nathan tried to catch the second strap to help, but Josh twisted away from him.

Maybe Issy would like a backpack to carry things, too. His head pounded a little harder.

Outside, Josh pulled away, but Nathan caught both kids' hands. "We don't cross the street unless we're holding hands."

That was what Cheryl would want. He wasn't *that* stupid.

"Nathan?" A woman crossed the street and stopped next to them. "Nathan Forester?"

The blonde looked familiar, but he couldn't dredge her name. His brain was full of holes.

"Hey, darlin'," he said to cover up.

"You forgot my name?" She rolled her eyes. "It's Tammy."

"Of course I haven't forgotten you." He eased back. They'd been partners, sort of, in high school—selling drugs. "How's it going?"

"I heard you were back." She stared at the two kids. "What are you up to?"

"Back in the family business." He wrapped a protective arm around the kids.

"I thought you hated construction." She pulled out a cigarette and held it in her lips, flicking her lighter.

Nasty habit.

Issy whimpered and tucked herself behind his legs.

"Why don't you join me for a drink?" She jerked her head at the bar. "We can catch up."

His mouth watered, almost tasting the beer, but he shook his head. "I have to get the kids home and fed."

"Pity." She ran a manicured nail down his bicep. "I'm still in the business. Maybe you want to make a little extra cash?"

"Nope." He stepped away from her. *Hell, no.*

She blew out a stream of smoke. "We were good partners. Think about it."

After she walked away, he took the kids' hands again. "What do you guys think about pizza for dinner?"

"Pizza's for Saturdays with my mom." Josh's chin stuck out.

"Well, it's dinner tonight." He didn't have the energy to fight with the kid. Nothing he said would make Josh happy.

"That lady stank. Like a skunk," Josh said.

"Josh," he warned. But Josh was right.

"Smoking will kill you." Josh scuffed his toe and caught a rock on the sidewalk. "You have icky friends."

"She's not a friend." Nathan didn't have friends. He didn't let anyone get that close.

The street was clear, so Nathan stepped off the curb. Josh dug in his heels. "Don't cross in the middle."

Nathan bit back a retort. The kid was only six. He backtracked and they headed to the crosswalk.

As they approached Fitzgerald House, Nathan asked, "What's your favorite pizza topping?"

"Green olives." Josh let go of his hand.

Nathan hated olives. He knelt in front of Issy. "What do you like?"

She pointed to Josh.

"You like Josh?" He wanted her to talk. "We can't cook him on a pizza."

She giggled.

"No." There was a *you dummy* in Josh's tone. "She likes green olives."

And the small ray of hope that Issy's smile had kindled evaporated like the winter fog. Josh wouldn't understand he was trying to get her talk. This mute stuff was getting old.

"Is that what you like?" Nathan asked her.

She nodded.

"What about pepperoni?" She shook her head. "Sausage?" Another head shake.

In their apartment, he went through a list of ingredients, getting only one more yes. "Cheese and olives?" He couldn't keep the disgust out of his voice.

She nodded and ran to her bedroom. And came back dragging her ragged blanket. At least it was clean.

He ordered a large pie and made the kids' half

cheese and olives and his side a meat-lover's. Since the delivery person wouldn't be able to get into the building, he left his cell phone number. He would have to go outside when the guy called.

He missed his simple life. It might not have been normal, but it had been easier. In Atlanta he hadn't worried about much, just hiding his dyslexia. Here he worried about every damn thing.

"I'm hungry." Josh plopped into one of his kitchen chairs.

What the hell did he have that wouldn't ruin their appetites before the pizza arrived? Nathan grabbed the last banana. It was a little soft, but it would do. He snapped the banana in two. A trick he'd learned in high school.

Josh's eyes were wide. "How'd you do that?"

Breaking a banana was the way to get through to this kid? Since this was their last banana, he put the two pieces together and showed Josh how to break it. "I learned that trick years ago." And Daniel had never mastered the art.

"Can I try?"

"This is the last banana." And if they manhandled it too much, the kids wouldn't get a snack. "Next time."

He grabbed a plate for the slices and set it between Josh and Issy's chair. Then he picked her up. "Go ahead."

"I don't eat bananas." Josh smirked. "They're mushy."

Nathan wanted to beat his head against the door frame. He pulled out a bag of carrots. Thank goodness

Issy had pointed at them when they were shopping. He added a few to the plate. "These aren't mushy."

Issy held up her hands. Shoot. Kids needed to wash their hands before they ate. "Hit the bathroom before you touch anything."

He helped Issy down and she and Josh ran down the hall.

His phone buzzed in his pocket. The letters held in place long enough for him to decipher the readout.

"Hi, Kerrianne."

"I need to double-check Quint's hours. You have him working seventy hours last week on the Fitzgerald House project."

"Seventy? Hang on." Not possible. He checked on the kids as he headed to his bedroom. After Issy arrived, he'd moved his desk there. He flipped through the paperwork looking for Quint's time.

Q. Q. Q, he reminded himself. There. He pulled the sheet. Scanned the numbers. "Twenty. He worked twenty hours."

"That makes a lot more sense," she said.

"Anything else you need?" Had he screwed up more numbers?

"No, that was the only question. Have a good night."

"Yeah." Didn't he wish.

In the kitchen, he opened the fridge and pulled out a Southbound IPA. Popping the cap, he let the cold liquid slide down his throat. His eyes closed, his head rocked back.

What he wouldn't give to just leave. Head to a bar. Forget all the crap filling his life.

Footsteps sounded in the hall. Issy's quick ones. Josh's dragging steps. He took another swallow.

Josh stood in the doorway, his arms crossed. "You're not supposed to drink beer."

"I'm an adult. I can do what I want." Boy, was that a lie.

"My mom said no drinking."

He finished the bottle. "There. Done. Eat your snack."

At the snap in his tone, Issy sidled to the wall, shrinking into her little body.

"It's okay." He moved to put her in her booster chair, but she cowered.

"Don't hurt her!" Josh scrambled over and took her hand, as if he could protect her from a man his size.

He knelt in front of the two kids. "I would never hurt her."

Tears filled Issy's brown eyes. She trembled like she was in a blizzard without a coat.

He reached out but didn't touch her. "I'll never hurt you, sweetie."

Her thin lips shook. Her mouth opened, as though she might speak, but nothing came out.

The kid was breaking his heart. He opened his arms and she stumbled into his hug. He inhaled the sweet berry scent of her shampoo. "How about finishing your snack?"

She nodded against his shoulder. He set her in her chair. Josh hopped into a seat.

Nathan checked the clock. If he was lucky, Cheryl would arrive before bedtime. It couldn't be soon enough.

CHERYL STARTED THE dishwasher and then wiped the cart and the counters.

She couldn't stop smiling. It was nice having Abby's kitchen to herself, to be trusted with the wine-tasting preparation and cleanup. Well, she could do without the cleaning, but it came with the territory. All the Fitzgerald sisters cleaned when necessary.

Life might have been different if she'd had a sibling. Maybe her mom would have been a better parent. Maybe she would have been loved.

She grabbed the bottle of Jameson and topped off the cut-glass decanter in the library. It was part of the service Fitzgerald House provided, but she turned up her nose at the smell. Mom would have finished off the bottle, not caring that the whiskey cost a fortune. It was all about the buzz.

Cheryl locked the butler's pantry and the swinging door into the kitchen. She'd waited for a late check-in, but she could finally head home.

Halfway across the courtyard, she glanced at her apartment. It should be empty, but lights glowed from the window. She froze at the bottom of the steps. Who was in the apartment?

Josh was safe with Nathan. Threading her keys through her fingers, she crept up the stairs.

She set her ear to the door. Nothing. No footsteps. No voices. She slipped the key in the door. She couldn't quiet the metallic click of the lock, but at least the door didn't squeak when she pushed it open.

She tiptoed into the room. The hallway light was on. Had she forgotten to turn it off?

No. Which way should she go? Over to Nathan's or to check out her own apartment?

Josh. She needed to make sure Josh was okay. Her heart pounded as she kicked off her shoes, hoping her bare feet would be quieter.

The kitchen door was propped open and so was the door to Nathan's apartment. Had they been robbed? Creeping in, she strained to hear anything. There was the buzz of the television. And…snoring?

With her back against the wall, she slid closer to the living room. The noises grew louder with each step. She closed her eyes, took a deep breath and peered around the corner.

Nathan was asleep in his recliner. The television showed a ball game. And two beer bottles sat on the coffee table.

Her teeth snapped together. Hadn't she told him not to drink around her son?

She headed to his bedroom, stomping a little. Nathan didn't move.

The bed was empty. Her heart twisted in her chest.

Maybe Josh had slept with Isabella. She hurried to the little girl's room, running to the bed.

Only Isabella.

She gasped.

Racing back to the living room, she shoved Nathan's shoulder. "Where is he? Where's Josh?"

"What?" He opened blurry red eyes. "What's wrong?"

"Where's Josh?" she wailed.

Nathan rubbed the heels of his palm into his eyes. "Asleep."

"I checked your bed and Issy's." She punched his shoulder. "He's not there."

"Give me a minute." Nathan shook his head like a dog.

"I don't *have* a minute." She rushed to the open door. Would Josh have wandered into the construction zone? Was he hurt?

"Hang on."

Bare feet padded behind her. Nathan grabbed her arm before she headed into the dark recesses of the carriage house. "Josh is sleeping in his own bed."

"You left him alone!" She changed direction and rushed through her open kitchen door.

Skidding to a stop outside Josh's room, she tiptoed next to his bed. She climbed the ladder, needing to touch her son.

"Mom?" Josh murmured when she stroked his leg.

"Just me, baby. Go back to sleep."

"Mmm-hmm."

She half slid, half crawled down the ladder. Her heart pounded in her ears.

Nathan waited in the hallway. His arms crossed over his chest. "He refused to sleep in my bed."

"So you left him in an empty apartment?" She got in his face and caught a whiff of beer. "And you were drinking. I told you not to do that around my son."

"I had a hell of a day. Everyone is safe." He handed her the monitor. "I would have heard if he'd woken up."

"Over your drunken snoring?"

He glared at her. "Lighten up."

"And you grow up." She pushed against his chest and he flattened his hand on hers, holding it against his warmth.

Something flashed in Nathan's eyes. "I'm sorry."

He stepped so close their legs brushed against each other. He stroked her cheek. "I didn't mean to worry you."

Her anger deflated and desire filled the space it left. Why him? He was the opposite of Brad. Brad had been her hero.

She tried to escape but her legs wouldn't move. He cupped her cheek and she closed her eyes, savoring the feel of his hand on her face. It had been so long since a man had touched her.

"I had a crappy day." He leaned in. "I'm sorry."

He was going to kiss her. He tipped her chin, his face drew near. And the scent of beer assaulted her nose.

She stumbled away from him. She would never

trust a man who drank because he was having a bad day. "No."

He held up his hands like she'd pulled a gun on him. "I just…" His voice trailed off. His eyes searched her face, but she refused to look at him.

"I need to…study." She stared at the floor.

"Cheryl." His voice scolded her. "Can't we—"

"No." She shook her head. Ashamed that her body wanted him to stay.

He backed away. "I can't help wanting to kiss you."

"Yes, you can." Her heart thumped. "We're not going to complicate this."

He headed to the kitchen. "We already have."

NATHAN DUMPED LAST NIGHT'S beer bottles into the recycling bin. He should have picked up the place after Cheryl had kicked him out. Instead he'd had another beer.

He would never admit it to Cheryl, but he had a slight hangover. What had happened to his tolerance?

Miss Temperance League had happened. *No drinking around the kids. No this. No that.*

"Issy, time to get up," he called.

At least it was Cheryl's morning to feed the kids and get them to day care. Assuming she hadn't changed her mind.

He got Issy ready, taking her to the bathroom to strip off her wet diaper and encouraging her to sit on the toilet. Then he handed her underwear. Thank goodness she was adept enough to pull them on herself.

This was his life now. Potty training and dealing with a silent kid. Sometimes he wondered if this was karma for all his troublemaking years.

"What do you want to wear?" He opened her dresser drawer. Everything went together—because everything was pink.

He held up a shirt with some princess on it and another shirt with a different character.

She pointed to the princess shirt.

"Say the words, short stuff."

She giggled but just pointed again. He sighed. Parents deserved a lot more credit than he'd ever given them. He pulled out shorts and handed them to her.

With her dressed and his water bottles filled, he took her hand. "Let's go see Miss Cheryl and Josh."

She turned the right direction in the hallway and waited while Nathan knocked.

"Who's there?"

He rolled his eyes. "Nathan."

The door snapped open. Cheryl stepped back so Issy could step in.

Was she still mad? Cheryl's golden-brown eyes didn't give anything away. Had she reconsidered their arrangement?

"We're having pancakes, Isabella. Does that sound good?"

Issy nodded and walked in.

Cheryl started to shut the door but he stepped inside. The look she shot him was poisonous.

He touched her arm. "I need to make sure we're okay."

"*We* aren't anything," Cheryl stated.

"I mean…" He puffed out a breath, stalling. "You wouldn't take your anger out on Issy, would you? It's fine to be mad at me, but Issy…" He held up his hands.

"I would never take my anger out on a child." Her shoulders drooped. "You don't have to worry about that."

"Thanks."

He helped Issy into the booster chair Cheryl kept for her. "Have a good day, short stuff."

She giggled again. At least it was something.

"Thanks," he whispered as he brushed by Cheryl. "I'll see you tonight."

How could the man think she would take her anger out on an innocent child? Cheryl gritted her teeth. A child who'd been forced to live with a father she'd never met.

And what about the girl's mother? Why hadn't she told Nathan about Isabella? When she'd ended up in rehab, she'd had to leave her child with a stranger.

Cheryl scooped up pancakes and put a couple on Isabella's plate. "Josh, come eat while they're hot."

Her son dragged himself into the kitchen. "I'm tired."

"How late did you stay up?" she asked.

"I don't know." A sly look crossed her son's face. "Mr. Nathan just kept drinking."

Her stomach twisted. How many beers had Nathan had?

"Why didn't you sleep in his bed?"

"It smelled…funny."

What did that mean? She'd never smelled anything funny. But then she'd never put her head on Nathan's pillows.

"It was almost as stinky as the woman he talked to on the street. She stank, right, Issy?" He wagged his head. "He called her *darlin'*." Josh dragged the word out.

Isabella nodded but kept dipping pancakes in syrup and stuffing them in her mouth.

He'd almost kissed her last night and he was calling another woman darlin'? Anger twisted in her gut. "Did the woman come to his apartment?" she asked, trying to sound normal.

"No." Josh took a big chunk of pancake and crammed it in his mouth. "He had to leave us alone when the pizza arrived."

She blew out a breath. First he talked to some floozy. Then he ordered pizza and, third, he left a four- and six-year-old alone in the apartment. Her fingers tightened around the pancake flipper. She would give him a piece of her mind. These were basic childcare rules. Even he couldn't be this stupid.

She stewed while walking the kids to day care. Stewed while prepping salads and sides for a luncheon in the Fitzgerald House ballroom.

"Are you okay?" Amy, one of the Fitzgerald House staff, asked as they cleared dishes from the luncheon.

"What?" Cheryl shook her head.

"Are you all right?" Amy asked.

"Fine."

"You look like you want to take someone's head off." Amy shivered. "I was glad you weren't serving today. You might have thrown the food in people's laps."

"Do I look angry?" She bit her lip.

"I've worked with you for over a year." Amy shrugged. "You usually smile. Today you've got furrows between your brows."

Cheryl set the last plate on the cart and dropped her head back, trying to relax her forehead. "I'm—"

"Upset?"

She didn't know what she was. "Yes. I need to yell at the person who upset me." And who put her son in danger.

"Do you want to talk about it?" Amy pushed the loaded cart to the elevator.

"No." This was between her and Nathan.

"I'm here for you." Amy patted her arm.

She and Amy weren't far apart in age. Amy was twenty-four and worked at the B and B part-time while going to college. Cheryl had just turned twenty-nine, but listening to Amy's tales of work and school made her feel ancient. Amy visited bars and picked up guys. Things Cheryl had never done. The only time she'd even been in a bar was to find Mama.

"Are you setting up for the fiftieth wedding anniversary?" Amy asked as they loaded the dishwasher.

"I'm prepping appetizers for both the B and B and

the party." After she found Mr. Nathan Forester and gave him hell.

"You're frowning again."

Cheryl chuckled. "You're sure worried about my mood."

"Well, yeah." Amy raised her eyebrows. "If you're grumpy, how can I ask you for a favor?"

Cheryl dried her hands. "What do you need?"

"Marion scheduled me to serve for that wedding on the Fourth of July." Amy rolled her eyes.

Marion was the B and B's head of housekeeping and had given Cheryl her first shot at a job. "Marion's always fair."

"But this is a holiday. Who gets married on the Fourth of July?"

"A patriotic couple?"

"Yeah, yeah." Amy swallowed. "Could you sub for me?"

"I'll check with Abby and see if I'm cooking for the wedding."

"Would you?" Amy grabbed her hand. "My boyfriend wants us to go to South Carolina with his family. It's the first time I'll meet them."

"You make me feel old," Cheryl blurted out.

"You're not old."

"I'm a widow and have a six-year-old."

"If you let me dress you, people wouldn't think you were old."

Cheryl's eyes went wide. "I dress old?"

"Like my mother." Amy slung an arm over her shoulder. "But I can help with that."

Cheryl looked at her polo shirt and shorts. "What's wrong with these?"

"You have great legs, but you wear shorts that come to your knees."

Cheryl shook her head. "I'm a mother. I guess it makes sense I'd look like one."

"We'll shop." Amy grinned. "And you'll be a hot mama."

"Right." She rolled her eyes. "I'll check with Abby about the Fourth of July."

Cheryl started working on the appetizers. She'd made the pesto and tapenade crostini plenty of times. Now, she took out her frustration at Nathan on the garlic, bashing the cloves with the flat side of her knife. She blended, added ingredients and tasted. "That's good."

She set the bowl in the fridge and then worked on the tapenade. She hated to think what all these Kalamata olives cost. She'd priced them in her grocery store and they weren't in her budget. She measured out the ingredients and squeezed fresh lemon juice over them, inhaling the wonderful scent. The food processor ground away, reducing everything to a paste. She tasted, seasoned and tasted again. She'd have to wait for Abby to see if there was anything missing.

She finally took a break and grabbed the afternoon snack Abby had set out for Nathan's crew.

In the carriage house, a saw buzzed from behind

the central staircase. She placed the container on the table. The tray from lunch was still here, but all the sandwiches were gone.

"What kind of cookies do we have today?" Nathan's voice carried from the back of the building.

She checked. "Lemon bars."

Nathan stopped next to her, smelling like freshly sawed wood. She tried not to inhale, but she loved his scent too much.

When no one else wandered over, she asked, "Are you the only crew?"

"The crew was here this morning, but Jed and one of our helpers headed over to another site. Just me now." He stuffed a bar into his mouth, closed his eyes and chewed. "I *love* lemon."

She rolled her eyes. "I need to talk to you."

"Sure. You smell like lemons today. Did you make the bars?"

She sniffed her fingers. "I squeezed lemons for something else."

He caught her hand and pulled it close to his nose. So close, his stubble tickled her fingers. "You smell great."

"How can you flirt with me like this?" She spat the words at him.

"Because…" He touched her cheek. "I like you."

"Don't." She wrapped her arms around her waist. "Do you flirt with every woman? Did you flirt with the *stinky lady* yesterday?" Her words were fast and clipped, not masking her hurt. Hurt she had no right to feel.

His eyes narrowed. "I wasn't flirting with anyone."

"You called her darlin'."

"What kind of lies does your kid tell you?" Nathan's face darkened with anger.

She'd seen that look on Levi's face too many times. She scrambled back.

"I won't hurt you!" His hands formed lethal fists.

She jumped, knocking over the table. The bar container slammed to the floor and she fell on her butt.

He swore, kneeling in front of her. "Are you okay?"

Everything inside her crumpled. She was acting like a…a fishwife. "Josh told me about last night."

"What was there to tell?"

"You were drinking." Her head snapped up and she looked him in the eye.

"I had one beer before dinner. The others were after they went to bed."

"You left them alone in the apartment."

"How else could I get the pizza? Josh and Issy stayed in your apartment while the pizza guy came up the front steps."

She dropped her head into her hands. "I didn't think about that."

Nathan sat next to her on the floor. "Your son doesn't like me."

She shrugged helplessly. He was right.

"You acted drunk when I came in to get Josh. And I

couldn't find him." Her throat went dry. "You let him sleep in an empty apartment."

"He refused to sleep anywhere else. And I'm not drunk on two beers. Or even three." He took her hand. "I was exhausted, that's all. I'm having trouble getting Issy to sleep through the night. She keeps waking up screaming."

"Still?" She squeezed his fingers. "Has she said anything? Did you take her to the doctor?"

"Yeah. There's nothing physically wrong with her." His arms hung down from his knees. His head drooped. "She gets scared if someone yells."

"I noticed." She couldn't stand his dejection. She touched his arm. "Do you have next steps?"

"Dr. Sanders gave me the name of a…" He waved his hand, as if he couldn't remember the word.

"Psychologist?"

"Yeah." He leaned against her shoulder. "Thank you for everything you've done for Issy and me."

She nodded, her breath catching in her chest.

"You've helped…lay out my blueprint for parenting." He turned toward her. His eyes were as warm as melted chocolate. "You don't know what that means to us. To me."

"You're welcome." This was the nicest conversation they'd had.

He cupped her chin. "I really want to kiss you." His voice came out in a rasp.

Her body heated up like a pan on high flame.

"I…" There were plenty of reasons why she

shouldn't kiss him. "I…" Her breath whispered out. She couldn't think of one.

He inched closer. And waited.

Leaning in, she kissed him. Her forehead knocked off his hat.

He pulled her against his chest. She laced her arms around his neck, her fingers burrowing into his hair.

His tongue, flavored with sugar and lemon, brushed hers. His lips toured her face, stopping at her ear and trailing down her neck to her collarbone. She squirmed as desire bloomed in her every cell.

He tugged her closer until she straddled his legs.

"Ooh." Her nipples tightened and her legs wanted to clasp his hips and never let go. Warmth rushed through her, filling and thawing body parts that had been frozen since Brad had died. Dizzy and unbalanced, she clung to Nathan.

His tongue traced a path from her collarbone to her shirt. His stubble brushed the top of her breasts, sending fire down her spine. "The kids are in day care. Let's go upstairs."

The kids. Josh. Her job.

She had responsibilities, to her son and to Fitzgerald House.

Pushing on Nathan's shoulders, Cheryl wiggled back.

He groaned. "God, you feel good."

"Stop." This wasn't about feeling good. She had to put an end to this. "I have to get back to work. What if someone walked in?" Like one of the Fitzgeralds.

Her face flushed with embarrassment and not the fire that Nathan had kindled in her body.

"I'm really attracted to you." The low growl in his voice sent shivers through her.

"This can't happen. You know that." She scrambled off him, scooting on the dirty floor, and stood, locking her knees so she couldn't crawl back to his lap.

"Why not?" He pushed his hair back from his eyes. "Seemed like we were getting along just fine."

"I have responsibilities. This is stupid—"

His gaze darkened. "You think I'm too stupid to date?"

"No." That wasn't what she meant. "It's the middle of the day. I have to work. You have to work."

"So, tonight?" He towered over her. "You want to get it on tonight? My place or yours? Or maybe neutral ground. The hallway?"

His crudity was a slap in the face. "I can't believe you said that."

"I can't believe you'd stoop so low as to kiss someone you think is *stupid.*"

"I didn't say that!" She threw her hands in the air. "Stop putting words in my mouth. It's stupid for us—" she waved her hand between them "—to ignore our responsibilities."

He leaned down. "I'm sure you've heard the rumors. I'm the irresponsible brother. If you'd wanted responsible, you should have hooked up with my twin."

Shaking, she backed away. "I can't talk to you right now."

"Run away like you always do."

His voice was so soft, she wasn't sure she heard him. But she ran.

CHAPTER EIGHT

NATHAN SLAMMED THE hammer down, forcing the nail through the board with two strikes. Cheryl thought he was *stupid*. Sure, she'd backtracked, hemmed and hawed. But the word that had come out of her mouth was *stupid*.

She was just like everyone else in his life. Why did he bother trying? No one thought he could succeed. He worked twice as hard as normal people to accomplish the same amount.

At least she hadn't changed their arrangements with the kids. Although the last three days of handoffs had been downright frigid.

Hard to believe she'd been plastered to his body as they'd kissed. He closed his eyes. He *was* stupid. He wanted to kiss her again. He wanted to do a hell of a lot more than kiss.

With the door frame finished, he tossed the hammer toward his toolbox. His father's voice echoed in his head. *Take care of your tools.*

"Jed, let's lay out the kitchen. I want Abby to see her workspace."

Marking off where appliances and equipment would sit helped owners visualize their space. And he loved seeing the plans come to life.

Since this was a two-man job, Jed measured and Nathan placed tape. Blue for the kitchen islands. Red for appliances. In the dining area, they measured out the wait station and the base of the bar.

"How big of an overhang will the bar have?" Jed asked.

"Abby wants a wood top." He had a surprise for Abby. "How wide are the old carriage doors?"

Jed measured and called out the number.

"Let's use a quarter of that width."

"You're making the bar top out of the doors?" Jed asked as he measured.

"I thought it would be a great combination of the old with the new." Nathan grabbed a piece of paper and sketched out his idea.

"You should have been a designer." Jed grinned, his white teeth gleaming against his mocha-colored skin. "Miss Abby will love it."

"I'm a glorified carpenter." But Jed's comment soothed some of the tension Nathan was carrying from his fight with Cheryl.

"You're more than that. You pull this off, you'll be an artist."

Artist? Nope. "Just don't tell anyone." Nathan rolled his shoulders. "It might not work."

"Sure thing."

They finished and stepped back. "What do you think?"

Jed scratched his head. "I'm good with houses and buildings, but I've never built a restaurant. Can't quite picture how the tables and chairs will fit."

Nathan could. He was good at visualization thanks

to his dyslexia. "Once we pull the doors, I think she'll want to run tables along those windows."

"That, I can see."

"But I'll suggest booths along the wall."

"You've got a good eye."

"Let's see what Abby thinks." He pulled off his cap, pushed back his hair and yanked the cap back down.

He cut through the courtyard. Two couples sat near the frog fountain, sipping cold drinks. He'd better hydrate. The temperature and humidity were high enough to start worrying about heat stroke. That was Savannah for you.

He knocked on the kitchen door and walked in, the cool air-conditioning shocking after the heat.

Abby and Cheryl had their heads together. They turned at the slap of the door and Cheryl's smile evaporated when she saw him.

He wished he was surprised.

Abby looked over and grinned. "Is my restaurant done?"

He chuckled. She'd been asking the same question for two weeks. "Not quite. Wondering if you'll take a look at the layout."

"I already approved the plans."

"You did. But Jed and I taped it off." He shifted on his feet. "I'd like you to see the equipment layout before we drywall."

"Absolutely!" Abby pushed away from the table and grabbed Cheryl's hand. "Let's see what this looks like."

"I can start on what we discussed." Cheryl didn't look at him. Wouldn't want to get too close, would she?

"I want to see what it feels like with people on the line." Abby pulled off her apron.

Nathan held the door. Cheryl brushed by, giving him a whiff of her apple scent.

Abby waved to the couples in the courtyard, but dragged Cheryl down the path. "I'm so excited." She walked in the door and stopped, not saying a word.

Nathan rubbed his neck. She hated it.

"This is the bar?" Abby moved through the opening they'd left.

"Yeah. That's a pass-through." He shrugged. "Unless you want to leave one end open."

She pretended to pour a beer and hand it to Jed as he stood on what would be the patron's side of the bar.

Jed toasted her with the make-believe mug. "This will go down nice today."

She grinned. "Cheryl, come back and help me serve."

Cheryl walked through the planned opening. The women moved back and forth.

"How long can you leave the tape in the space?" Abby asked.

"Until the electrician comes to lay the coils for the heated floors." Nathan thought about the schedule. "Thursday."

Abby nodded. "It feels good to me, but I'd like one

of the bartenders working the event tonight to swing by and tell me what they think."

She looked at the end of the bar. "Will we be able to get a stool here? It's so close to the wall."

He stepped over. "I thought you could have a server station."

Cheryl inched away as he moved next to her. He gritted his teeth. Would she ever stop cringing near him?

Abby spread her hands as if she was holding out a tray. "Will people run into the wall, Cheryl?"

Cheryl skirted around Nathan, pretending to hold a tray. "They'd always have to turn left. It could work. What if the bar was round here instead of squared off?"

"We could try." Nathan wasn't sure if the old wood would take a curve. "Maybe the bar should stop here. We'd leave an opening without a pass-through on this end." Nathan grabbed the dark blue tape and made the adjustments on the floor.

"That's better." Abby tapped her lip.

In the kitchen area, Abby walked around the marked-off spaces. "This is all flattop?"

He nodded, pulling out the plans so she could match them with the space.

"Cheryl, stand here," Abby ordered. "Nathan and Jed, I need you, too."

He and Cheryl stood back to back.

"Can you both bend over like you're grabbing something from the shelf underneath?" Abby asked.

He bent at the same time as Cheryl and they bumped butts. He'd had his hands on her tight cheeks just last week. Cheryl inhaled. Her gaze shot to his and she took a step sideways. "It's tight."

"Too tight?" Abby chewed her lip and moved next to Cheryl. "I want all the work surface possible, but it makes the aisle really narrow."

She had them crowd around different spots in the kitchen.

"What are you thinking?" Nathan asked.

Abby and Cheryl sat on overturned buckets.

"I think the space between the lines is too narrow." Abby sighed. "I've worked in kitchens that packed their chefs in like sardines. I don't want that, but I hate giving up table space."

"What if the dishwashing station was in the kitchen?" Cheryl asked.

Abby grimaced. "I like the idea of keeping water away from a high-traffic floor."

"Let's move everything a foot and see if the dining area's too small." Nathan headed back to the kitchen. "This is why we're doing this, so you have the space you want."

Abby and Cheryl helped moved the tape over a foot. Then Abby had them go through the same bending exercises. Nathan missed the brush of Cheryl's butt. She was probably ecstatic.

"We could add tables so you could see that, too." Nathan moved to the center of the dining area.

"There are tables upstairs in the storage room, right?" Jed asked.

"Yes," he and Abby said together.

"Kemper will be here tomorrow morning. We can bring down tables." Jed checked the time on his phone. "I need to get over to the Chatham project."

Cheryl shifted on her feet. Was she nervous because he'd touched her? Disgust ate a hole in his stomach.

She turned to Abby. "Have you thought about how food will get up to the second floor? Especially during parties?"

He relaxed a little.

They moved to the central staircase.

"The stairs are a showpiece, but I sure couldn't climb the spiral with a heavy tray." Jed shook his head.

"What about the dummy system we use at Fitzgerald House?" Cheryl chewed her lip.

"I've been so focused on the kitchen design, I didn't think about second-floor service." Abby looked over at Nathan. "Can we get a dumbwaiter in here?"

"How wide do you want it?" he asked.

She and Cheryl looked at each other.

"Can you show Nathan the system we use in Fitzgerald House? I have to meet Dolley at the attorney's office."

Cheryl crossed her arms so tightly, he worried she would cut off her air supply. "Of course."

He and Cheryl traipsed across the courtyard in silence. Her hands twisted as they headed to the dumbwaiter built into the side of the kitchen.

"This is it." Cheryl pulled open the door. He took out his tape measure and notebook. Not that he used them much when he couldn't trust his brain to interpret what he saw. Handing the notebook to Cheryl, he asked, "Can you write down the measurements?"

"Sure." She gave him that look again. The one that said she didn't believe he could read.

He snapped the tape out, angry with…everything. Then he barked out the numbers as he measured.

He took the notebook back, intentionally letting their fingers brush. She snatched her hand away and tucked it behind her back.

"Really?" he asked.

"What?" Her gaze caught his. Her eyes were as big as spools of cable.

"You hate it when I touch you." He shook his head. Why did he punish himself like this? He frightened her. "Forget it."

He pushed past her. Time to leave.

"That's not it." She grabbed his shoulder. "I…"

He waited. Her apple scent flooded the air around them.

"Sorry I bumped you earlier. It wasn't intentional." He willed his feet to move but her hand still held him.

"It's not that I don't like your touch," she whispered.

He should leave. He didn't need to be humiliated. "Right."

"I was thinking about our kiss."

His head snapped up. Her face was bright pink.

He turned toward her. Their bodies were in each

other's space. And she wasn't pushing him away. "So was I."

"I just…" She took a deep breath. "I can't stop thinking about it."

As if she were a piece of glass, Nathan slowly cupped her chin. He paused, waiting for her to bolt.

She didn't. She leaned into his hand, closing her eyes. "I miss being touched."

He slid his thumb along her cheekbone. Her sigh warmed the space between them.

Stepping close, his other hand stroked her bare arm. Her taut muscles relaxed under his touch.

He cradled the back of her neck and tilted her head. He dropped his lips so they almost touched hers. "May I?"

"Please."

He kissed her with a sigh. A soft brush, so she didn't run.

A flick of his tongue on the seam of her lips and her tongue darted out to meet his. Sparks built between them and flared to life. He tugged her close and her arms wrapped around his neck like kudzu.

"Don't let go," he whispered.

His hands dropped to her butt, pulling her tight. A hip roll brought her into perfect alignment but didn't ease his growing ache. He spread kisses across her cheek, up to her eyes. When his teeth scraped her earlobe, she squirmed.

Pain and pleasure stole his breath. He buried his head in her neck, his breath blowing in and out like a bellows. His hands found their way to the delicate skin under her shirt. He smoothed and stroked, wishing he could pull the thing off.

She dropped kisses on his neck and up to his ear. Her touches were tentative, but grew bolder as she used her teeth and tongue.

A buzzer blared.

Cheryl broke away, gasping. "Shoot. I have to get that."

She tugged down her shirt and straightened her ponytail. "Do I look okay?"

She looked rumpled and sexy. Fabulous. Her lips were swollen and pink. Probably not what she wanted to hear.

"You're beautiful."

She looked panicked.

"Don't worry." He touched her cheek.

Her face lost most of its color. "My job is on the line."

The buzzer sounded again.

She rushed away. "Shoot. Shoot. Shoot."

He took deep breaths, trying to get his body under control.

He'd decided to stay away from Cheryl, but kissing her was a much better plan.

CHERYL CHECKED THE TIME. Again.

Nathan should be bringing the kids home any minute.

She touched her lips. Were they still puffy from this afternoon's kisses? Every breath she took carried his woodsy scent. Her skin still tingled from the touch of his hands.

She shouldn't have kissed him. He had too many problems already, but, Lordy, she wanted to kiss him again. It had been so long since she'd felt like a woman.

She pulled out extra plates, silverware and glasses. Would Nathan accept a dinner invitation? It was just chicken, salad and fresh green beans.

Would it look too obvious if she set the dishes on the table? She left them on the counter, ready to grab if he and Isabella accepted her invitation.

Footsteps pounded on the outside steps. Josh. Cheryl grinned, wishing she had a small portion of his energy. She opened the door as he hit the landing.

He grabbed her around the knees. "Mom. Mom."

"Josh. Josh."

He shoved his backpack into her hands. "I got to feed a bunny. Can we have a bunny? Please, Mom, please?"

Nathan came up, carrying Issy. He smiled at her, a little tentatively.

She smiled back and held the door open.

"What's this about a bunny?" Mama had always said no to pets.

"He was big and fluffy. I know we can't have a dog. But a rabbit stays in its cage most of the time. We let it out and it hopped around the room and right to me. And it ate lettuce from my hand. He was so soft. And I want one." Josh spoke so quickly her head spun.

"It was a really cool rabbit." Nathan jiggled Issy is his arms. "Right, short stuff?"

She nodded.

"What did you like best about the bunny, sweetie?" he asked.

Issy stroked Nathan's hair. And Nathan's smile dimmed. "Can you use your words?"

She buried her face in his neck. He sighed but headed toward the kitchen.

"You got to see this marvelous creature?" she asked, not wanting them to leave.

"Mom." Josh tugged on her shirt. "Can we have one?"

"I'll think about it." She handed his backpack back to him.

"That means no." He scowled. "I never get anything."

Nathan stopped walking and started to open his mouth.

She shook her head. This was her battle to fight. "I said I would think about it. I don't know how much a rabbit costs and what they eat."

Josh stomped off to his room.

"That was fun." She rubbed her arms.

"He's a kid."

Nathan set his daughter down. She leaned against his legs. The way she clung to Nathan reminded Cheryl of how Josh had acted after they'd run from Levi. Something to discuss with Nathan when Isabella wasn't around.

"The bunny was cute," Nathan said. "Long fur. Not sure what breed it was."

"I wish Abby had a no-bunny rule in the lease."

He stepped a little closer, brushing a finger down her cheek. "Are you okay?"

She swallowed. "Yes. You?"

"Worried."

"Why?" He didn't seem like the kind of man who worried about anything.

"I'm afraid you'll rethink what happened today."

She shook her head. "It was…lovely."

His eyes sparkled. "More than lovely."

"I was wondering if you and Isabella wanted to eat dinner with us."

"Oh, yeah." He stepped a little closer but didn't touch her. "I'd like that a lot."

Her body trembled at being near Nathan without touching him. This didn't make any sense.

"Issy and I will just drop her stuff off." When he stepped back, Cheryl missed his heat. Clearly, she was losing it.

"Maybe playing with Issy before dinner will help Josh's mood." While they were gone, she set the table and added the flowers she'd splurged on at the grocery store. "There."

"How come there's flowers on the table?" Josh tromped back into the kitchen. "And why are there extra plates?"

"Because flowers are nice and we're having guests for dinner."

He crossed his arms. "We don't have guests."

"Mr. Nathan and Isabella."

"Don't leave me with *him* again. Please." His tone was equal parts panic and sadness.

"Mr. Nathan helps us. A lot. I want to help them."

"I want it to be just you and me." He was full-on whining now. "Like it always is."

She knelt, holding out her arms.

He hugged her tight, his cowlick tickling her nose. Her son tried to be strong, but he was still her little boy. "I love you."

"Then we can eat dinner." He tugged on her arm. "Just you and me."

"I've already invited Isabella and Mr. Nathan." She stood, still holding him. His legs dangled down to her knees. She twirled in a circle. He giggled. She pretended to stumble, weaving around the kitchen. He giggled harder. Finally she slid to the floor.

"Mom. Mom." Josh patted her face, part of their game. "Are you okay?"

She eased him to the floor and tickled him. "I'm wonderful."

The kitchen echoed with his laugh and her demented cries.

"No more. No more." He scuttled on his butt away from her. "I give."

Jumping up, she raised her hands in the air. "I'm the champion. I'm the champion!"

"Of what?" Nathan's deep voice called from the open kitchen door.

Cheryl turned, grinning. "I'm the champion of the family. Now Master Josh has to do everything I ask without complaining the entire night."

Nathan's eyebrows arched so high, they were hidden in his blond hair. "Can I get a piece of this action?"

"Nope." The thought of Nathan holding her pinned to the floor seared her body.

Issy stood behind Nathan, her arm wrapped around one solid thigh. Her blanket was clutched to her face and fear filled in her eyes.

"Are you okay, sweetheart?" she asked.

The little girl looked at Josh. Then looked at her.

Nathan scooped her into his arms and tipped her upside down. An anemic squeak erupted that could have been a giggle. But it was nothing like Josh's belly laugh.

Cheryl may have made mistakes in her life, but running away from Levi and ending up in Savannah was the smartest thing she'd ever done. Here, Josh felt safe enough to be normal.

She needed to be strong, for him.

"Josh, you and Issy can play for a few minutes," she said. "I'll call when dinner's ready."

"She's a girl." Josh rolled his eyes.

"And you're a boy. And I'm the queen of the family right now."

He sighed but held out his hand.

When Issy took Josh's hand, Nathan's gaze followed them out of the room.

Cheryl moved to the stove to stir the chicken.

"Something smells good." Nathan's breath made the hairs on the back of her neck flutter. His hand snuck around her waist and pulled her back into his chest. "And dinner smells good, too."

"If you distract me, I'll overcook the chicken." She gave him a nudge. It was strange having a man in the kitchen. Even when Brad was alive, he'd spent his time training or overseas. The moments they'd had together had been precious but few.

She pushed away her sadness. "Would you get the salad out of the fridge?"

While Nathan moved behind her, she tested a piece of chicken and a potato.

"What kind of dressing?" His head was in the fridge.

"The balsamic."

Bottles and jars scraped and rattled as he searched. "Can't find it."

She put the lid back on the pot and joined him. Their hips bumped as she pushed around the bottles he'd moved. "It's homemade. Sorry. I should have warned you."

"I don't mind." He wrapped an arm around her waist. "It got you over here, didn't it?"

She saw the kiss coming. His lips brushed and teased. She couldn't wait for him to press his mouth more firmly to hers.

Instead he pulled away. "I need to pace myself. You're potent."

"No one has ever called me that before." She liked it.

As they waited for the potatoes to cook, she asked, "Have you figured out why Issy is so jumpy?"

"Jumpy?"

"Loud voices. Angry words make her—pull into herself."

"I wish I knew." He sat at the table. "She won't say a word. I've tried to find Heather. Called the few friends I remember her having, but they haven't seen her in years. Didn't even know she had a kid."

"She moved?"

"Yeah. I even tried the county on Issy's birth certificate. Nothing."

"Have you looked her up on the internet to see where she got her DUI?"

"Tried." He shook his head. "I'm always running short of time."

"I could help."

Relief warmed his eyes as he stood. "Let me get my laptop."

When Nathan brought the computer in, he started to open the cover, but she held up a hand. "Dinner's ready."

He nodded. "I'll get the kids."

"We can search after dinner." And maybe she could check her grade on the quiz she'd taken last week.

It was nice having the craziness of feeding two kids and a man at her table. This is what life would have been like if Brad hadn't died. She touched her stomach. Maybe they would have had another child.

She watched Nathan cut Isabella's chicken. There wasn't a second child in her future, but she could help Nathan with his daughter. Eventually, Nathan and Issy would move on, both physically and emotionally. But she could help for now.

"I cut the potatoes," Josh told Isabella.

Issy forked a potato and smiled at him. A pixie with dandelion fluff for hair and her father's heart-breaking brown eyes.

Cheryl brushed the hair out of Isabella's eyes. "Is it good?"

The little girl nodded.

"I love it." Nathan grinned.

Josh shot him a glare. And the bubble broke. They weren't a family. She was just helping out a semi-clueless father with a damaged daughter.

As dinner wound down, Isabella set her milk too close to the table's edge and the plastic glass dropped to the floor.

"Issy." Nathan's voice was sharper than normal, but he didn't yell.

The little girl cringed anyway. Her shoulders curled up to hid her face. A whimper erupted as she bent in two.

"It's okay. It's just spilled milk." Cheryl hurried to the other side of the table. "Josh, can you please grab paper towels? We'll have this cleaned up in no time."

Isabella was frozen. Cheryl stroked her back and she jerked. "Nathan, I think she's done."

Nathan took the hint and picked up his daughter. She wrapped her limbs around him like a vine.

"It's okay." Josh handed a wad of towels to Cheryl. "Sometimes I spill, too. Mom never slaps me."

"Slaps?" Nathan said. "Issy?"

The girl tucked her head deeper into Nathan's shoulder, shaking her head.

Josh covered his mouth.

"Josh?" Cheryl wiped the floor, trying to keep everything nonchalant. "Has Isabella talked to you?"

"I can't tell." Josh looked at Issy. "I promised."

Nathan's face darkened. His hand reached out. Cheryl knew he wouldn't physically hurt her son, but her reaction was automatic. She pushed off the floor and moved between Nathan and Josh, tossing wet paper towels into the garbage. She brushed by Nathan and whispered, "Don't."

He hefted Isabella higher on his hip. "But…"

"Wait." She kept her voice soft. Louder she said, "Let's get the dishes cleared. Issy, would you throw the napkins in the garbage?"

Nathan set her down.

Cheryl assigned small tasks to Issy, praising her as she completed each one.

"Thank you, everyone," Cheryl said when the kitchen was clean.

"Can I play?" Josh asked.

"I think you're forgetting something."

Josh looked at Nathan and Issy. "Not in front of them."

She tickled him. "Oh, yes, in front of them."

"Mom."

She crossed her arms, grinning.

Josh exhaled a breath as strong as a hurricane. "May I go play, Queen Mother of Mine?"

She ruffled his hair. "Yes, you may, my slave."

He hugged her legs and ran to the living room.

"Issy, you can go, too," Nathan said.

After the kids left, he ran his hand through his hair. "She talked to Josh."

"Sounds like it." Cheryl wiped the table.

"She doesn't trust me, but she trusts him." Nathan shook his head. "I want to know what she said."

"I'll ask." Her heart ached for him. "Give her time. Josh is a kid, like her. Not scary."

"But I'm her dad."

"And you've known her for five weeks."

"This…sucks." At least he was cleaning up his language.

She pointed to the computer. "You were going to check for Isabella's mother's arrest records."

"Right. Right." He pulled his laptop off the counter and sat.

Cheryl updated her grocery list.

"Shoot. The county only lists the arrests in the past twenty-four hours. Holy cow, what's wrong with all these people?"

She leaned over his shoulder. "Is there another way to find her?"

"I'll try a few more searches."

Cheryl watched him type. He entered Heather's name three times before he spelled it right. "Do you want me to type for you?"

"I'm good." He shook his head, not looking at her. "I'm typing too fast."

He wasn't, but she didn't argue. If he wouldn't seek help, there was nothing she could do.

He clicked out a few more searches, using different combinations of her name.

"There. I found her." Excitement laced his voice. "People blog about arrests? Sick."

They read through. He frowned. "This was two years ago."

"Maybe you can call the county?"

"Yeah." He typed away. "Can I have a piece of paper?"

She ripped one off her pad and he wrote the phone number down. She was close enough to see he'd transposed the numbers. "It's seven-six-three"

"What?"

"You reversed the numbers." She pointed to the paper. "It's seven-six-three."

His jawbone jutted out. "Right."

He said the numbers as he wrote. "Seven, six, three." But he wrote 6-7-3. Twisted.

Her mouth dropped open. "You're dyslexic."

His face tightened and he stared at her, as if trying

to read her mind. His Adam's apple moved up and down. He nodded.

"May I?"

He handed her the paper and she made the correction.

"It's why you had trouble with the measuring tape." Clues started to fit together. "Do you want me to enter the number in your phone?"

"Sure. Whatever." He unlocked the phone and shoved it at her. "I'm stupid. I get it."

"You're not stupid." She should have guessed earlier. "My best friend in high school was dyslexic. I helped her study."

"You pitied her." His movements jerked as he packed his computer.

"Of course not. She had to find a different way to learn." Cheryl set a hand on his shoulder. "I read textbooks to her. That helped."

And she'd been able to stay away from home. From Mama.

The rasp of his computer bag zipper filled the silence. He set his fists on the table. "Too bad I didn't have you as a friend in high school. I might have done better."

"You had a brother."

He snorted. "We weren't close."

"Daniel didn't help you?" Wasn't that what family was for? To help you through the tough stuff? "Your family's nice."

"Well, I was a challenge."

"I can't imagine how tough life was for you." Her heart broke for him. "But you've adapted."

He snorted again. He set the bag and his phone on the table. "I'll get Issy and get out of your hair."

She couldn't let him go like this. He was beating himself up. "Hey."

He slid the chair he'd been sitting on back into place, refusing to look her in the eye.

Shifting, she blocked his path to the living room. "Nathan."

"Can you move?" he snapped.

She did. Right into him. Pressing herself against his chest. "Is this good?"

His arms hung at his sides. He didn't move for a moment. Then he wrapped his arms around her, burying his face in her hair. "I...I hate my brain."

Her arms pulled him close enough to feel his heat through their clothing. "Don't."

"I'm so...so...effed up. I'm one big flaw. Stupid."

"Language," she murmured into his hair. Hair that smelled of his woodsy shampoo. She inhaled and the scent ignited her body.

He pulled back and cupped her face. "I don't like people knowing. I don't want their sympathy."

"I don't feel sorry for you." But she did. Because he wasn't stupid and someone had made him feel that way. "I'm angry at all the people who didn't help you conquer your disability."

His eyebrows arched over brown eyes glittering with gold flecks. "Thank you."

They stared, drowning in each other's gaze.

His mouth closed and settled on hers. Their tongues danced a sensuous, slow tango. She clutched at his shoulders, needing to get closer.

His hands cupped her butt and he slipped a leg between her thighs. Unashamed, she rubbed against him, her breath coming in little pants.

Nathan's hand slipped under her top and smoothed a path to her breast.

Touch me.

He chuckled. "Oh, yeah."

His hands molded and massaged, and her nipples sprang to life. A moan filled the kitchen.

"Shush," he whispered and kissed her again.

Then there was nothing but the press of his body to hers, his lips and tongue and his marvelous hands. She wanted more, so much more.

"Leave my mom alone!"

Footsteps hammered behind her. She pulled away from Nathan.

Josh launched himself at Nathan. His fists pounded on his thigh, back and knees as Nathan stumbled away.

Cheryl tried to grab Josh, but he kept punching. "Joshua Bradley, stop now!"

A wail erupted in the living room.

"Let go of my mom, butthead." A flying fist accompanied each word. Nathan pinned Josh's arms to his sides.

"Let go!" Josh kicked and wiggled.

"Stop it. Stop!" Cheryl tried to pry Josh out of Nathan's arms and got a fist to the side of her head.

"No more!" Nathan roared. Everyone in the kitchen stopped, but Isabella screamed louder.

"Done?" Nathan squeezed Josh's arms.

Cheryl pulled on her son's shoulders. Her hands shook so hard, she could barely hold him.

"Don't hit," Nathan warned.

Josh glared.

Nathan ran to the living room. "Issy."

"What were you doing?" Cheryl held Josh on her lap.

"Saving you from the butthead like I did uncle Levi." Tears and fury filled her son's eyes.

She gasped, pulling him into a tight hug. "I was fine."

"He was hurting you." Tears dripped off his eyelashes. "I saved you."

"Mr. Nathan didn't hurt me. He kissed me."

"Uncle Levi tried to kiss you and you screamed." His little face scrunched up. "He's a butthead. I hate him."

"Don't say that." Her heart pounded.

Isabella's screams had quieted. Nathan carried her into the kitchen. "Everything okay in here?"

"Get out!" Josh yelled.

"Joshua!" Cheryl's breath hitched. "Go to your room. We'll talk about this later."

Josh stomped away. Cheryl sagged into the chair.

Nathan crouched next to her, Issy clinging to his shoulders. "Are you okay?"

No. Her son had just attacked Nathan. "I'll be fine. Take care of Issy."

She set her hand on the girl's back, but Isabella flinched.

How had everything imploded?

Nathan brushed a kiss on her cheek. "I'll come over after she's asleep," he whispered.

"I need to calm Josh down." She shook her head. "Tomorrow."

Nodding, he closed his eyes. His knees popped as he stood. "Get some sleep."

How could she sleep? She trudged down the hall, pausing at Josh's door. A rhythmic thump came from his room. She knocked and walked in.

Josh sat on the bottom bunk, heels bouncing against the bed frame. Tears streaked his face.

Sitting next to him, Cheryl took his small hand. "Why did you attack Mr. Nathan?"

"He can't touch you." His chin shot out. "I had to protect you."

Protect her? She'd been so weak, her six-year-old son had become her guardian. Josh believed he needed to save her, and that was wrong. That was her responsibility.

"I hate him." The bitterness in her little boy's voice made her squeeze his hand.

"But he's kind to you."

Josh shook his head. "He can't touch you."

"Honey, he's very nice."

But nothing she said changed her son's mind. Josh hated Nathan.

CHAPTER NINE

"LET'S GO SEE Cheryl and Josh," Nathan said.

Issy yawned, holding up her arms. He hefted her up. He couldn't force her to walk. He was too dadgum tired. The catastrophe with Josh had triggered two nightmares.

At Cheryl's door he stopped. What would he find behind door number one?

His stomach churned. He'd finally found someone who didn't think he was dumb and her kid hated him. He had bruises on his shins to prove it.

Pop would have swatted his bottom if he'd done that when he was a kid.

He doubted Cheryl would punish her son. She let everyone walk over her. Maybe even him.

"Go ahead and knock," he encouraged Issy.

It was a quiet knock, but they heard footsteps on the other side of the door. Cheryl opened the door and smiled at Issy. "How are you, sweetheart?"

Issy didn't say anything.

Cheryl held out her arms for Issy. "I've got her." She wasn't letting him in the door. Wasn't even looking at him.

"Cheryl."

"I'll get the kids fed and to day care." She set Issy on her feet. "Go hop in your seat. Your cereal's poured."

She started to close the door but he stuck his foot out.

"It was a long night," he said. "Because of Josh, she had two nightmares."

Cheryl's head rested on the doorjamb. "It wasn't his fault."

He leaned in. "Why didn't you return my call?"

"I didn't know what to say."

The churning in his stomach turned into a full-blown storm. "Say we'll have dinner tonight. Say we'll talk."

She swallowed. "That isn't smart."

Was that a crack about his dyslexia? "I'd say it was the *right* thing to do."

She shook her head. "We can't see each other like that anymore."

"Are you kidding me?" His voice grew louder. Sleep deprivation played havoc with his self-control. "You're letting a six-year-old dictate who you see? Who you sleep with?"

She jerked back. "I never said anything about sleeping with you."

"Don't run, Cheryl." The plea ripped out of him. "Don't let a six-year-old control your life."

"He *is* my life." Cheryl's lip trembled.

She let the door close. It banged on his work boot.

He slid his foot out of the way and pulled the door shut. The hell with this.

GIVING NATHAN UP was the right thing to do. Cheryl opened the vanilla extract for the heavy cream she was whipping. There'd been too much turmoil in Josh's life already.

You're letting a six-year-old dictate who you see? Nathan's words rang in her head.

He didn't understand what being a parent meant. He'd only had Issy for a few weeks. He hadn't nursed her through a fever or told her that her father was dead. Cheryl rubbed at an ache in her chest. Or carried her nine months and loved her every single minute.

Not upsetting Josh was important. He was her life. But she ached at the idea of never kissing Nathan again.

"Are you adding the vanilla or waving it over the bowl and hoping it picks up the flavor?" Abby joked.

"Sorry." She poured in a teaspoon and restarted the mixer.

Nathan couldn't interfere with her work. She had a goal. That meant concentrating on getting a job in Abby's restaurant.

"How's class?" Abby asked.

The question forced her to pay attention to what she was doing. Abby peppered her with questions.

"Your skills are improving each week." Abby folded her recipe book. "The bride finalized her wedding reception menu for the Fourth of July."

"What did she decide on?" Cheryl had prepped some of the tasting menu for Abby.

"Red, white and blue food. Strawberries and blueberries on the wedding cake."

"I like your design." Cheryl checked the peaks on the whipped cream and pulled the bowl out from under the beaters.

"It's time you made your first solo wedding cake." Abby pulled ingredients out of the coolers.

"Me?" Cheryl's voice squeaked. "I've only ever assisted."

"You've got a good feel for cake making and decorating." Abby touched her shoulder. "You're ready. This is a small reception, perfect for your first cake."

"You mean, if I screw up you'll have time to swoop in and fix it." Cheryl couldn't hold back her grin.

"That's not what I was thinking." Abby chuckled. "I started with small cakes, which gave me the confidence to move on to bigger ones."

"I can't wait." This was a huge step. She'd worked on all the components—cake, fondant, flowers and decorations—but she'd never been responsible for the whole thing. "Thank you for believing I have the skill."

"You've earned this." Abby pointed a finger at her. "Don't mess it up."

Cheryl laughed. She wanted to tell Josh and Nathan about getting the opportunity.

Nathan. The good news didn't feel quite so good anymore. He wouldn't want to talk to her again.

Pushing the thought aside, she left the kitchen and peeked inside the business center. Empty. It would only take a minute to check her quiz score. She hadn't had a chance to check in because of last night's chaos.

After logging into her student account, she checked on the grade: A-. She'd have to go over her notes to see what she'd missed. She exited the website and, since she hadn't checked her email for a while, did that.

"Lord, why do I get all these ads?" She deleted ad after ad. She didn't have the money for their offers. No one did.

At the top of her inbox was an email address she didn't recognize. The message was sent a couple of days ago. She clicked.

Cheryl,
I need money.

Money? Then she saw the name.

Levi Henshaw.

The last time she'd seen Levi was in the courtroom after sentencing. He'd gotten thirty-six months for extorting her survivor checks. It had been embarrassing to take the stand and tell the judge how weak she'd been. How she'd let Levi force her to sign over her checks. Gray and Abby had stayed with her throughout the trial.

She straightened her shoulders. She'd vowed to be stronger. Hitting Reply, she typed. NO.

DANIEL'S RINGTONE BLARED out of Nathan's phone. "What?" he snapped. All he wanted was to work alone. He had enough on his plate.

"Whatever bug crawled up your ass, don't take it out on me," Daniel growled.

"Bad night." Bad morning, too. But he and his brother weren't into sharing. "Issy has nightmares."

"Sorry." There was a squeal of a saw on Daniel's end, along with the sound of hammering.

Nathan inhaled, trying to lose his bad mood. It didn't work. Cheryl had screwed that. Wouldn't even stand up to her bratty six-year-old. For all her motherhood experience, she wasn't doing the kid any favors.

"Did you need something?" Nathan asked.

"I'm waiting on the engineer over at Abercorn and he's late. Can you cover the Chatham inspection?"

"What time?" He glanced at the electrician laying the copper wire for the heated floor. Jed could handle pouring the polymer once the electrician was finished.

"Thirty minutes."

Thirty minutes? He'd barely get there. Nathan hung up, had a word with Jed and hustled to his truck. He glanced over at the Fitzgerald House kitchen. Couldn't stop himself. Cheryl and Abby worked together at one of the counters.

His fingers clenched into fists. Was their attraction so easy for Cheryl to forget? Or did she just not want to deal with someone who wasn't normal?

He'd admitted he had dyslexia to a woman. And she'd dumped him at the first opportunity.

Lesson learned.

He headed to the Chatham spec home. A car waited on the dirt driveway. Damn, he hoped it was one of the crew. He parked and moved to the door.

The man sitting in the car hopped out. "About time someone showed up."

Nathan sighed. Inspector, then.

"My brother asked me to meet you. He's tied up." Nathan liked the image of his brother tied up. Then he could torture him for not calling sooner. "Sorry."

"I had problems with one of your properties last year." The inspector pointed a finger at Nathan. "I hope this isn't going to be the same situation."

"No, sir." Nathan wanted to crack off a salute, but being a smart-ass wouldn't help the company.

He found the key and held open the door. "What time was the inspection set for?"

"Two." The inspector walked in.

Nathan peeked at his phone. He had two minutes, but he wouldn't bring that up.

He followed the guy around. It was like the inspector wanted to fail them.

"You're missing a ground default in here," the inspector said, examining the kitchen.

Nathan opened the door under the sink. "This one?"

The inspector glared. "Right. Okay."

After that, he got pickier and pickier.

Nathan sent Daniel a text.

This guy is trying to fail us.

At least, he hoped that's what he'd sent. Texting was iffy. Even before he tucked the phone back into his pocket, it dinged.

Anything need correcting?

Not yet. Day's young.

But they got through the inspection. The man handed him the preliminary approval. "Next inspection, be on time."

"We will. Thank you," Nathan said through gritted teeth.

The inspection had taken so long, his crew was gone by the time he got back to Fitzgerald House. He left his truck there and headed to the day care on foot. He'd pick up the kids early. Maybe buy them ice cream. By watching the kids have fun, his mood might improve.

"Mr. Forester," the receptionist called as he came in. "The director would like to talk to you. Let me call her."

Now what? He swore under his breath. He'd written the weekly check—hadn't he?

"Mr. Forester." The director came through the locked door. "Good to see you."

"It's Nathan. What's up—" he checked her name tag "—Sally."

"It's Sarah." She frowned. "Come on back to my office."

He followed her to a space that barely fit a desk, credenza and a couple of chairs. He could reorganize. By building shelves and getting rid of the credenza, they could use more of the wall space.

"Is there a problem?" he asked, dusting his pants in case construction debris clung to him.

Sarah laced her fingers together. "Are you aware of any traumas in Isabella's life?"

"Nothing more than what I've told you." He leaned forward. "Has she talked?"

"No. She did draw this." Sarah opened a drawer, pulled out a drawing and passed it to Nathan.

Red. A stick figure with red scribbled all over it. Black hair sprouted from the head. A smaller figure with blond hair stuck out from under the other figure. "What is it?"

"We're not sure." Sarah rubbed her forehead. "I asked her if this was blood and she curled into a ball."

"Blood? Jesus."

"I know there isn't anything physically wrong with her voice. She mutters in her sleep during naptime. But maybe you need to get her some help."

"I've set up an appointment with a psychologist." He rubbed his eyes, but couldn't push away the brewing headache.

"Take this with you. Maybe the doctor can find out what it means."

He stood and had to lock his knees so he didn't collapse.

When he walked into Issy's classroom, she ran and hugged his knees. He swung her into his arms and kissed her. Tears swam in his eyes. "We're in this together, kid."

"You're early," Josh said when they went into his classroom.

"Yup." Nathan refused to engage. He had bigger problems than bratty six-year-olds.

"Anyone want ice cream?" he asked as they passed the shop on their walk home.

Issy bounced in his arms. Josh glanced at him, surprise making his mouth form an O. "Maybe."

In the store, they sampled flavor after flavor. Josh chewed his lip. "I'll take Superman ice cream."

The girl at the counter piled a cone way too high.

"Issy, what do you want?"

She pointed to the far end of the counter. Then Nathan played the guessing game, pointing and describing until she settled on strawberry.

"Make her cone smaller," he whispered to the clerk. "And I'll take praline-pecan."

Issy wiggled and he set her down to pay their bill.

The clerk started to count out his change. "Wait. You gave me an extra ten dollars."

"Thanks." It had been a hell of a day. He was surprised he hadn't given her an extra hundred.

They headed home. The ice cream dripped from the kids' cones faster than they could lick.

"Let's sit in the square." That way maybe their clothes wouldn't be completely filthy before they finished their treat.

Josh and Issy sat next to each other in the shade. Nathan knelt next to the bench, letting Issy taste his cone. It was a habit he'd always thought gross. Now it was natural.

"What's the drawing?" Josh scoffed, pulling out the

paper Nathan had tucked into his back pocket. "Gross. Did you draw this? This is like baby stuff."

Nathan shook his head. He couldn't do anything right in this kid's eyes.

"Issy?" Josh held the paper in front of her. "Did you draw this?"

She nodded.

"Is this what the bad man did?" Josh asked.

What the hell? Nathan froze.

Issy nodded, no longer eating her ice cream.

"Then it's good your mom brought you here."

Bad man? Nathan took a deep breath. "She talked to you?"

Josh covered his mouth, but Nathan grabbed the kid's arm. He knew something. "What did she say?"

"Hey!" Josh fumbled his cone. Ice cream dripped on both of them.

Nathan took a deep breath. "I need to know what the picture means."

Issy pushed her ice cream at Nathan, tears filling her eyes. She curled into a ball and rocked back and forth.

Nathan jammed the mess into the garbage can. "Josh, did Issy talk to you?"

Josh held out the picture and scooted off the bench. Even before Nathan could tuck the paper back into his pocket, Josh headed toward the B and B. "Yeah, she said stuff."

Nathan's chest shook with the hope bubbling inside. Or was it resentment? Why would she talk to a smart-ass kid and not her own dad?

He picked up Issy. "It's okay, short stuff."

Catching up to Josh, he said, "I need you to tell me what she's talked about."

Josh shook his head. "It's a secret."

"What's in that drawing shouldn't be a secret."

"You can't make me tell you. 'Cause Issy can't talk about it."

She tucked her chin into his shoulder. So much for not adding to his problems. Cheryl had better make Josh talk.

CHERYL UNLOCKED THE apartment door, dreading another confrontation with Nathan.

Maybe she'd been too harsh. But after tossing and turning most of the night, she'd decided it was better to forget the chemistry between them. She didn't understand dating. Shoot, they hadn't dated. They'd kissed.

She took a five-minute shower, washing off the smell of sautéed onions. Since she needed to rescue Josh, she ran a comb through her wet hair and pulled it back into a ponytail.

In deference to the heat and the window air conditioners that couldn't keep up, she pulled on shorts, a bra and a tank top. It was time to face Nathan.

"It's open," Nathan yelled when she knocked.

She couldn't live the way Nathan did, leaving his door unlocked. But she wasn't over six feet tall with muscles as big as Josh's and her waist combined.

"We're in Issy's room," Nathan called.

She found Issy sitting cross-legged on the floor, watching Josh and Nathan.

Nathan and Josh drew on large pieces of brown paper that had been taped to the bedroom's windowless wall.

Cheryl crouched next to the little girl. "What are they doing?"

Issy just cuddled a stuffed unicorn under her chin.

"We're drawing pictures for Issy's wall." Josh bounced as he spoke.

"You are?"

"It's a mur-mur—" Josh looked at Nathan.

"Mural. A drawing on the wall." Nathan tipped his head but never looked at her.

"Isn't Issy helping?" Cheryl asked.

"I hope she will." His eyes finally locked on hers. "Maybe you want to look at the picture she drew at school. It's in the kitchen."

Her head spun in confusion. Why would a picture make Nathan look so serious?

"Do you want to come with me?" she asked, but Issy pointed at the wall.

In the kitchen, a plate with apples and string cheese sat on the counter next to a turned-over piece of paper.

She flipped it over. Red. On a...a...person? She couldn't tell whether the stick figure was male or female. Her stomach churned. What had Issy drawn?

A small figure with yellow hair stuck out from the figure covered in red crayon. She didn't want to say blood. She didn't want to acknowledge what this could be.

Cheryl turned the paper over again, not wanting to look at the gruesome picture. Setting her hands on the counter, she exhaled. If only Issy would talk.

Heavy footsteps moved down the hall and into the kitchen. Nathan.

"That's…awful." She shook her head.

"I know." He stopped behind her.

She caught his scent, her body melting. She gripped the counter so she wouldn't turn around and pull him into a hug. "I don't suppose she said anything?"

He snorted. Even though Cheryl couldn't see him, she pictured him shaking his head.

"Not to me." He touched her shoulder. "She talked to Josh."

"Josh?" She spun around.

Nathan's face could have been carved from rock. "Yes."

"She talked to Josh?" She couldn't take it in. "That's good."

"Did you see the picture?" He paced to the stove and then back. "What four-year-old draws something like that?"

Her hand covered her mouth. "After Levi hurt Josh, his pictures got pretty dark."

"Like this?" He shook the paper.

"No." Cheryl leaned against the counter. "What did she tell him?"

He stepped closer, his hands resting on the counter on each side of her waist. "Josh won't tell me."

"He wouldn't tell you what Issy said?"

"It's a secret." He leaned in, his eyes sparking with unyielding determination. "I need you to get him to talk."

She shivered. This wasn't the man who'd kissed her. Every muscle was frozen and she was back in Mama's apartment, not knowing where to run. Did she flee outside or into her bedroom with no lock? Mama's latest boyfriend might catch her in the hall. She didn't like the way the man looked at her, as if she was naked. Or did she face Mama's drunken wrath? Mama was probably the lesser of two evils. She would just shake her.

"Cheryl." Nathan voice was a low growl. "Will you talk to your son?"

She pulled up her trembling hands and pushed him back so he didn't loom over her.

"Hey." Nathan reached out to touch her but she jerked away from him. "Where did you go?"

She held up her hand, trying to control her body.

"I…I didn't mean to scare you." Nathan eased away, bouncing a fist off his forehead.

"'S'okay." She was proud she didn't stutter.

Nathan let out a sigh. "Someday you'll tell me why you're afraid."

She didn't say anything. She'd never told Brad. He'd guessed Mama had hit her. Guessed she'd been afraid of one or two of Mama's boyfriends.

Living with Mama had made her afraid to move. Because if Mama had to chase her, the hits were harder.

She pushed away the past. "I'll…I'll talk to Josh."

As she brushed past Nathan, he caught her hand. "I need to know."

"I understand. Your child is more important than anything, even…" She trailed off.

He paused, looking at her for a long minute. Then he nodded. Maybe he understood. She'd sacrificed a relationship with Nathan for Josh's well-being.

AT BEDTIME NATHAN tried again. He held the awful drawing. "Can you tell me what the picture is about, short stuff?"

Issy stared at her bright pink comforter and shook her head.

"Whatever you say, I'll believe you. You can tell me everything. Anything. Please."

She picked at the bow on her bear's neck, not looking at him.

"No one will ever hurt you," he promised.

But was that true? What would happen when Heather came back? How would he protect her then?

Tears dripped down Issy's face. She threw her arms around him.

"I'll keep you safe," he whispered. An ache filled his chest. Somehow he would keep that promise. Setting Issy back onto her pillow, he brushed a kiss on her forehead. "I'll protect you."

Once he left her room, he tucked the drawing in a file. That foul thing wasn't going on the fridge. After opening a beer, he puttered around the apartment. Paid a couple of bills. Put Issy's toys in the toy box he and Pop had built.

Because he was thinking of Pop, he called his parents in Texas. "How's this treatment going?"

"About the same." Weariness filled his mother's voice. "The nausea keeps him from eating, but I force protein shakes down his throat." Mom sighed. "He's sleeping."

"He's in bed already?" It was just after seven in Texas.

"He was worn out from pushing around his dinner."

Nathan laughed at her sad joke.

"How's my granddaughter? I loved the photo you sent yesterday."

"She's good. Just went to sleep." He'd wanted to talk through his fears with his parents, but they were dealing with their own problems. He took a deep drink of his beer. Maybe he should call Daniel.

A month ago that thought would not have crossed his mind.

"Is she talking yet?" Mom asked.

Nathan walked her through their visit with the pediatrician. "Josh says she talks to him. I'm hopeful." Hopeful he could find out why she was afraid.

"That's a start." His mom yawned loudly enough for him to hear. "Send more pictures."

"I will. Are you getting any sleep?"

"A bit. But your father tosses and turns."

Why couldn't life be easy? Maybe this was what normal was like.

After saying good-night to his mom, Nathan shut off his phone and finished the beer, tossing the empty bottle. The recycling was full, so he grabbed Issy's monitor and took the bag down to the can.

Two couples sat at a courtyard table, sipping wine and laughing, a half-empty bottle on the table between them.

A longing for something normal like a night out drinking with a pretty woman walloped him. He and Cheryl might have been able to have something like that. Except for Josh.

He stuffed the bag into the container a little harder than he should. Nothing but static came through the monitor, so he headed up the outside steps to Cheryl's place. She hadn't told him to stop using their kitchen door, but he'd gotten the *stay away* message this morning.

Through the living room window, he saw lights on in the kitchen. He knocked. Not hard, because Josh would be in bed. He waited. Nothing.

He turned to leave, but stopped himself. Issy was important. Finding out what she'd said to Josh couldn't wait.

He knocked louder.

This time he heard footsteps. He steeled himself. When Cheryl had walked into his apartment earlier, he'd wanted to rush over and hug her. That wasn't happening. He'd never hold her again.

The footsteps paused at the door. Then the chain slid and the lock clicked open. Shoot. The sound reminded him that he hadn't locked his door. Someone would have to go through the interior of the carriage house, but still... Issy was alone.

He had to trust that he'd hear if anyone went in.

"Hi." Cheryl held the door open and he walked in. She gestured to the living room.

"Could we talk in the kitchen? I want to open the door to listen for Issy."

Cheryl nodded and led the way into the kitchen. It was wrong, but he watched her butt.

Throwing open the lock and propping the door open, she asked, "She's in there alone?"

Her accusation was like ice water, cooling his attraction. She still didn't believe he was a good parent.

"I had to take out the recycling." He patted the monitor. It wasn't like she hadn't done the same thing the evening she'd helped him measure the restaurant space. "Did Josh tell you anything?"

She nodded, pulling out a chair. "I think you should sit."

He couldn't. Instead, he grabbed her arms. "Was she molested? Please tell me she wasn't hurt."

"I'm sorry." She touched his cheek.

"God." Who could do that to a child? "I'll kill whoever touched her."

"No. No." She pulled his hands from her arms and

held them. "She wasn't molested. Not that she told Josh."

She led him to a chair. His heart beat as fast as a cement mixer. "What did he say?"

She sat facing him, still holding his hands. Her willingness to touch him should have made him happy. Instead he couldn't breathe.

"Bear in mind that this is coming from a four-year-old, interpreted by a six-year-old. From what Josh said, the man with the blood is her other papa."

Other papa? Nathan hadn't known his heart could hurt any more than it did. "Okay." He drew the word out.

"But a bad man hurt her other papa. There was yelling. Guns. Her mom told her not to talk to anyone."

"Not to talk to anyone?" What was Heather hiding?

Cheryl squeezed his hands. "Are you sure her mother is really in rehab?"

He shook his head. "I can't find her. I called the county where she was arrested two years ago, but they don't know anything."

"Maybe you can find this other papa." She touched his cheek. "If there was a shooting, there might be a police report."

"I don't even know who to look for. Or where to look." He leaned closer. "Can Josh get a name?"

She shook her head. "Issy didn't say."

He swallowed, but the lump blocking his throat didn't move. "How can I help, if I don't know what happened?"

"Oh, Nathan." She touched his cheek. "You can help by holding her and telling her you love her. By being there. Maybe a therapist will be able to break through."

"What if that's not enough? She has to start talking sometime. Otherwise, what will happen to her?" He dropped his forehead to hers. "I know what it's like to be stupid. I don't want that for my daughter."

Her hand cupped the back of his head. "You're not dumb. You know that, don't you?"

"That's what my mom always told me." His hands rested on her shoulders. "But she didn't have kids laughing at her when words screwed with her brain."

"You survived." Cheryl's second hand stroked his cheek. "You need to show Issy she's loved."

How could she stay positive? How could she keep going?

"How do you do it?" Nathan asked. "You've struggled, but you put me to shame. You know what you want. I'm sinking."

She laughed. Her minty breath lured him closer. It was as if last night hadn't happened.

"I'm the opposite of together. I'm scared. All. The. Time. I freeze. I want to hide, but because of Josh, I can't. He makes me a better person. He's the one who gets me through." Her lashes fluttered closed.

He lifted her onto his lap and she curled into his arms. The tension in his chest eased. "We're quite the pair." He buried his face in her hair, not wanting to ruin this moment. He wanted her. And he wanted her help with Issy.

"What do you think I should do next for Issy?"

He didn't want to ask about them.

"Ask what happened to her mother and other papa."

"I'll try." He wasn't sure how to get his daughter to talk.

"When is her psychologist appointment?"

"After the Fourth of July." Her silky hair soothed his cheek. "Thank you."

"I didn't do anything."

"You talked to Josh. Got more information than I've gotten in weeks." His arms tightened around her. "And you've given me…" Damn, words wouldn't come.

"Help?"

"Yes, but…support. You're supporting us. Issy and me." It still didn't feel like the right word but it was better.

"This isn't one-sided." Her voice was almost too low to hear.

His heart skipped a couple of beats. "What do you mean—not one-sided?"

"You're helping me, too. I couldn't go to school without you. Abby won't consider me for a restaurant job if I don't take classes." She tipped her face. "And what you and I have together, it's not one-sided."

She closed the distance between their mouths. Her kiss was a little awkward, bumping his nose with hers, and too short. It was also everything he wanted.

He slanted her head with his hand and urged her mouth open.

Her fingers gripped his hair, tugging him closer. Her aggressiveness stole his breath, making his heart race. He licked her mouth, tasting mint and Cheryl's sweetness.

Eventually she eased away. "I need to breathe." But she laughed.

Nathan hugged her, relieved. And there was no reason to feel any relief. Issy was traumatized. Cheryl hadn't made a commitment. Hell, before Issy, the word *commitment* had never crossed his mind.

She wiggled closer. "I guess the best way to approach this is to…keep our relationship from Josh."

His relief soured a little. She wanted to sneak around.

"You could just tell him."

"Let's give this some time." She sighed. Her breasts brushed against his chest. "I'm sorry about this morning."

"Me, too." He pulled her closer. "If I'd known I could talk to you about Issy's picture, I might not have freaked out as much. You keep me…grounded."

"I wish I hadn't reacted so badly."

"This is nice. Making up is nice." He kissed her again.

"I hope Issy sleeps through the night." She traced a finger under his eyes. "You need sleep."

"I know this isn't perfect timing, but could we go

out sometime? No kids." He set her on her feet, trying to make his question casual.

"Like a date?"

He nodded.

"Wow. I didn't think I'd ever go on one of those again."

"You haven't dated?" Heat surged through his chest. He was the first man she'd considered dating. "I'd love to…have dinner, go to a movie. Even take a walk."

Her fingers traced a pattern on his chest. "I'd like that."

"Let's see how Issy does." Because she was number one in Nathan's life. "Just in case, when's your next night off?"

"The night before July Fourth."

He cupped her face. "I'll find a sitter."

CHAPTER TEN

CHERYL BRUSHED MASCARA ON, smiling at her reflection. In less than an hour she would go on her first date in…she didn't know how long. She and Brad had lived frugally, not making big deals of anniversaries or birthdays. She hadn't minded making a special dinner for him instead of going out, or watching a movie at home instead of going to a theater.

Which was why she would enjoy the thrill of her first date. Her body hummed with anticipation. Nathan's kisses had her so wired, she had trouble thinking. For the past few days, she'd worried about cutting her finger or dropping a tray at work.

Issy hadn't said anything more to Josh and had had only one nightmare. So this date was a go.

Nathan hadn't told her where they were going or how to dress. She twirled and the skirt flared on the light blue sundress she'd found at a vintage store.

Exhaling, she collapsed on the side of the bathtub. Would she sleep with Nathan? Whenever he kissed her, she wanted to take the next step. But now? Her stomach did a backflip.

They were so different and this was a dinner date. She didn't have to sleep with him. There was no reason to rush anything.

There was a pounding on the bathroom door. "Whatcha doing?" Josh yelled.

"Inside voice, please." She opened the door.

Josh barged in, dropped onto the toilet seat and stared at her dress. "I thought I was getting pizza tonight. Are we going someplace?"

"I told you last night, *I'm* going someplace."

"You never wear a dress." He crossed his arms. "Where are you going?"

Sometimes she wished Josh wasn't quite so observant. "Out."

"Where?"

"I'm not sure. It's a surprise."

"Then who will be with me?" He pouted.

"Remember? Mr. Dan and Miss Bess are watching you and Isabella."

"Yeah." Josh's eyes narrowed. "Why are they watching Issy, too?"

"It's a favor." She didn't want him to press her. She wouldn't lie about going out with Nathan, but she didn't want Josh freaking out, either. "Why don't you draw a picture of Carly for them?" Josh loved their dog.

"Okay." He frowned, but left her alone.

She swished on blush and spritzed perfume. "Done."

When the doorbell rang, butterflies invaded her belly. She pushed back her curled hair. Since her hair was fine and stick-straight, the style wouldn't last long in Savannah's humidity, but she'd made the effort.

Josh was in the living room, waving a paper in Bess's face. "Did you bring Carly?"

"She's in the greenhouse." Bess looked over at Cheryl and her eyebrows went up. "You look gorgeous."

"Thanks." A blush heated her face.

"Where's Mr. Dan?" Josh tugged on Bess's hand to get her attention.

"He's getting Issy." Bess ruffled Josh's hair. "We're going to Abby's house to make pizzas. Then we'll cook them in the outdoor pizza oven."

"I helped make the oven." Josh's chest stuck out. "I laid the first brick, Mom."

"I know." The Fitzgeralds were so kind to them.

Bess held out her hand for him. "Why don't we go see what Abby's got for pizza toppings? Daniel and Issy are meeting us there. It's going to be a party. Dolley and Liam and Mr. and Mrs. Forester are all coming."

"Thank you," Cheryl said. "I can't believe you're doing this."

"You're welcome." Bess gave Cheryl a quick hug. "I'm doing this because you're part of our family," she whispered.

Cheryl's mouth dropped open. All along, she'd thought the Fitzgeralds had invited her to their celebrations because she was on her own, not because they cared about her personally. "Th-thank you."

Bess pulled away and grinned. "Besides, I'm hoping Issy and Josh will wear Carly out and she won't crawl on our bed tonight."

Cheryl laughed at the image of a dog that out-weighed Josh climbing into bed with Daniel and Bess. "I hope they can."

"Have fun." Bess waved. "Daniel's got a key so we'll get the kids into their beds." Bess swept Josh out.

Cheryl was alone. Now her stomach did swan dives. What was she thinking? She was a mom. Putting her needs before Josh's made her a *bad* mom. She should stay home. Make sure Josh knew he was the most important thing in her life.

There was a knock on the door. Maybe Josh was sick or hurt. She yanked it open. Nathan filled the doorway and everything melted inside her.

He wore khaki shorts, a silky-looking polo shirt and boat shoes. For once, his hair was tamed. She missed his messy hair.

She swallowed. "I'm overdressed."

"You're perfect."

His face lit up as his gaze took a leisurely trip from the top of her head to her toes. Toes she'd painted a dark purple. She never wore nail polish. What was Nathan doing to her?

"I don't get to see you in a dress very often. You look good enough to eat." He held out his hand. "Let's run before the kids spot us."

She grabbed her purse and locked the door behind her. Her sandals clacked on the wooden steps.

Instead of Nathan's truck, he led her to a vintage Mustang.

"Is this yours?" she asked.

"Daniel lent it to me." The engine roared as Nathan started it.

"He's a nice man."

"He lectured me on not hurting you." Nathan glanced over. "Did you and my brother ever have a... thing?"

"Never." She grinned. "You sound jealous."

He reached across the console and squeezed her hands. "I think you might be right."

"No one's ever been jealous over me."

"Not even your husband?" He stared out the windshield. "Unless you don't like to talk about him."

"Brad? No, he was never jealous." She shrugged. "He knew I'd never look at another man."

"You're kidding."

"Once I met Brad, that was it. For both of us, I think."

"Tell me about him."

She squeezed her fingers together. Could she tell Nathan about the boy she'd loved for most of her life? "I was a freshman in high school when we met."

"A freshman?"

She nodded, but he was looking at the road. "I was quiet. I didn't like people noticing me."

"I would have noticed you."

"You would have been with the popular crowd."

"That was Daniel. I was with a crowd you wouldn't have hung around with."

Maybe she should ask about Nathan instead of talking about herself. She'd heard about the trouble he'd gotten into, drugs being the worst. But other than alcohol, there hadn't been any signs of that since he'd moved in next door.

"I worked in the library after school," she said. "I'd stayed later than usual, reshelving books. By the time I left, football practice was over and a couple of players hassled me."

She shivered. Even after all the years she could still feel the hot breath on her neck as they caged her next to her locker. Every time someone frightened her, she froze. "Brad saved me. They were his teammates and he stood up to them."

"You started dating that long ago? You were how old? Fourteen?"

"Fifteen." Her chest ached with the loss of the boy she'd loved. "Brad was a junior. He left school two years before I did. Headed to boot camp."

"When did you get married?"

"After I graduated. I took a bus to his base. He'd just come back from overseas. We were married in the chapel."

"Did your mom go with you?"

"No!"

He glanced over at her. "Not a fan of Brad?"

"She was…" Nathan had fantastic parents. How could she explain that her mother resented her only child? "She was an alcoholic. My existence ruined her life. She…hit me."

"I'm sorry." He reached for her hand again. His touch was warm and comforting. "Too bad you didn't have my parents. I made their life miserable. It would have been better for me to be born to your mother than burden mine."

"I'm sure they don't feel that way." She'd witnessed the Forester family bonds. She'd wanted that kind of connection growing up. She hoped she was making it with Josh.

"In high school, I was…wild," he said. "I gave them gray hairs and sleepless nights."

"But you've changed, right?"

He turned into the marina. "Absolutely."

"Where are we going?"

"Out on the water."

She sighed. "That sounds nice. I've only been out once since we arrived in Savannah."

"Have you been on Daniel's boat?" he asked.

"Josh talked Gray into taking us out with him and Abby last summer."

"Well, that's where we're headed." He parked in the lot. "I was kind of hoping you hadn't. I'd like to be your first something."

She turned and touched his hand. "You are. My first date."

"Cool." He grinned. "Let's have fun."

"I'm game." She slipped out of the car. He grabbed a basket from the backseat.

"I saw Abby packing that," she said.

He wrapped an arm around her shoulders. "Well, I couldn't ask you to make a picnic supper."

She bumped her head into his shoulder. "I would have done it."

He hurried up the gangplank and held out a hand to help her aboard. A marina employee cast the lines to Nathan.

He fired up the engine and steered them out of the docked boats, sending her to the bow to check his clearance.

"To the left," she called.

He adjusted.

"This is incredible." She sucked in a breath filled with the brackish scent of the river. "Thank you."

He stood at the wheel, looking like a captain. Who was this man who wanted her? He looked perfect building the restaurant. He looked at home playing on the floor with Isabella. And when he'd talked about shading and perspective with Josh as they'd sketched in the mural, he'd looked perfect there, too.

Why did he want to have anything to do with her? It didn't make sense.

"A storm passed over your face. What's wrong?" His smile slipped. "Where do you go when that happens?"

She stared at the rocking deck. "I was thinking about you. How…comfortable you are with work and Issy and…everything." She looked back at him. "I don't understand why you're interested in me."

His mouth dropped open. "Come here, please."

She did and he took her hand, reeling her in until she was tucked under his arm.

"I'm not sure who you're talking about. I'm out of my element with Issy, with work, with you." He brushed a kiss on her forehead. "I can't compete with your hero husband. I'm the family screw-up."

"You are not." She planted her hands on her hips. "If you were a screw-up, you wouldn't have taken in your daughter. You wouldn't be helping me. You wouldn't know how to make Abby's dream come true."

He shook his head and the wind caught his hair. "I have a daughter who's afraid to talk. I'm helping you out because you're helping me. And construction is all I know."

"You're an artist. I've seen the mural you're making for Issy." She poked him in the chest. "Stop running yourself down."

He blinked. She'd made him speechless. Not a bad thing.

"You're amazing." She straightened his hair. And then ran her hand down his chest. "What's for dinner?"

NATHAN TOOK A deep breath and inhaled the scent of apples and something spicy.

Cheryl thought he was amazing.

His heart beat faster than it did the few times a week he ran. Well, he hadn't run since Issy arrived.

"You're hungry?" His voice cracked like he was a teenager.

Her smile warmed him. "Yes."

"I'll…" He looked around. They were coming up on

an island whose name he couldn't remember. "Let me park…" That wasn't the right word. "Anchor. Let me anchor the boat. We can eat. Have something to drink."

She nodded.

"I have soda and champagne. Just in case you wanted to…" God, was he blushing? "I'm not trying to take advantage of you. I saw you have a glass at Abby's wedding." The words flooded out.

She tipped her head back and laughed. Her silky hair brushed his arm. He wanted her hair to curtain his face as she rode him.

The boat lurched.

Shoot. He'd yanked on the wheel. "You. Stand—" he waved his hand "—next to the railing. I don't want to crash."

He concentrated on moving into a small bay, one without other boats. It took some maneuvering. Too many people were already celebrating the holiday.

He nosed the bow where he wanted, shut off the engine and dropped anchor. "Okay."

He spread a blanket on the deck. "Let's eat."

"Great." She pulled over the picnic basket.

"No. I want you to relax."

"I was only—"

"Taking care of everyone but yourself." It was his turn to spoil her.

"Oh." She sat and arranged her skirt in a circle covering her lovely legs. Pity.

"Hang on. I forgot something." He ran to the galley and came back with a cooler. "Champagne?"

She chewed her lip. "A small glass."

He twisted off the closure and popped the cork. Then he tipped the golden wine into her glass. He'd never made such a big gesture for a woman. Was he doing this right?

He poured his own glass and licked a drip off his hand. Her gaze followed his tongue.

"If you keep looking at me that way, I'm going to have trouble staying on this side of this blanket."

Her eyes flared open. "Ooh."

Holding up his glass, he asked, "What shall we toast to?"

Her shoulders relaxed. "Our children."

Did she mean *ours* in a joint way? Like, together *ours*? This was their first date, but it was like they'd dated for…weeks. Touching his glass to hers, he repeated, "Our children."

He wanted more than the kisses they'd shared. He wanted to bury his nose in her apple-scented hair and stroke her soft skin. And he couldn't help wanting to bury himself in her body until they were one.

He gritted his teeth. There was no rush. Even though his body was primed, he planned to enjoy his first adults-only dinner in over two months.

The sun set fire to the sky as he fed her cold fried chicken. She dangled asparagus in front of his lips as the stars popped out. And they shared potato salad off his fork when the moon rose.

"This is nice." Cheryl bit a plump chocolate-covered

strawberry and popped the rest into his mouth as his head nestled in her lap. "It's like a dream."

"It is." Nathan urged her to join him on the blanket, and they lay face-to-face. There was a salty bite in the air and the boat rocked gently on the waves. "Life doesn't get much better than this. If I'm dreaming, don't wake me."

Her eyes sparkled in the moonlight. "I don't want to wake up, either."

They moved together. Petal-soft lips met his. She tasted sweet. Not just of the fruit and chocolate, but Cheryl—all Cheryl.

Rolling her onto her back, he settled between her thighs, biting back a moan at the sheer rightness of being with her. Pushing up on his elbows, he stared.

Her blond hair, fanned out on the blanket, shimmered white in the moonlight.

"How did I...?" Get so lucky to be with someone as wonderful as Cheryl?

She touched his face. "What's wrong?"

"Absolutely nothing." He slid a finger down her cheek. "Despite what Issy is going through, being with you has made this the best summer of my life."

She swallowed. "Nathan."

She didn't say anything else. Didn't tell him she felt the same. Was that pity in her eyes?

He couldn't bear her pity. Dipping down, he kissed her. Not a sweet kiss like before. This was a kiss of possession.

She buried her fingers in his hair and held him close, sucking his tongue into her mouth.

He cupped her breast, flicking a thumb over her nipple. She arched up into him and his hips surged into her softness.

She tore her mouth away. "Wait."

He froze, easing his hand back to the blanket when it wanted to cradle her breast. "I'm sorry. I shouldn't have…"

"Nathan," she scolded. Reaching behind her neck, she undid her halter straps.

His heart pounded with the explosive force of a nail gun. He smoothed away the fabric. Moonlight danced on her pale breasts. He stared, unable to wrench his gaze away. "You're beautiful."

"I'm not." Her voice trembled.

"I'm the one looking at you." He trailed a finger from her collarbone to the tip on her nipple. Then showered the same attention on her other breast.

Cheryl squirmed under him, rubbing against his groin.

"Touch me," she whispered. "Please."

"I will." For once he didn't worry about words, numbers or directions. He was focused on one thing— Cheryl's pleasure. Because she was giving him a gift. He was the first man to touch her since her husband died.

He brushed kisses against the soft skin of her breasts. "You smell like strawberries here." He nosed his way to her ear. "And apples here." Then nuzzled into her neck. "And spicy here."

She wriggled against his groin. "It's my body wash, shampoo and perfume."

"It's you." He swirled his tongue around the tight peak, his fingers rolling her other nipple.

Cheryl's head thrashed, knotting her hair on the blanket. She yanked on his shirt. "I want to touch you."

Pulling away, he ripped the shirt over his head one-handed. Easing back down to her, he brushed his chest against her breasts, skin to skin.

"This is incredible." She nudged up with her hips.

Groaning, he rolled to his back, willing to do anything she wanted.

She rose like a goddess, straddling his thighs. With tentative strokes, her hands explored his biceps, slid to cover his pecs and then his obliques. "You're amazing."

She kissed his nipples, abrading them with her teeth. His fingers tangled in her hair, holding her there.

"I want you naked," she whispered.

They were *so* on the same page.

Music echoed across the water, reminding him that they were exposed up on the deck. Grinning, he rolled her back under him and kissed her. "We should move into the cabin."

Cheryl wedged a hand between their lips. "Nathan."

He kissed her palm. "Cheryl."

"That's your phone."

"Phone?" He sat. The music stopped then started again. Daniel's ringtone.

He pulled his phone out of the picnic basket. "What's wrong?"

"Sorry," Bess said. "Issy had a nightmare. She's keeps rocking and whimpering. We tried to get her back to sleep, but she won't stop crying."

Issy. Damn. "Let me talk to her."

"Here she is," Bess said.

His little girl whimpered.

"Hey, Busy Issy. Daddy's coming home right now." His hands clenched into useless fists. "Don't worry. Don't cry. I'll be there soon."

Cheryl nodded, retied her dress straps and had packed the food and blanket before he disconnected.

He raised anchor and started the engine, backing away from the island. "I'm sorry."

She wrapped an arm around his waist as he steered the boat back to the marina. "Don't be. Issy comes first."

He kissed the top of her head. "Thanks for understanding."

"Of course." She handed him his shirt.

He tugged it over his head. "This wasn't how the evening was supposed to end."

It was a quiet drive back to Fitzgerald House. "Issy hasn't had a nightmare since the day she drew that awful picture," he said, breaking the silence.

She linked their hands together. "It's probably just the change in her routine."

"I hope so." Worrying about his daughter didn't stop him from remembering Cheryl's reaction to his confession that being with her was the best time of his life. She'd been married. It made sense she didn't feel the same way.

He pulled into the parking lot and they hurried up the stairs. Daniel opened the door before they hit the landing. He held a finger to his lips. "She just fell asleep."

Bess sat rocking Issy.

Nathan gathered his daughter in his arms and she tucked her head on his shoulder and sighed in her sleep.

Cheryl headed to Josh's bedroom.

"She calmed down after she heard your voice," Bess whispered. "You might have been able to stay out."

"I'm glad you called." It had been too soon to leave his daughter. "Thank you for watching them."

Bess joined Daniel by the door. His brother wrapped an arm around his fiancée's shoulders. "We had fun. Sorry your evening ended early."

Cheryl came back into the living room. "We had a lovely dinner on your boat. Thank you."

She didn't come stand next to him. What had happened to their new togetherness?

"See you and the kids tomorrow," Daniel said as he and Bess headed out.

"Do you want Issy to sleep here tonight?" Cheryl crossed her arms, her body stiff and uninviting. Reluctance poured off her like rain off a roof.

"I think she'll be better in her own bed."

Relief flashed through Cheryl's eyes. "If you think that's best."

He didn't, but he couldn't argue. The closeness they'd had on the boat had vanished.

Maybe it really had been a dream.

CHAPTER ELEVEN

"KIDS—" NATHAN SNAGGED the bag Cheryl had left "—let's go ride the sailboat."

Issy caught his hand and headed out the door with him.

Josh dragged behind. "Does my mom know about this?"

"Of course she knows. She packed your bag."

"But she's not here." There was a pout in the kid's voice.

Was it going to be this kind of day? "She's working. Let's have fun. I don't want you spoiling the holiday for my parents."

"Mr. Dan's dad and mom will be there?"

Nathan rolled his eyes. "They're my parents, too."

Josh muttered something under his breath. The only word Nathan caught was *butthead*.

"What did you say?"

"Nothin'." Josh clattered down the carriage house steps while Nathan locked the door.

Through gritted teeth, he said, "Right."

If he admitted his brother would be on the boat, Josh would be over the moon. It was petty, but Nathan refused to tell him.

Why was he falling for a woman whose son hated him? Who had that kind of luck?

Today's goal would be to get along with Josh. Nathan wanted to replace Daniel as Josh's favorite Forester.

He buckled Issy into her seat and double-checked that Josh was strapped in. Crouching, he stared him in the eye. "Let's have fun today."

Josh shrugged. "I don't have my drawing stuff."

"There'll be plenty to do." He'd thrown fishing gear into the back of the truck for the kids. "Give me a chance."

Nathan shut the door. He didn't want to see another shrug. He wished Cheryl was here. This morning he'd stepped in to give her a hello kiss, hoping she'd remembered how good they had been together, but Josh had barreled into the room. Cheryl had jumped back so fast it was like he had the plague.

He glanced at the kids. Issy's blanket was tucked next to her face. Josh stared out the window.

How could he change Josh's attitude? Buying him stuff hadn't worked. He'd tried to help him with his drawing, but the kid said his art teacher was teaching him how to draw.

He flipped on the music station Issy liked. Josh rolled his eyes, but his foot kicked the back of Nathan's seat in time with the song. Issy rocked back and forth. Wouldn't it be something if she sang?

Nathan sang, "Hot dog. Hot diggity dog."

Issy rocked faster.

"Sing with me." He smiled at her in the mirror.

The words weren't hard to remember, they were mostly *hot dog*. Josh was too cool to sing along. Issy mouthed the words. Maybe mouthing was a start. Her appointment with the psychologist was next week. It'd be great to go in there and tell the doctor she'd made progress.

Traffic heading to the marina was heavy, but they finally pulled in. He unlatched Issy. Josh climbed out of the seat. "Hang on," Nathan said.

Josh tapped his foot in the dirt as Nathan grabbed the fishing poles. "Can you carry these?"

Josh frowned. "Those are baby poles."

"They're for kids. For you and Issy."

Josh took the poles, still frowning. "What will we do with them?"

"See if we can catch dinner." Nathan grabbed the bait. "Issy, can you carry this?"

She grimaced and carried the container of live shrimp in her outstretched arm.

"What are those?" Josh asked.

"Shrimp." Nathan grabbed the bag. "Red fish love them. We'll have fun."

"We're gonna be a Dr. Seuss book." Josh laughed. "One fish, two fish, red fish, blue fish."

"You got it." Nathan smiled.

They headed to Daniel's slip. Nathan called, "Ahoy, the *Savannah Queen*."

"Young slaves to help sail this ship," Bess yelled. "Excellent."

Issy snuck behind Nathan legs, wrapping her arms around his thigh.

Bess strode down the gangplank. "Let me carry her."

Issy clung a little tighter.

"Could you carry the bag instead?" Nathan asked.

Bess smiled at Issy. "Sure."

"Josh, hold my hand," Nathan said.

"I can do it myself," the boy complained.

"And your mom will have my head if you fall in the water." He hoisted Issy onto his hip and held out his hand.

Josh glared but obeyed. Together they moved up the narrow walkway.

"There's my crew," Daniel called. "Are you ready to swab the decks?"

Josh shook Nathan's hand away, tossed the fishing rods onto the deck and ran to Daniel. His brother swung the kid in the air, making him laugh.

"I didn't know we were going with you and Miss Bess." Josh gave Daniel a big bear hug. "This is awesome."

"I'll even let you steer." Daniel set Josh down.

"Let's go!" Josh bounced on his toes.

"You and Issy need to wear life jackets," Nathan called.

He sat Issy on a bench and opened the storage area where he'd stowed the jackets last night. He handed the correct size to Josh then outfitted Issy.

"Do I have to?" Josh asked Daniel.

"Yes," the brothers answered together.

"Carly has to wear hers." Daniel pointed to the dog sitting next to the helm.

"I guess." Josh stepped into the leg straps. Nathan started to zip him up.

Josh wiggled away. "Mr. Dan can do it."

"Mr. Dan is getting the boat ready to leave the marina." Nathan gritted his teeth and zipped Josh into the jacket.

Mom came up the stairs from the galley with Pop following behind her.

Nathan hugged his parents. As always, when Pop came back from his grueling week-long chemo treatments, his body seemed thinner and frailer than before.

"There's my angel baby." Mom gave Issy a hug and a kiss. Issy hugged her back. Then Mom grabbed Josh in a hug. "How's handsome Josh?"

"Great!" Josh said. "Mr. Dan said I can steer the boat."

Pop sank onto a bench, huffing and puffing.

"How's it going?" Nathan asked.

"I'm on the right side of the grass."

Nathan laughed but he hated that joke. It was a reminder that Pop could lose his cancer battle. He wanted the vibrant man his father had been, not this scarecrow wearing Pop's face and clothes.

Bess reeled in the lines and Nathan went to help.

"Are we ready?" Daniel called.

"Yes! Yes," Josh shouted.

Daniel started the engine and navigated out of the slip and into the busy river.

Nathan stood next to the two kids. "Grab the railing." He held Issy and made sure Josh hung on.

"Sorry about last night." Bess put a hand on Josh's shoulder.

"We had fun." He smiled. "Thanks."

Bess glanced at Josh. "We had fun, too."

"Where were you?" Josh asked, suspicion in his voice.

"I…" He wouldn't lie to the kid. "I came to the boat and made sure everything was shipshape."

"But Mr. Dan was with me last night." Josh chewed on his lip. "This is his boat."

"And I was here." Nathan patted the railing.

The boat hit a speedboat wake and rocked. Issy squealed, clinging to his neck. "That fool shouldn't be going this fast near the marina," Nathan said under his breath.

"Let me hold Issy," Mom said.

Nathan kept his stance spread as he walked to his parents. He tickled Issy as he set her on Mom's lap. "Don't let her dive in the water."

Mom nuzzled Issy's neck. "I won't."

Daniel waved him over. "I didn't have a chance to ask how last night went."

"Great." Except for Issy's nightmare. "Thanks for letting us use the boat."

"Just remember what I said about hurting Cheryl," Daniel warned.

"We went through this when I asked you to babysit." Nathan rolled his eyes. What about Cheryl hurting him? "With the kids, it's hard to get time together."

"Yeah, yeah. The puppy was a date killer for a while." Daniel rubbed his foot on the dog lying near his feet.

"Carly's an angel." Nathan rubbed her head.

"You've never cleaned up after she gets into the garbage."

"Want to talk about messy things?" He nodded at Issy. "She's still having trouble with potty training."

Daniel held up a hand. "I'm not ready for that."

Nathan laughed. "As soon as you're married, Mom will expect grandchildren."

"She's got a good one now."

"If only Issy would talk."

"She will. You're good with her." Daniel didn't look at him.

Compliments from his brother were rare. "Thanks." His voice cracked a little.

"You stepped up for her and you're getting the help she needs. When does she see the psychologist?"

"Next week." He hadn't stepped up for her in the beginning. He'd wanted to pawn her off on Mom or Cheryl.

"I'm looking for a best man." Daniel tipped his head and looked at him. "You interested in the job?"

Best man? Now he really was choking up. He'd been shocked when Daniel had asked him to be a groomsman. "I'd…I'd be honored."

"Good." Daniel's eyes sparkled in the sunlight. Was he choking up, too?

Nathan cleared his throat. "Next we'll be hugging and doing each other's hair."

Daniel punched him in the arm. "No way."

Nathan punched him back.

"Bess wants Issy to be a flower girl." Daniel rubbed his arm.

They both looked at the kids and their parents. "That can be arranged."

Nathan checked on the kids as Daniel steered the boat through traffic. His brother's best man. Cool.

"Hey, crew," Daniel said. "Can someone secure those fishing poles?"

Since Bess had her hand on Josh's shoulder, Nathan stowed them.

After they cut through the surf and into the ocean, Daniel hollered, "Lower the mainsail!"

He and Bess moved to the lines.

"Captain Bligh needs an eye patch," she whispered.

"Are you sure you want to spend your whole life with Mr. Control?"

Bess's face softened. "Oh, yes."

Together, they hoisted the sail. The sheet billowed and caught the wind. The boat leaned into the wind.

"Beautiful." Nathan stood next to Josh, making sure he was hanging on. "What do you think?"

"I love this!" Josh's eyes sparkled.

"Hey, Josh," Daniel called from the helm. "Ready to steer?"

Josh skidded across the deck to the wheel. "Yeah."

The kid's grin was bigger than Nathan had ever seen. He pulled out his phone and shot pictures of Josh standing with his feet spread, hands on the wheel. Cheryl would love to see this.

He wasn't sure he'd get cell coverage out here, but he sent Cheryl the picture anyway. Then he took some of Pop, Mom and Issy.

His daughter was growing so quickly. Her face had filled out and her cheeks had more color than when she'd arrived. He should buy a camera.

He dug through the bag and squirted sunscreen into his hand. "Short stuff, we need to get you covered up."

"I'll put Josh's sunscreen on," Bess volunteered. "All this helping with kids is kind of fun."

"Thanks," he said, squirting more in his hand and handing her the bottle. At least Josh liked Bess.

Around lunchtime, Daniel anchored near an island. Nathan helped the kids into the dingy and they headed off to play while the adults set up the meal.

"Lunchtime, Issy, Josh," Nathan called out. When they didn't come running, Nathan searched. "Where are you guys?"

Issy dragged herself out of the brush. Carly tumbled after her.

"You're supposed to wait until I found you." Josh came out of the other side of the brush. "That's what hide and seek means."

She shrugged.

"Let's eat." Nathan pointed to where the food was set up.

Josh scratched his tummy. "I'm not hungry."

Josh toyed with his sandwich. Issy wasn't much hungrier. Nathan handed the kids water bottles. "It's hot. Make sure you drink plenty of water."

After lunch, they played in the surf and searched for shells. They fished, sailed some more, ate dinner and then headed into the harbor for fireworks.

As they waited, Issy sat on the deck near his chair. Nathan finished his beer.

"When do we eat my fish?" Josh asked, rubbing his stomach.

"You barely ate dinner." Nathan frowned. Josh usually had a great appetite. "I cleaned it and put it on ice. We'll take it back to your mom and she'll decide."

"I caught the biggest fish," Josh bragged.

"You sure did, slugger."

"Thanks for helping me bring in my fish." Josh scratched some more.

"You're welcome." Nathan grinned. The kid's thank-you was…gratifying.

Issy scratched her back.

"Did you kids get bit?" Sand fleas could be vicious. He checked their ankles, but didn't see any bites.

"It itches." Josh reached down to scratch, but Nathan stopped him.

"Let's see if there's something in the bag." He pulled out a pink bottle of calamine lotion. "Your mother packed everything." He pretended to dig some more. "Yup, there it is…the kitchen sink."

"It's a mother thing. You might need to start carrying a bag." Mom laughed. "I'll grab paper towels for the calamine."

Daniel handed Nathan another beer and sat in the lawn chair next to him.

"Thanks." He sipped the ice-cold drink.

"Mom says you shouldn't drink." Josh crossed his arms, a miniature version of Cheryl.

"It's a holiday."

Daniel changed the subject. "I want to go back and talk about the idea of you carrying a man bag."

Pop huffed. "Forester men don't carry purses."

"I carry a backpack." Josh frowned. "Is that wrong?"

Pop patted Josh's head. "Backpacks are approved."

"I can be a Forester man?" Josh looked at Daniel with more longing than a kid at Christmas.

"We'll name you an honorary member," Nathan said so his father didn't step into the trap Josh was setting for him.

The kid wanted Daniel as a dad. Good choice. Who would choose Nathan Forester? Poor Issy hadn't had an option.

What would Josh do if Nathan asked his permission to date Cheryl? Spit in his face?

Mom handed him a paper towel and he and Bess dabbed pink liquid on the kids' ankles. "Does it itch anywhere else?"

Issy pointed to her calves. He dotted more of the liquid there. She kept pointing and he kept dabbing.

He finally bounced a dot on her nose. "I think it doesn't itch in all those places. I think you just want me to paint you pink."

She giggled. He pulled her onto his lap, getting pink streaks on his arms and shorts.

The first set of fireworks exploded. Issy screamed.

"Honey." Nathan clutched her to his chest.

She kept screaming.

"It's fireworks." He rocked her back and forth. "Only fireworks."

She trembled, burying her face deep in his shoulder.

"Issy." Josh patted her head. "Don't worry."

"It's nothing bad. I won't let bad things happen to you. This is just…" Nathan couldn't think of the words.

Mom knelt next to his chair, stroking Issy's back. "Oh, baby, fireworks are just colorful lights that make a big bang."

Her sobs came out in shuddery gasps.

"I'm here. It's all right." Nathan repeated the words, rocking back and forth. His heart ached for his daughter.

"Talk to me, Issy," he begged. "Tell me why you're afraid."

She shook her head, frantic.

"Oh, honey." Nathan's mother stroked her hair. "Your dad will make everything better."

Issy's sobs eased. Her back, stiff as a two-by-four,

softened. Nathan wanted to rip her pain away. Was this what it was like to love someone? Love your child?

"Should we leave?" Daniel asked.

Issy clung to him but she'd stop crying. "Are you okay?"

She nodded.

He turned her around and pointed to the sky. "Watch, honey."

She snuggled into his arms, but her eyes were open.

"It's only noisy lights." He jiggled his knee.

A massive bang echoed across the water. Issy whimpered, but the fireworks exploded into a golden waterfall.

"Isn't it pretty?" he asked.

She pointed at the sparks as they fell into the water and faded. He hugged her close. He had to get the bottom of her fear. Then maybe she would finally speak.

"Look at Josh steering the sailboat!" Cheryl held her phone out to Abby.

"He's a natural." Abby brushed a wisp of hair off her cheek with her shoulder. "How's the reception going?"

"Dinner's done." She bit her lip. "The cake's been cut."

"I popped in as they cut the cake." Abby poked her shoulder. "You may have found a new calling. They were raving."

"Really?" Cheryl leaned against the counter.

"I tasted it. Fabulous." Abby blew on her nails and

polished them on her chef's coat. "You must have had the *best* teacher."

"I did. I do."

"How are classes going?" Abby asked.

"Really well."

"I can tell. Your skills improve every day."

"Thanks." Warmth filled her chest. "I want to work full-time in your restaurant."

"You're doing all the right things," Abby said but didn't commit to hiring her.

Cheryl's phone dinged. "Nathan's sent another picture."

This time Josh's ankles were covered in pink dots. "Oh, no."

"Bug bites?"

Cheryl shrugged. "I hope he's okay."

"He'll be fine." Abby loaded the last of the dishes. "How was your date? We've been so busy, I didn't get a chance to ask."

"A dream." She smiled. Nathan had said this was the best summer of his life. What did that mean? "The food and setting were perfect."

"And was Nathan perfect?"

"Until Bess called." Then everything had gotten weird. He'd looked so hurt when he and Issy had left last night. "Issy had a nightmare."

"The poor kid."

The phone call had been a reality check and had kept them from having sex. It had reminded her she couldn't ignore her real life. In the moonlight, she'd forgotten how much Josh despised Nathan.

Abby wiggled her eyebrows. "I wouldn't have paired the two of you, but you're like puzzle pieces. You fit."

"You might be right." But Cheryl wasn't sure they could ever fit together properly. Josh despised Nathan. "I think I'll take more coffee to the ballroom and make sure they don't need anything."

"I'm done here. If you need anything, call." Abby dried her hands. "I'm going to watch the fireworks from my balcony with Gray. Come over if you get a chance."

Cheryl nodded and filled the coffee urn.

Josh was watching fireworks with the Foresters. Too bad she'd let Amy talk her into working. Sitting on a boat with Nathan and his family would have been wonderful.

Mama had never taken her to a fireworks display. The one good thing about Mama was that she wouldn't drive drunk. And by the time it was dark enough for fireworks, Mama was at the stage of her evening where she'd stayed put.

Brad had been appalled she'd never watched fireworks. He'd taken her one summer and they'd made out on a grassy hill while fireworks glittered. When Josh had been two, they'd gone as a family. Her chest ached at the memory of how innocent she'd been to all the pain that was coming.

She pushed through the swinging kitchen door and

headed to the ballroom. Next year she would make a Fourth of July family memory for Josh. She would develop a backbone and stand up for herself. She had seniority at the B and B and should be able to have holidays off if she wanted.

In the ballroom, everything was running like clockwork. She checked with the bartender and brought him more ice.

The glittering chandeliers reflected off the mirrors on the walls. She wanted to salute all the red, white and blue draping. The newlyweds had been in the navy, stationed near Norfolk.

The patio doors were open and guests milled around the terrace, staring into the sky at the same fireworks her son watched. If only the reception would end. She could go home and cuddle her boy. And maybe cuddle Nathan. She drew in a shaky breath at the memory of him kissing and touching her.

But what about Josh?

Back in the kitchen, she pulled out Nathan's computer. She had a paper to finalize for her history class and wanted to get it in a couple of days early.

Why she needed a history class—actually two of them—when she was going for a Culinary Arts Associate's degree, she'd never understand. She just wanted to work in Abby's restaurant. But she wouldn't let her grades drop. She hoped to get an academic scholarship to help pay for her remaining classes.

She began editing. If she had to write about ancient history, it would have a food twist. She'd picked the history of nutmeg. Who knew the Dutch had controlled the spice? A couple hundred years ago, the bag of nutmeg in her cupboard could have made her a wealthy woman.

She reread the paper, checked her references and sent it to her professor. Done.

Since no one needed her in the ballroom, she opened her email. She'd take a couple of minutes to clear out the junk.

There was an email from a J Smith. More junk? But the subject line said DO NOT DELETE. She took a chance and clicked on the message.

A mutual friend wanted me to send this to you. If you don't deposit the requested money, this goes to the Fitzgeralds. You have the instructions.

What? She hesitated, then opened the attachment.

It was a video showing a blonde woman bouncing on a man seated in a chair. A naked blonde. It was—porn. She shivered. As Josh would say, *gross*.

She slid the cursor over to stop the disgusting video, hoping she hadn't infected Nathan's computer with a virus. Before she could, the camera panned around and zoomed in on the woman's face.

Cheryl's hand froze. *Her* face?

The woman's eyes were closed, her hair wild around her head.

Cheryl's hand shook, making the cursor jump.

"No." Acid burned the back of her throat. The camera shifted and focused on the guy.

"How?"

It couldn't be. She didn't recognize the man, the room or the body. But it was her face on the woman.

She slammed the computer shut, swallowing back bile.

It wasn't her. She'd never been that busty. Her hair hadn't been that long for a couple of years. She rubbed her throbbing head. What should she do?

What if J Smith sent this to Abby? Would her boss believe the disgusting images weren't her? How would it affect her job?

What if Nathan saw this? Or Josh? She wanted to curl into a ball. Oh, God. What would this do to her son?

Her breath came in raspy gasps. She couldn't move. Her life was just coming together. Now this.

NATHAN LIFTED A sleeping Issy out of the car. It broke his heart that she'd been so scared.

Josh's feet dragged as they headed up the stairs. The kids were up way past their bedtimes.

Laughter floated from the ballroom into the courtyard. The wedding guests at the B and B were still partying.

He'd hoped they'd be gone. Then he could spend the last of the holiday with Cheryl. Just holding her would be nice. He wanted to get back to the connection they'd had on the boat.

He'd missed her today. Hopefully next year she'd have the holiday off and they could celebrate together.

Next year?

His heart jolted. He'd never thought that far ahead with a woman. Never wanted to date beyond a month or two. It was just too hard hiding his flaws.

But Cheryl already knew. She knew and hadn't booted him from her life.

He unlocked her apartment. Setting down the bag, he said to Josh, "Go brush your teeth and hop into your pajamas."

Both kids should probably wash off the sand and salt, but it was more important for them to get to sleep.

"I'll be right back." He planned to let Issy sleep in Josh's bottom bunk until Cheryl came home. He stripped her down, checking her ankles. No bites that he could see.

Grabbing her toothbrush, he carried the sleepy girl to Cheryl's place.

Josh was putting his toothbrush in the holder.

He helped Issy onto the stool and applied toothpaste to her brush. "Here you go."

"That's my toothpaste." Josh crossed his arms.

Nathan refused to engage. "And next time you brush your teeth in my place, you can use Issy's."

He wet a washcloth and wiped it over Josh's face and then Issy's. He said to Josh, "Why don't you hit the sack and I'll tuck you both in."

Josh shuffled into his bedroom and Nathan guided

Issy into the bottom bunk, pulling the blankets around her chin. "You're snug as a lightning bug."

Please don't let her have nightmares from the fireworks.

"I want a book." Josh pointed.

The kid could read better than he could, but Nathan picked up a well-loved book and opened the page to the marker. He stumbled through the story.

Josh closed his eyes. Issy drifted off.

He'd put himself to sleep, listening to his crappy reading.

Relieved they were both asleep, Nathan turned off the light. The night-light glowed from the corner.

He propped the door open in case Issy had a nightmare. He should have put a Pull-Up on her. Lately, they'd stopped using them. But she'd just had a screaming jag over fireworks.

He flipped the television on, searching for a movie. And found *Independence Day*. Appropriate.

Laughter erupted from the ballroom terrace. He stared over at the partiers. Sparklers wove patterns in the dark. They didn't sound like they were going home anytime soon.

He checked on the kids. Then he got a beer from his fridge. It was a holiday. He could have a couple of beers—well this might be his third or fourth, but he'd spread them throughout the day. Before Issy, he would have gone through a case on a holiday.

The cold brew soothed as it slipped down his throat. He stepped out onto the small landing, leaving the door open. Over the hum of the movie, fireworks exploded. Bright gold and white showers flickered above the trees. Firecrackers popped somewhere. He leaned on the railing and stared at the ballroom. *Go away. Let Cheryl come home. To me.*

Everyone around him was hooking up—permanently. At least, all the Fitzgerald sisters. Abby and Gray were married. Dolley and Liam lived together. Daniel and Bess's wedding was coming up fast. He smiled. As best man, he would be in charge of the bachelor party.

Bess would castrate him if he got strippers. The woman was strong and could probably do it. And his brother would hold him down.

He could ask Gray for ideas. He was a groomsman and pretty classy. Nathan leaned over and stared at Gray and Abby's carriage house. Light gleamed from a window. He'd check with Gray about planning the party.

Back inside, he watched the movie. After a long day of sun, surf and chasing kids, the beer had him nodding off.

He jerked awake. Listened for the kids. All quiet. Will Smith dragged an alien across the sand on the television screen. Footsteps rattled on the stairs. A smile cracked his face. Cheryl.

His knees clicked as he stood. He opened the door. She jumped back, setting her hand on her chest. "Hi."

He pulled her into a hug. "Hi back atcha."

She was stiff for a few minutes, then melted. He loved the way her body fit with his.

"How was the wedding?" He didn't give her a chance to answer. He angled her face and brushed a kiss on her upturned lips.

She sighed. How could one of her sighs make him feel ten feet tall?

He eased his tongue into her mouth, savoring her. Until she stiffened and nudged him back.

Hell. She'd remembered Josh.

He brushed one more kiss on her lips. "I missed you tonight."

"I wish I could have been with you, but the wedding was fun. Very...patriotic."

"I saw the guests swinging sparklers." He led her to the sofa.

"Oh. I should check on—"

"Josh is fine," he interrupted.

She settled into his shoulder. "Thanks for including him in your family party. I'm glad he didn't have to hang around the B and B."

"He had fun." Maybe not with Nathan, but Josh loved being around *Mr. Dan.* "He caught a red fish. He's expecting you to make a feast with it. It's in your fridge."

"Do I have to clean it?" She shuddered. "I know how. I just don't like to."

He nuzzled her neck. "What would you do for me if I cleaned it for you?"

She turned into his body and grazed her lips along his chin. "I might think of something."

"Sexual favors?"

"Sexual favors?" Her voice sounded weird. Goose bumps covered her arms. "Um. Maybe."

"You okay?"

"Just a long day." She leaned her head against his chest. "But the bride and groom loved the wedding cake I made."

There was something off about her enthusiasm. "Congratulations."

"Thanks." She pulled away from him. "What time did Josh go down?"

"Late. About ten."

"Wow."

"Issy's asleep in the bottom bunk." He pulled her ponytail out and combed his fingers through her hair. "Want to fool around?"

She groaned as he massaged her scalp. "Want to. Can't."

He knelt, slipped off her shoes and massaged the balls of her feet.

She arched her back. He tried not to watch the way her shirt pulled around her breasts. His body was hoping for more of her tonight.

Then she went wet-noodle limp. "Oh. Oh, my."

He chuckled. "You like that?"

"*Yes*. No one's ever massaged my feet." She groaned. "If you do this every night, I might work on those sexual favors."

She'd never had a foot massage? "But you were married," he blurted out.

The tension sprang back into her muscles. "It wasn't something Brad did."

He wanted to kick his own ass. "Well, I don't mind giving you one."

He worked his fingers until they ached, not wanting to stop touching her.

"That was amazing." Her foot slipped out of his hands. "But I need sleep."

Here's your hat. There's the door. "Do you want me to take Issy home?"

"She's fine."

He caught her hand and pulled her to her feet and into a hug. If she'd been a wet noodle before, now she was a stiff board. What was going on? He tried to keep it easy. "I'll lock up behind me."

He bent to brush a kiss on her lips. Her head turned and his lips landed on her cheek.

"Night," she muttered.

Was she done with him already?

After locking the door, he slumped against the hallway wall. What had he done wrong?

CHAPTER TWELVE

CHERYL SIPPED HER coffee and grimaced.

She rarely made coffee, but the apartment had a coffeemaker. She'd hoped the caffeine jolt would help her figure out what to do about the video.

She tapped her finger on the mug. If the Fitzgeralds or the Foresters saw that awful thing, she would die. Would anyone believe it wasn't her? Her stomach burned. She tipped the mug into the sink. The coffee wouldn't do her any good if it made her sick.

As much as she hated the thought, she needed to see the video again.

The last time her hair had been that long was after Brad died. They'd lived with Levi. She shuddered. He must have taken pictures of her sleeping and had them superimposed on the actress's face in the video. Could he have done this from prison? Was he J Smith?

To clear her mind, she pulled out the makings for oatmeal pancakes. It was the only recipe her grandmother had passed down to her.

Life would have been better if she'd grown up with Grandma. From what she remembered, her grandmother had loved her, but she'd died when Cheryl was nine.

After pulling the ingredients together, she threw bacon into her cast-iron pan. It was Saturday. She would invite Nathan and Issy to join them.

Maybe she shouldn't. If something happened and

this video came out, she didn't want to see the disgust on Nathan's face. He'd been kind last night and she'd pushed him away.

Josh came into the kitchen, rubbing his eyes. "Mornin'."

"Good morning to you."

"I smell bacon." He yawned.

"And oatmeal pancakes," she said. "I thought we'd have our own Fourth of July celebration."

"Okay." He didn't have any enthusiasm. There were pink dabs on his legs and ankles.

"Did something bite you?"

"I dunno." He scratched his tummy. "Bess put stuff on me."

She'd never seen him so tired. What had he gotten into? "Why don't you brush your teeth, shower and get dressed?"

"Issy's in my room."

"You can dress in the bathroom."

"'Kay."

She started turning the bacon, but a soft knock at the back door interrupted her. Hurrying over, she flipped the lock and rushed back to the pan. "Come on in."

Should she tell Nathan about the video? No. He had enough to worry about with his daughter. He didn't need to take on her problems, too.

"Did everyone sleep all right?" Nathan wrapped his arms around her and brushed a kiss on her neck.

Since the shower was still running, she gave herself a minute to enjoy his hug. With his arms around her, she could forget about everything else. "The kids didn't make a peep."

"I was worried Issy would have another nightmare. She freaked out during the fireworks."

"Oh, no."

"I got her calmed down. But she jumped at every explosion."

She turned to look at him. "How did you and Josh do?"

"He had fun with the family." He exhaled. "I don't know why he hates me. I'm trying. I just…" He raised his hands and let them drop to his thighs.

"I'd hoped things would get better." She flipped the bacon.

"You and me both."

"Josh is itchy. What did he get into?"

"We weren't sure." Nathan pulled out plates. "Both he and Issy were scratching and didn't eat much. We thought maybe sand fleas."

"Ouch."

"I didn't see any bites. We put on calamine." He stroked her back. "I missed you yesterday."

She set the tongs down and kissed him. And longed for more. But she still had to deal with Levi's foulness and Josh's dislike.

Nathan brushed back her hair and touched the circles under her eyes. "Didn't get much sleep?"

She tried to joke it off. "Are you saying I look old and tired?"

"Just tired." He smoothed his thumb between her eyebrows. "What's wrong?"

"I tossed and turned last night." She flipped the bacon, even though it didn't need turning. "I shouldn't have sampled the wedding cake. I can't eat sweets that late."

He headed to the coffeemaker. "Mind if I…?" He waved his hand.

"Go ahead." At least it wouldn't go to waste.

"You don't usually make coffee." He took a sip. "And this is good coffee."

"I only like the smell." She pulled out the griddle.

"You've got a lot of food here." He leaned against the counter. "Need help eating it?"

"Are you inviting yourself to breakfast?" She kept her tone playful, but maybe she should put some distance between them. If Nathan saw the awful video, he might push her away.

"Am I invited?" Nathan asked.

"You and Issy are invited. It's my famous oatmeal pancakes."

"Need help with breakfast?" he offered.

"You could set the table and check on Issy."

She flipped another strip and stared into the pan. "Can I borrow your computer again?"

"Sure. Didn't finish your paper?"

"No." She hated lying, but she had to watch the video again.

For Josh's sake, she had to stop letting people

take advantage of her. That meant figuring out what to do about Levi's blackmail.

"HEY, SLEEPYHEAD." NATHAN rubbed Issy's shoulder. "It's breakfast time. Pancakes."

He hadn't tried his hand at pancakes yet. Life would be simpler if poor Issy had two parents who lived together. Then each parent could focus on their strengths. Cooking definitely wasn't his. He needed to find Heather—not that he wanted to co-parent with her, but he was still drawing a blank locating her.

He wouldn't mind parenting with Cheryl.

Issy opened her eyes and shook her head. Nathan put a hand on her back. Was she warm? "Come on, let's get you up."

Thank goodness the bed was dry. He took her into the steamy bathroom. "On the pot, kiddo."

Josh was at the table by the time they entered the kitchen. But the boy cradled his chin on his hand.

"I must have kept them up too late. They're exhausted," he whispered.

Cheryl set a plate of pancakes on the table. "They slept in, though."

She brushed Josh's hair back. "You're a little warm."

They both put bacon and pancakes on the kids' plates, cut everything and added syrup. "Eat up."

Nathan dug in. "These are great."

The kids barely moved.

"Come on, Josh." Cheryl picked up his fork and fed him. "These are your favorite."

Nathan did the same with Issy. It was like the kids were zoned out. He rubbed his neck. "Maybe they had too much sun yesterday."

Cheryl looked at Issy and then Josh. "No one's sunburned."

"And I made sure they drank plenty of water."

Issy gave up after eating half a pancake. Josh didn't each much more than that. He asked, "Can I watch TV?"

"Sure." Cheryl chewed her nail. "Take Issy with you."

Josh held out his hand. He and Issy made a sweet picture as they walked into the other room.

"Do you think they're okay?" Cheryl asked.

"I have no idea." He had so much to learn about kids.

"I don't understand." Cheryl picked up plates and scraped the remains into the garbage. "Josh always eats at least four pancakes."

"Maybe they should take it easy this morning. Issy and I are going to my parents' house this afternoon." He stacked juice glasses in the dishwasher. "Mom wants a quiet picnic at the house. She invited you and Josh."

"Maybe."

"You needed to use my computer?" He pointed to the laptop on the counter.

Cheryl looked at the computer like it was evil. With a sigh, she flipped open the screen. "You should have a password."

"Not me. You know…" He tapped the side of his head and circled his finger.

"What?" She frowned.

"My brain doesn't work right."

Her mouth dropped open. "That's not true. You just learn differently."

"Right." He didn't need a pep talk.

"Stop tearing yourself down." She pointed a finger at him. "You're talented. Other people can't create what you do. Can't love your little girl the way you do. Can't draw the way you do."

Now it was his mouth that dropped open. "No one has ever stood up for me."

"Your family loves you."

"Yeah." But they hadn't stood up for him. He'd been angry at the unfairness of his world and burned too many bridges. "I may not have earned the right to have my family defend me."

"Well, they should. And if they didn't, that's on them. Not you."

"You're good to me." He pulled her out of the chair and pressed his lips to hers. "For me."

She stiffened, then relaxed and wrapped her arms around his neck.

"I think we should tell the kids," he whispered, holding her close. "Tell Josh."

"I know you do." She took a deep breath. "I want to wait."

"Mom?" Josh called. "Can I have a glass of water?"

"Sure." She eased away and pulled two glasses out of the cupboard. "Maybe they both need water."

"I'll take it in." He needed space. Otherwise he would press Cheryl for more than she was willing to give. She was the first woman he wanted to be with and she wouldn't tell her son about them.

"I'll finish this." She waved her hand at the computer. "Then we can see how the kids are before deciding on the picnic."

She stared at the laptop like it was a snake ready to strike.

Something was off. He released a breath. That was his world. Something was always half a bubble off plumb.

"How's it going?" he asked the kids, handing them the glasses.

"I feel funny." Josh rubbed his back against the sofa. "Issy does, too."

Nathan leaned forward. "What did she say?"

"Not words." Josh squirmed.

Nathan moved to Issy. "You're not feeling well?"

She shook her head. That could mean anything. He checked her ankles. She had dried dots of pink from the calamine lotion. He checked Josh. Was his skin red?

"Did anything sting you when you went swimming?" he asked. Jellyfish?

Josh and Issy shook their heads. Nathan pushed back Issy's hair. She might be a little warm.

The pancakes sat like rocks in his stomach. Had he screwed up yesterday? "Let me know if you feel worse."

She nodded but focused on the television. Josh shrugged. Of course.

Nathan headed back to the kitchen, stopping in the doorway. Cheryl stared at the computer screen, her hand over her mouth. All the color had drained from her face and her freckles stood out like brown paint on her pale skin.

"What's wrong?" he asked.

Her head jerked up. She looked back at the screen, clicking off whatever had horrified her. "Let me just send this last note."

Her fingers flew over the keyboard. Then she clicked everything closed and shut the laptop. "Done."

He poured the last of the coffee into his mug. Probing, he asked, "Was that school stuff?" Would she trust him with the truth?

"Yes." She brushed the crumbs from the table and then grabbed a wipe and scrubbed. "I told you about my nutmeg paper."

She was lying. The pancakes did another turn in his stomach. Why?

Whatever she'd been looking at had scared her badly. He had to find out what it was.

"THE KIDS AREN'T perking up." Cheryl tossed the last paper plate in the garbage can next to the Foresters' deck.

She, Nathan, Bess and Daniel were cleaning up

from the picnic. Debbie and Samuel held hands as they swung on the glider.

Nathan shook his head. "I don't know what's wrong with them."

She pointed at the tree house where the kids were coloring. "Are you sure that's safe?"

"Pop built it. Daniel and I both checked the flooring before letting the kids climb up." He threw an arm around her shoulder. "They're safe."

"I'm just—Josh is never this quiet," she said. "Plus, they're scratching even more."

Bess came up behind Cheryl and Nathan and set a hand on both of their shoulders. "You're watching those kids like hawks. What's up?"

"They're not acting normal." Cheryl sighed.

"They had a big day yesterday." Bess squeezed her shoulder. "Lots of running, swimming and sun."

Both kids raked their fingers across their calves.

"I wonder." Nathan headed over to the tree and up the ladder. "Guys, can you come down?"

He hoisted Issy into his arms and Josh followed them down the ladder.

"Oh, no." They both had a rash on their legs. Cheryl pulled up Josh's shirt. Red bumps covered his belly. "Does it itch?"

Josh nodded. "I can't stand it."

"Don't scratch," she said.

"That looks like chicken pox." Debbie moved closer and touched both kids' heads as they sat on the edge of the deck. "I'll grab the calamine."

The screen slammed shut as she headed into the house.

"Where would they have gotten chicken pox?" Daniel asked.

Nathan and Cheryl turned to each other. "Day care."

Pop stopped next to the kids. "You're looking multicolored there, you guys."

Cheryl grabbed his arm. "Have you had chicken pox?"

"When I was little."

Daniel shook his head. "You should check with your oncologist before getting too close to them, Pop."

Cheryl set her hand on Josh's forehead. "He's been warm since this morning."

"My head hurts," Josh whined.

Issy pointed at her head. "Does your head hurt, too?" Cheryl asked. Issy nodded, her bottom lip quivering.

Debbie came back with a bottle and cotton balls. "Let's cover what itches."

She shook the bottle, loaded up a cotton ball and handed it to Cheryl.

"It feels like I should do more," Cheryl said.

Nathan and she dabbed at all the red, blotchy skin.

"Let's head home," Nathan said, glancing at his dad.

"When Daniel and Nathan had chicken pox, I gave them oatmeal baths," Debbie said.

"I've got oatmeal." Cheryl wanted to get Josh home and comfortable.

They packed and buckled the kids into the truck. Nathan helped Cheryl into the front seat, suggesting, "If you don't mind, maybe we could take care of them together."

"I'd appreciate the help." With Brad overseas, she'd raised Josh mostly alone. She'd dealt with teething, illnesses and just plain grumpiness. It would be nice to share the burden. "Issy can sleep in the bunk bed."

"And me?" he whispered. "Where will I sleep?"

She was worried about her son and he was worried about where he'd sleep? "I can't think about that right now."

NATHAN GRABBED HIS phone when it rang. Finally. He'd been waiting for the on-call doctor from the clinic to call back.

"Mr. Forester, I understand you might be dealing with chicken pox cases."

"That's what we think, but we don't understand," Nathan said. "Both Josh and Issy have been vaccinated."

"I looked up their immunization records. It's possible Isabella was exposed before she got her first vaccination. Hopefully Josh's vaccination means he'll have a milder case."

Great.

"Keeping them comfortable is about all you can do." The doctor rattled off a list of instructions. "Keep them isolated until the pox crust over. That can take up to two weeks."

She gave Nathan recommended antihistamine doses for Josh and Issy. He carefully wrote down the amounts and then read them back. He couldn't screw this up. The kids and Cheryl were counting on him.

Nathan stuck his head into the bathroom where Cheryl was supervising Issy's bath. "Dr. Sanders called back."

He ran through the conversation and then said, "She recommended antihistamines and lotion."

Cheryl poured water over Issy's hair. "I planned to search online, too."

"I'll do it." He should be able to handle that, right? If he had trouble, he'd bring the laptop to her to double-check.

He opened the computer. And remembered Cheryl's worried face this morning. He wanted to find out why she'd looked so frightened, but that would have to wait. Issy and Josh came first.

It took him three tries to get the correct spelling of chicken pox. Damn his fingers and brain not working together. He finally found a website. "Calamine. Aloe vera. Lavender infusions. Tea tree oil. Oatmeal baths and witch hazel."

When he went to tell Cheryl, she was drying Issy off. He quickly related what he'd found and let her know he'd be back soon.

After a trip to the drugstore and a conversation with the pharmacist, Nathan returned home with two full bags.

When he entered the apartment, the kids each sucked on a Popsicle. "That looks tasty."

"I thought they could use the water." Cheryl touched Josh's forehead and then Issy's.

He set the bags on the table and pulled out bottles, tubes and cotton balls. "I talked to the pharmacist, too. She confirmed everything I bought."

"They're both running low-grade temps." Cheryl wrapped her arms around her stomach. "I don't like this."

"Are they over 102 degrees?" The doc had said to call if that happened.

"No."

Josh held out his stick. "Mom."

"Yes?"

"I'm done."

Cheryl brushed Issy's hair back. "Hey, short stuff. I wish you would tell us how you feel."

Issy rubbed her eyes.

"Don't rub, sweetie." Nathan pulled her hands away. "I know it itches, but you can't rub."

Issy whimpered. He picked her up and she tucked her head under his chin. "I wish I could take away the itches."

Josh scratched under his T-shirt.

"Let's get the antihistamines in them." Nathan grabbed the paper with the doses.

He handed the note and box to Cheryl. "You'd better check that I wrote down the right amounts."

She checked the back of the box and the amounts he'd written down. "These are right."

"I bought two boxes. Can we mark each dropper with the right dose and keep them separate?" Then he wouldn't worry about screwing up and hurting the kids.

"Good idea." She touched his back before getting a marker to indicate the right dose. "We'll keep Josh's in the bathroom and Issy's in the kitchen."

They dosed the kids and covered the spots with aloe vera.

"I bought a…" He couldn't find the damn word. Instead he handed Cheryl the box.

"An infuser?"

He shrugged. "A website said we could use lavender oil to keep them calmer."

"You're a good man." She started to fold the bag, then shook it. "What else did you get?"

"A few things to keep them occupied." A couple of movies and coloring books. Chutes and Ladders. Matchbox cars. He'd loved those as a kid.

"Do you want to watch a movie?" Cheryl asked the kids.

"Sure." Josh pointed at the action movie. Issy pointed at the princess movie.

Cheryl held up the princess movie. "Issy first then Josh's pick."

Josh's face looked like a thundercloud had rolled in. "Mom."

"Josh."

It would be a long day.

"I GAVE JOSH his antihistamine." Cheryl stretched her arms over her head. Everything ached. She hadn't carried Josh this much in years. "He's asleep."

"Issy went out like a light. I hope they don't scratch all night." Nathan sat on the sofa, his head bouncing a little on the back cushion. "Thanks for letting her sleep here tonight."

"They comfort each other." She chewed on her lip. She should make a bed for Nathan on the sofa.

"Come here." He patted the spot next to him.

Sitting next to him, she heaved a sigh. "I'm glad we're…together in this."

"Me, too." He kissed her forehead. "I'd be fumbling without you."

He shifted so they sat sideways on the sofa, her back to him. Then he kneaded her neck.

Her head dropped forward. The warmth of his touch released the tension in her shoulders. "Don't stop."

Chuckling, he worked his hands as if kneading dough.

"Lie down." His warm breath caressed her ear.

She sank into the cushions.

Nathan worked his amazing hands down her back. His weight shifted and he massaged her thighs and feet. The fridge hummed. The fan oscillated, blowing against her skin. None of that mattered. There were only his hands on her body and the incredible intimacy of his touch.

His movements slowed. Instead of massaging, he

stroked. His hand slipped under her shirt and wrapped around to caress her breasts.

Her breath stuttered, awareness shooting through her body. Everything yearned inside her. For Nathan. She wanted this. Wanted him.

He pressed his lips against her neck and lingered. Each stroke of his tongue sent energy coursing to her core.

"I do better work in bed." His words were warm pulses in her ear.

"Massage?"

Flipping her over, he hauled her into his arms. "That, too."

She laughed, but his lips stopped the sound. His kiss swept away her stress. She clutched at his soft hair. No more chicken pox, rashes or cranky kids. She tucked away the worry that Josh despised Nathan.

Their tongues stroked and played. His hands cupped her butt and tugged her up, swinging her so she straddled his lap.

She tightened her legs around him and their bodies aligned. The seam of her shorts rubbed in all the right places. His magical hands slid her tank top and bra straps down her shoulders. As he kissed his way to her breasts, she moaned.

They shouldn't be out in the open like this. Josh or Issy might wake up.

Her hips rocked with his. "We should…"

He rolled a nipple between his fingers and took the other in his mouth. She forgot everything but the sensations ricocheting through her body and converging between her legs. Heat. Fire. Pulsing need.

The world jerked and shifted. Nathan carried her down the hall. "I need you. Now."

She pressed the door closed as he carried her into the bedroom. Then it was a scramble to shed their clothes. Even the air-conditioning on her bare skin didn't cool her fire.

His shorts jingled as he dug for his wallet and pulled out a condom. She should keep condoms in the nightstand.

"Let me." She took the packet and rolled it on, staring into his eyes.

"Are you okay with this?" he whispered, pulling her on top of him.

She flung a leg over him, like a cowgirl. "Oh, yeah."

Settling on top of his erection, she rolled her hips. Tingles ignited in every muscle.

"I plan to drive you crazy." She ran her teeth along the shell of his ear. His groan rumbled under her lips.

"Just looking at you makes me crazy." His breath feathered her hair. "I want to be inside you."

"Not yet." She undulated her hips.

His fingers tightened on her butt. It would be her fault if there was bruising, but she didn't care. She wanted him mad with desire.

"Cheryl." He lunged and took her nipple in his mouth. His small bite took her to new thresholds of pleasure. Then he did the same to her other breast.

She jerked up and slid him home.

"Oh, oh, oh, my." Her words tumbled out.

He held her in place. "Hang on."

"Nathan." She wanted to ride him into oblivion.

"Wait," he groaned through gritted teeth. "Please."

She tightened around him.

His fingers clenched around her hips. "You're pushing me over the edge."

She grinned.

"Kiss me," he demanded.

Her hair fell around their faces. Just leaning forward changed the pressure into something…more. Her breath quickened.

His kiss was rough, carnal and everything she wanted. She tried to move, but he kept one hand on the small of her back and one locked in her hair.

When the kiss ended, she gasped for air. "I need to move."

She should be in control. But she wasn't. He manipulated every slide, keeping them slow and steady. She wanted speed. She set her hands beside his head. "Please."

"I don't want this to end."

She would die from sexual frustration before she came.

Finally they moved. Their bodies slid apart then joined together. Each stroke took her higher. Her breath caught in her chest and stars glittered at the edge of her vision.

"Breathe," Nathan whispered.

She gave in, gave Nathan control.

He reached between them and she combusted at his touch. Nathan gripped her hips, thrusting higher, and followed her into orbit.

Her muscles melted like ice cream in July. She collapsed onto his chest.

"I've got you." Nathan stroked her back, pressing her close. "I've got you."

What energy she had evaporated. It was all she could do to roll with him to her side. Her breaths came in deep gasps.

They lay together on the same pillow, face to face. He brushed a kiss on her lips. "That was... You are..."

"Unbelievable." She found enough energy to touch his cheek. "Thank you."

"Thank you." He grinned. She could see the carefree boy he must have been once.

Nathan kissed her slowly and tenderly. When he pulled away, her breath stuttered out and her heart pounded.

He sighed. "I'll be right back."

She burrowed deeper under the sheet. In a few minutes she would get up and find Nathan the extra blanket and pillow she'd bought. Get him set up on the sofa.

A few minutes to enjoy the aftershocks of her orgasm. Who would have guessed Nathan was so wonderfully thorough?

And she drifted to sleep.

CHAPTER THIRTEEN

"GET AWAY FROM my mom!"

A small fist punched Nathan in the back, jolting him awake. A flurry of punches smashed into his kidneys.

"You butthead!"

"Hey!" Nathan rolled and grabbed for Josh's hands, but they were a blur.

"Joshua Bradley," Cheryl clutched the sheet under her arms. "Stop!"

Josh aimed a punch at Nathan's nose. It grazed his face, but only because Nathan bobbed out of the way.

Nathan caught Josh's shoulder and pulled him against his side, clamping the kid's hands and arms together.

Shit. He was naked. He glanced over. So was Cheryl.

Josh kicked, almost nailing him in the groin.

"Cut it out!" Nathan roared.

"Get away from my mom. You butthead. Get out of her bed!" Tears filled Josh's voice. "Don't you hurt her."

"I'm okay." Cheryl grabbed for Josh, but even in the low morning light, Nathan saw her distress as the sheet slipped. She tucked the covers under her arms and slid over to where he held her son. "He's not hurting me. It's…like Issy sleeping in your bedroom."

"But…" Josh slumped in Nathan's hold.

Cheryl juggled the sheet while pulling her son to her lap. "Nathan, can you…?" She made a walking movement with her fingers.

"Not a good plan." He glanced at his chest and raised an eyebrow. His bare chest wasn't the worst. He'd planned to pull on his boxers last night, but instead had curled up next to Cheryl.

"Oh." She slapped a hand on her mouth.

"Yeah. Oh." How the hell would they get out of this?

She bit her lip, but kept stroking her son's shoulder. "How are you feeling, honey?"

"I'm itchy." Josh glared at Nathan. "All over."

"Why don't you head into the bathroom and I'll fix breakfast?"

"I'm not hungry." Josh slipped out of Cheryl's hug and tugged on her hand. "Come with me."

"Go…watch TV." Desperation laced her voice.

Josh frowned. "Mommy, now."

"Obey your mother," Nathan said. It was Pop's words coming out of his mouth. When had that happened? "Would you check on Issy, please?"

"I don't have to do what you say," Josh shot back.

"Josh!" Cheryl tugged his chin up. "You will apologize to Mr. Nathan. And you will be polite."

"Mom—"

"Now."

"Sorry," the kid snarled. Under his breath he added, *"Butthead."*

"Close the door when you leave." An egg could cook on Cheryl's bright red face.

Of course his couldn't be much paler. He'd never had a kid walk in on him like that before. This was effing complicated.

Josh stomped away, slamming the door.

Cheryl whirled on him. "Why didn't you sleep on the sofa?"

"What?"

"You should have slept on the sofa." She rushed to her dresser and pulled on underwear.

"This is my fault?" He hauled his boxers off the floor and yanked them on. "There were two of us here last night."

"This is the worst thing that could have happened." She pulled on a bra and tank top, then grabbed shorts.

"Wow. Sleeping with me goes down as the worst thing that's ever happened in your life." The bitter words rolled off his tongue. Last night had been possibly the best night of his life. Now this. He pulled on his T-shirt and shorts. "Issy and I will get out of your hair. Wouldn't want to ruin your *life*."

He grabbed the doorknob. Thank goodness it was Sunday. He had all day to figure out how to manage the construction project and take care of Issy. Alone.

"Nathan. Wait." She slumped onto the bed. "I didn't mean it that way."

He pressed his hand to the wood. "I think you did."

Soft footsteps padded from the bed to the door. He didn't turn around. Didn't want her knowing how deep her words cut him.

Cheryl's arms wrapped around his waist. She set

her cheek against his back. "I'm sorry. I just didn't want Josh to see us…" Her voice trailed off.

"Together? You're ashamed of me." The words ripped out, like knives slicing into his gut.

"No!" She pulled on his arm. "I've never done anything like this."

He should have walked out the door. Instead he faced her.

"I have to think of Josh first." Worry lined her forehead. "You understand that, right?"

"Yeah." Was he putting Issy first? He didn't know. But his heart ached at the thought of anything hurting his little girl. "What do you want?"

Her eyes closed. "I didn't want Josh finding us in bed."

"That ship has sailed." For the first time since the kids had gotten sick, he craved a beer. A really large cold one and it wasn't even eight in the morning.

Cheryl's head dropped to his chest. His arms wrapped around her, even though his head hollered at him to step away. She would never choose him. Josh would see to that.

He should be thinking about his daughter. How to get her healthy. How to get her to talk. "I should check on Issy."

She held him tighter. "Are we all right?"

"We're absolutely fine," he lied.

They could help each other with the kids, but he couldn't afford to let her tie him in emotional knots.

He just had to stop this falling-in-love shit.

ALL DAY, CHERYL and Nathan dosed the kids with anti-histamines, dabbed on calamine or aloe vera, entertained, cajoled and comforted. Apparently, misery did like company. It had taken forever to get them to sleep.

"The day care director's voice mail said two more kids got the chicken pox right before the holiday." Nathan set a bowl in the dishwasher. "A sister and brother. The boy's in Josh's room and the girl's in Issy's."

"At least we know where they got it." Cheryl wiped the counters, shifting Nathan's laptop. Shoot, with the kids sick, she'd forgotten about the disgusting video. She gnawed on the ragged edge of her thumbnail. What if whoever sent her the video had gotten frustrated and sent it on to the Fitzgeralds? "Can I borrow your computer?"

"You don't have to ask." Nathan headed to the living room. "I'm going to watch the ball game."

"Go ahead." She didn't want Nathan knowing what she was doing. If he was engrossed in a game, hopefully he wouldn't ask.

She turned on the computer and opened her email.

Another email with a DO NOT DELETE jumped out at her from the string of emails. With shaking fingers, she tapped the mouse to open the message.

Deposit money now or the video goes out.

The message was dated July fifth. Yesterday. Her fingers bounced against the keyboard. What if this…this…person had already sent the video to the Fitzgeralds?

The mac and cheese she'd made for dinner threatened to come back up.

Her fingers jabbed at the keys as she logged in to her banking site. Her hands shook so hard, it took three tries before she got it right.

The rent and car loan checks hadn't cleared. Once they did, she would have eighty dollars to spare until payday. She still needed money for groceries and gas.

But with the kids sick she didn't want to deal with Levi. It might be easier to just…give him something. She'd buy time to make another plan.

Cheryl dug out Levi's email and followed the instructions for sending money to inmates. Then she sent twenty dollars.

She swallowed and replied to J Smith.

I've sent twenty dollars. That's all I have. Josh is sick.

Clicking the send button, she slumped into the chair. The wooden bars ate into her back. She'd just given in to blackmail.

"ARE YOU SURE you're okay with the kids?" Cheryl asked Nathan.

She really wanted to ask what was wrong.

The past three days, everything had been—weird. Too normal. Too everyday. Too accommodating.

Nathan stayed away from her. No soul-searing

kisses. No touches. Just brief swipes of his lips on hers, even after the kids were in bed.

It was like Nathan had left her, even though the four of them had spent the past four days in the same apartment. Without her even asking, Nathan had slept on the sofa.

She wanted him to sleep with her. But how could she say that after freaking out last time?

"What did you ask?" Nathan turned from washing Issy's hands.

"Are you sure you're okay with the kids?" It was only midafternoon, but Abby needed her help for an anniversary party. She and Nathan had given the kids their undivided attention, but Josh and Issy had been getting harder to entertain.

"We'll be fine." He helped Issy off the stool, ruffling her hair.

"Is everything okay?" she asked.

"Fine."

She'd been getting the same answer for three days.

"Okay." She twisted her hair into a bun. "Issy's medicine is in the kitchen. Josh's bottle is in the bathroom."

He looked up from helping Issy dry her hands. "We've been doing the same routine for days."

"I know." She hurried over and touched his shoulder. "I'm sorry. I wish I could be here tonight."

"Mom," Josh whined.

"What do you need?" She squatted next to Josh as he drew.

"I don't want you to go."

She wanted to brush back his hair, just to touch him. But angry spots covered his face and scalp. If she could take them away, she would. "You and Mr. Nathan will have a good time. And Issy, too."

"We won't." Josh shot an ugly look at Nathan. The word he mouthed looked suspiciously like *butthead*.

Her stomach twisted. Josh's attitude—bad to begin with—had gotten worse since he'd found Nathan in her bed.

"We're working on Issy's mural. Then we'll watch a movie." Nathan smiled at her. A smile that didn't reach his eyes. "We'll be fine."

There was that word again. *Fine*. Between Nathan and her son, she was walking a tightrope with angry gators snapping at her heels. She didn't want to lose Nathan, but maybe she already had.

Nathan set a hand on her back and guided her to the door. "Go. Everything will be—"

She covered his mouth with her hand. She couldn't stand to hear the word again. "I get it. You'll be fine."

He grinned under her fingers. His first real smile since Josh had found them.

The coil of stress in her belly loosened. Maybe she and Nathan were still a team.

She took his hands. "I think it's time to tell Josh about us."

He swallowed. "Are you sure?"

Holding his gaze, she nodded.

Together, they could work out Josh's aggression.

Together, they could make Issy comfortable enough to talk. Together, they could overcome everything.

A light came back into Nathan's eyes. A light that had been missing the past few days.

"Sleep in my bed tonight. Please?" she whispered.

He grinned. "If that's what you want."

She curled her fingers around his. "I do."

She turned to go, her burdens a little lighter on her shoulders.

Josh stood in the kitchen doorway, hands on his hips. His spotted face twisted into a scowl.

"Be good for Nathan tonight." She waved. "I'll check on you when I get home."

She headed across the courtyard, a spring in her steps. Maybe the reason Josh had never liked Nathan was that he'd instinctively known Nathan threatened their status as a little family of two. She would make sure Josh knew he was loved, but her son would have to adjust. She wanted Nathan and Issy in their lives.

She'd never thought she would love again, but she did. She loved Nathan Forester.

As she pulled open the kitchen door, she did a little shimmy. Tonight she would tell him.

"Finish dinner and we'll head over to the other apartment," Nathan said to Josh.

Issy's plate was clean so he scooped her up and twirled until she giggled.

He couldn't wipe the grin off his face. Cheryl was finally going to tell Josh.

A couple of hours ago he would have said he and Cheryl were heading into the trash. Now? He took a deep breath, inhaling the scent of Issy's shampoo. He and Cheryl were officially together.

"I don't want to." Josh pushed broccoli around his plate.

"Well, that's the plan." He kept his voice mild. Somehow he had to crack the nut that was Josh. Somehow they had to connect. Art should be the ticket. "I thought you wanted to help me paint Issy's wall."

"It's dumb." Josh took his plate and scraped his dinner in the garbage. *Not a good sign.* It might be a long evening.

"Let's go," Nathan said.

Issy waited by the door, scratching her arm.

"Don't scratch," he whispered, unlocking the door.

He'd barely been in their apartment over the past four days. The place looked sad. It didn't have the life Cheryl's apartment had. It didn't have her energy.

His furniture might have been newer, his things more expensive, but Cheryl's apartment was a home. And that was what he wanted. He wanted to build a life with Cheryl, Issy and Mister Grumpy Pants.

Maybe painting Issy's mural would break through to the kid. He didn't care what the mural looked like, he just wanted Josh to contribute. Wanted Josh to know he was proud of his art.

"Can you get the drop cloths out of the kitchen closet?" he asked Josh.

"Why can't you do it?"

Nathan pulled Issy's bed away from the wall. "Because I asked you."

Josh muttered under his breath, but at least he headed to the kitchen.

Nathan should know how to get through to a rebellious kid. He'd been one most of his life.

Nathan set Issy on her bed. "Are you watching or painting?"

She pointed at her bed.

"Can you say *watch*?" he asked.

She held her fingers over her lips, shaking her head.

Josh dragged in a drop cloth. One. At least he'd done that. When they needed another, Nathan would ask again.

"Can you spread it against the wall?" He pointed, just in case he messed up telling his right from his left. Josh *always* caught those mistakes.

Nathan headed to his room to get the supplies he'd bought.

"Here's your palette, paints and brushes." He handed the materials to Josh.

"Wow." Josh's eyes were as big at the lids of the acrylic paint. He picked up a brush and stroked the perfect edge.

"You've been working on blending colors in your art class, right?" Nathan asked.

"Yeah." Josh chewed his lip. "When you say these are mine, do I have to give them back like at art school?"

"That's up to you and your behavior, slugger."

Josh's blond eyebrows came together in a frown.

"What do you want to start with?" Nathan asked.

Josh moved to the right side of the wall. "The castle."

Grays and tans. Nathan handed him the book with the picture of the castle. "In case you need a reminder."

He'd painted the wall an off-white before he and Josh had sketched the princess kingdom on the wall. "What color do you want the princess's dress to be?" he asked his daughter.

Issy scooted off the bed and grabbed her doll's dress, holding out the bright fabric.

He had to be patient, but couldn't she just say pink?

Nathan combined red and white to make the pink. It wasn't quite right, so he added a little blue and held up the color. "Is this good?"

She nodded.

Before he painted the dress, he checked on Josh. All was fine there.

Nathan hit the button on Issy's CD player and the *Frozen* soundtrack filled the room.

He stroked on the color, filling in the skirt. Then added more white to give the fabric folds and depth.

"How did you do that?" Josh asked.

He demonstrated. "Don't forget we're putting the sun in that corner."

"I learned about shadows in art class." Josh nodded.

The music played. Issy bounced on the bed and Nathan and Josh painted. Neither of the kids scratched. It was a win.

He'd just started painting a frog when his phone rang.

"Hey, Cheryl." He grinned.

Josh twisted around, a frown on his face.

"How are the kids?" Cheryl asked.

"Good. We've finished dinner and are working on Issy's mural."

"Let me talk to my mom." Josh tugged on his arm.

"Give me a minute." Nathan moved to the doorway. "How's the anniversary party?"

"The couple was a half hour late. We're backing everything up."

He sighed. "That's too bad."

"Don't wait up," she said.

"I will. I want to." He closed his eyes. "I've got things to tell you."

"Me, too," was her soft reply.

He'd never told a woman he loved her. Would she laugh? Tell him she could never love someone as dumb as he was?

No, Cheryl wasn't like that.

"I can't wait," he said.

"I want to talk to my mom." Josh's tone was belligerent.

There was a crash in the background. "I have to help Abby." Cheryl sounded frantic.

"Okay. See you later."

He disconnected.

"I wanted to talk to my mom!" Josh slammed down the brush and palette. Paint splattered across the floor.

"Hey!" Nathan shoved his phone into his pocket. "Look at the mess you made."

"You're a butthead." Josh kicked at the door frame. "You didn't let me talk to my mom. I wanted to tell her what I'd done. And you're too stupid to let me use the phone." The words spilled out of Josh.

Even with the kid sick, Nathan couldn't let this go. "You're done. And you won't be keeping the art supplies."

"You're mean." Tears sprang from Josh's eyes. "I'm telling my mom you're mean."

Issy cowered on the bed. Her thumb crept into her mouth.

"And I'll tell her what you did and said." He bent to pick up the stuff Josh had thrown. "Get paper towels out of the kitchen closet."

Josh stomped into the hall.

Nathan rinsed the brushes in the bathroom.

Josh tossed the paper towels at his feet and they unrolled.

"Once we clean this up, you're going to bed." Nathan grabbed the towels, wet some and handed them to Josh as they headed back to Issy's bedroom.

"I get to watch a movie." Josh scrubbed hard enough to swirl the colors together.

"Not now." Nathan cleaned up behind the kid. "You're going to bed."

Josh shot him dagger-filled glares but they cleaned up together.

"I'm going to *my* apartment." Without asking, Josh took the paper towels back to the closet. That was a good sign—maybe.

"We'll be right there." Nathan changed Issy into her PJs, then held out his arms. "Come on, let's brush your teeth."

He locked up. In Cheryl and Josh's place, the shower was running. In the kitchen, he got Issy's antihistamine ready. "Here you go."

Josh came into the room.

"Did you brush your teeth?" Nathan asked.

"After I take my medicine." Josh looked at him with big, innocent eyes. Too innocent. "Will you fill my dropper?"

Nathan filled it, then closed the bottle. "Put this back in the bathroom, please."

"Sure."

Josh was acting too cooperative. What was he up to? Nathan started after the boy, but Issy tugged him into the bathroom. He supervised her brushing and dabbed on calamine lotion. "Anything else itch?" He dotted as many spots as he could see.

She shook her head.

"Into bed. I'll be there to tuck you in in a minute."

She nodded.

He heard noises in the kitchen. What was Josh up to?

The kid stood in the middle of the room opening a can of beer.

"What the hell are you doing?" Nathan rushed over to him.

Josh jumped. The can dropped to the floor and sprayed the counters, the table, Josh and Nathan. The scent of beer filled the air.

Nathan swore. "Where did you get that?"

Josh backed away from him. "The closet."

Cheryl rarely drank. Grabbing a towel, Nathan wiped at the sticky pool on the floor. "Your mom had beer in the closet?"

Josh slithered closer to the table. "Your closet."

"What the hel—heck were you planning to do with a beer?"

Josh shrugged.

Nathan rinsed the towel and mopped up the spills. "You aren't supposed to touch stuff like that."

"I…I figured you'd want one." Josh scuffed his toe into the linoleum floor.

The kid was lying. But it didn't make any sense. Why would he take a beer?

"You need to wash off anything that splashed at you," Nathan said.

"I will."

"Do you need calamine?"

"I'll do it myself." Josh grabbed something off the counter and stomped out of the kitchen.

"Clean up and hop in bed."

He glanced up in time to catch Josh sticking out his tongue.

He let it go. Otherwise he'd be tempted to grab the kid by the collar and shake him. They'd all been locked in the apartment too long.

Nathan tossed the empty can in the recycling.

He washed his hands, but the room still smelled of beer. Great. Cheryl would have his head. She wouldn't be happy with Josh, either. He wiped everything again.

Josh crept into the kitchen.

"You're supposed to be in bed." Nathan wrung out the towel and hung it on the hook under the sink.

"I brought back my glass." It rattled as he shoved it on the counter. Issy's antihistamine bottle fell to the floor. Josh scooped it up and set it on the counter. "I didn't get to watch my movie."

Nathan took in a deep breath. "You lost that privilege when you threw the paint."

"You're not the boss of me." Josh shot out of the room.

Nathan wanted to sink into a chair and hold his head. No. He wanted Cheryl to come home. They could talk about the kids, sit on the sofa and just be with each other. She'd know how to deal with her son.

If they wanted to have a relationship, they had to defuse Josh's anger.

He pushed away from the counter and popped his head into the kids' bedroom. Issy was asleep. He didn't know about Josh, but at least the boy was quiet and still.

Exhausted, he headed to bed. He didn't care that it was early. Cheryl had invited him to sleep in her bed. He couldn't wait.

CHAPTER FOURTEEN

Cheryl rushed across the courtyard. She was tired of being cooped up with cranky kids, but she couldn't wait to get home. To Nathan. Somehow they were on the same page. She didn't know if he'd fallen in love, but she sure had.

Glancing up, she smiled. The TV's bluish flicker lit the living room. Tomorrow, she and Josh would talk about Nathan. She rolled her shoulders. The two of them had so much in common. She hoped painting tonight had helped them bond.

When she walked in, her smile turned into a frown. Josh was dozing in front of the TV.

"What are you doing up?" she asked, catching him under his arms.

"I was scared," Josh mumbled.

"Scared?" She groaned a little under his weight. "Why didn't you go to Nathan?"

"*He* scared me."

Her heart sped up. "What? How?"

"The beer." Josh hid his head in her shoulder.

"Beer?"

"Yeah." Josh shook his head. "I didn't want him to hurt me."

"Nathan wouldn't hurt you." But even she heard the doubt in her voice. Nathan would never hurt them, but he'd also promised not to drink around the kids.

Pain lanced through her chest as she carried Josh

to his bedroom, cutting as deep as a knife in a two-tiered wedding cake.

"Get some sleep." She set him on the ladder.

As he climbed to the top bunk, the odor of beer filled her nose. "Why do you smell like beer?"

"He threw it at me." Josh rolled over and fell asleep.

Nathan threw a beer at her son? Cheryl's knees wobbled and she sank onto Issy's bed. Had she misjudged Nathan and put her son in danger? There had to be an explanation.

But her mother had thrown beer cans at her all the time.

Issy rolled over. "Miss Cheryl?"

"Go back to sleep, honey." She stroked the little girl's hair, the only place not covered in spots.

Issy's eyes closed.

Cheryl's mouth dropped open. Issy had talked. Nathan needed to know.

She rushed into her bedroom. When she moved to Nathan's side of the bed, the stench of beer slapped her in the face. Josh had been telling the truth.

Cheryl backed away from the bed. She couldn't talk to Nathan now.

After everything she'd been through, how could she have fallen in love with a drunk?

She stumbled into the hall. Her elbow banged the bathroom door. As much as she wanted to throw Nathan out of her apartment, that might wake the kids. He could be a mean drunk like Mama.

The harsh bathroom light emphasized the shadows under her eyes. She set her hands on the counter and leaned on them. She'd thought they'd had something special.

A bottle slipped off edge of the counter. She picked it up. Had Nathan given Josh his antihistamine? She didn't want her son suffering because Nathan couldn't stop drinking.

She pushed the bottle back, then looked more closely and frowned. Why was Isabella's antihistamine in the bathroom? Had Nathan screwed this up, too?

She inhaled. What if Isabella had taken Josh's dose?

She started back to the bedroom to ask Nathan, then stopped. If he'd been drinking, would he even remember? Instead, she dashed into the kitchen and called Poison Control.

"Slow down, ma'am," the woman said. "Tell me how much you were giving each child."

Cheryl went through all the information, forcing herself to take deep breaths so she could be understood.

The woman's keyboard clacked. Cheryl's fingers drummed against the table. Both bottles sat in front of her. How could Nathan have done this to her? To them? They'd been a team. Her heart ached like he'd pounded it with his hammer.

"With the minimal difference in doses, one dose isn't a problem." The woman rattled off warnings.

"Thank you." Cheryl collapsed into the chair.

Everything was heavy. Her head. Her hands. Her

heart. Just shutting off her phone almost took more energy than she could summon.

Using the table for leverage, she pushed out of the chair and lurched into the living room. On the sofa she curled into a ball and pulled a throw over herself.

A tear slipped down her cheek. She had to cut Nathan and Isabella from her life. Tomorrow.

NATHAN OPENED HIS EYES, disoriented. He'd slept in too many places the past week.

Cheryl's bedroom. He grinned. Today would be a good day. He rolled to her side of the bed.

She wasn't there and the sheets were cool. Was she already up? She could have woken him. He wouldn't have minded.

He tugged on his shorts. Lord, they still stunk of beer. Then he peeked in on the kids. Still sleeping.

He should shower, but he would just have to put on his beer-sprayed clothes.

Why had Josh grabbed the can? Was it just a case of a kid wanting something he couldn't have? Or had Josh planned to make trouble?

Heading to the kitchen to start coffee, Nathan spotted Cheryl on the sofa. He stopped, drinking in her face.

In sleep, her worry lines were smooth. Her blond hair was a delightful mess, falling out of her bun.

She must have been so exhausted she'd crashed on the sofa. She did so much for everyone. Hell, she'd helped make him a father.

He knelt and smoothed her forehead with his thumb, stroking the hair off her face. Still she slept.

He loved her. He'd always made sure people didn't get too close, afraid they'd see his flaws. Cheryl had seen, embraced and accepted them. Amazing.

Leaning in, he kissed her. Her lips went soft beneath his and she gasped. He took advantage of her open mouth and explored. She tugged until he lay on top of her.

When he came up for air, he murmured, "I missed you last night."

"Mmm." Cheryl's eyes were still closed.

"Why don't we take this somewhere else? I'd rather the kids not get an eyeful."

"Nathan. Nathan?" Her eyes snapped open. She pushed on his chest. "You stink of beer."

"Yeah. There's a story behind that." But he didn't want to rat on her son. He wanted to make love to her. "The good news is, I want to get rid of both of our clothes."

He rolled to his feet and held out his hand. Instead of taking it, she wrapped her arms around her knees. "No."

"Kids are still asleep. I just checked."

She closed her eyes. "We're through, Nathan."

"What are you talking about?" Through kissing?

"You mixed up the kids' dosages."

"What?"

"Last night. Issy's medicine was in the bathroom." Her tone was flat.

"I…I didn't move anything."

"How would you know? You were drinking. Around the kids." She took in a deep breath. "We're done."

"I wasn't drinking!"

"Right." She sniffed. "Don't lie."

"I smell like this because your *perfect* son spilled the beer."

"You *were* drinking last night."

"No!" He clenched his fists. "Josh stole a can out of my closet."

She stood. "You're calling my son a thief?"

"Hang on." He wanted to stop the train that was barreling down on him. "Josh threw paint on the floor and got in trouble. He must have found the beer in the closet when I sent him to get paper towels."

"You were dumb enough to let a six-year-old in a closet that had alcohol in it? Are you stupid?"

Stupid. "I was thinking your brat of a son threw paint all over my daughter's room and needed to clean it up. Can I help it if he's so badly behaved he pulled out something he shouldn't touch?" He should stop talking. He was saying things he didn't want to say. But he couldn't shut up. Cheryl had called him stupid.

"Josh said you threw the beer at him." Her arms were crossed. Her face was stony. He'd seen love there just yesterday. Now he saw disbelief.

"He lied." He threw up his hands.

She flinched.

"Jesus. You think I would hit you?"

"No." She released a deep breath. "But I didn't think you would drink, lie and put my son in danger."

"*I'm* not lying. I thought we had something." He shook his head. "You were just waiting for me to screw up. If this is what falling in love is about, it stinks." He trudged into the hall. "I'll wake Issy and we'll get out of your life."

"Oh. Oh."

Her tone stopped him. He turned around, praying she'd changed her mind.

"When I checked on the kids last night, Issy spoke."

He grabbed the wall to stay upright. "What?"

"She said 'Miss Cheryl.' I almost didn't realize it." She curled a little deeper into herself.

"Good." His voice was full of gravel. He forced himself to walk into Josh's bedroom and scoop up his daughter.

He wanted to run and bury his head in Cheryl's hair and cry.

But he couldn't take any more rejection.

IT WAS THE right thing to do. Cheryl filled the coffee-pot. She wasn't in the mood for coffee, but since Nathan had been around, she'd formed the habit.

Josh wouldn't lie to her.

"I heard yelling," Josh said, yawning.

"Mr. Nathan and I were discussing something."

Josh's eyes went wide. Under the red spots, his face went pale.

"How are you feeling?" She put her hand on his forehead.

"I'm okay." Josh scurried out from under her hand and took his place at the table. "Hungry."

She gathered up a bowl and cereal. "You sure your stomach feels okay?"

He nodded, staring into his bowl while she poured his cereal and milk. "Where's Issy?"

"With her father," she said.

His eyes got bigger.

"Do you want toast?" Cheryl fought down a feeling of dread.

Josh nodded, shoveling cereal into his mouth.

"Did you throw paint in Issy's room?" she asked, biting her lip. She wanted Nathan to be the liar, not Josh.

"The bu—"

"Josh," she warned.

Her son's face twisted in a scowl. "You called and *he* wouldn't let me talk to you."

She set her hand on his shoulder. "I was working."

"I wanted to talk to you." The stubborn set of his jaw reminded Cheryl of Brad, adding one more layer of pain to the ache in her gut.

"Did anything else happen last night?" she asked. This time *she* didn't want to look at Josh. She headed to the coffeepot.

"No." The answer was abrupt.

"What about the spilled beer?"

"I…" He shoved a spoonful of cereal into his mouth. "*He* threw it."

Her heart banged in her chest. "Josh, did you take a beer out of Nathan's closet?"

He shoveled in more cereal. His eyes filled with tears. He shook his head so hard his hair flew around his face.

Cheryl scooted a chair next to him. She tipped his head up, forcing him to look her in the eye. "Telling a lie is the worst thing you can do, right?"

Tears spilled down Josh's cheek. He tried to turn his head, but she wouldn't let him.

Where had she gone wrong? How had she failed her son? She'd tried so hard to mold him into a good man.

She'd just pushed away another good man. Nathan. He'd told the truth.

"Josh?" She kept her voice even, though she wanted to scream.

"I took it. But…he made me mad."

"What happened?"

"I…" Josh crawled into her lap and buried his wet face in her neck. "I wanted him to get in trouble."

She hugged him, hard. "And Mr. Nathan never drank the beer? Never threw it at you?"

He shook his head against her neck. Oh, no—had Josh done something with the antihistamines?

"Did you touch the medicine bottles?"

"What?" Josh kept his face hidden.

"You heard me."

"Yes," came his tear-filled whisper.

"What did you do?" Cheryl's chest ached.

"I mixed them up." His shoulders shook.

Oh, God. The things she'd said to Nathan. The horrible accusations she'd made. "Did you take the right dose last night?"

He nodded. "I'm sorry, Mommy."

What was she supposed to do? He had to be punished. There wasn't much to take away. His art? Nathan might have ideas, but she'd burned that bridge. "You'll have to be punished."

"Mr. Nathan already took away my movie last night and made me go to bed."

She sighed. "That was because you threw the paint."

He rubbed his runny nose on her shoulder.

"I'll have to think about your consequences." She made him look her in the eye. "And you'll apologize to Mr. Nathan."

Josh stuck out his bottom lip. "Why?"

"What you did was wrong. I can't let that go." Josh wasn't the only one who'd been wrong. "I need to apologize to Nathan, too."

Would he accept their apologies? She wished she could turn back time. Too bad that wasn't possible.

NATHAN HOISTED ISSY a little higher on his hip. "Let's go check on Abby's restaurant."

He and Cheryl had planned to split time with the kids today. She would have watched them in the morning and he would have taken the afternoon. Of course, the plan to take both kids to Issy's psychologist appointment may have to be postponed because of the chicken pox. Calling the doctor's office was on the morning's agenda.

Swinging his daughter around, he carried her piggyback down the stairs. Stopping in the closest bathroom, he admired the wall tile. It was light gray and complemented the charcoal-gray flooring.

Jed looked up from where he was troweling. "Hey, Issy. You have pink freckles."

She giggled and held out her arms. Nathan hoped having her on his back kept her far enough from the other man that they wouldn't risk contagion.

"You're polka-dotted." Jed pointed. "Have you been playing in paint?"

She giggled again. "No," she murmured.

Nathan gasped. He swung her off his back and enveloped her in a bear hug. The pain in his heart eased a little. Issy *was* talking.

Something in his life had to go right. If he had nothing else, he had his daughter and his family. His parents and brother had never meant as much to him as they did now that he was trying to figure out how to be a daddy.

He and Jed talked through the day's work. "If you need me, call."

"We're good. I'll keep an eye on Eddie." Jed tipped his head to the other bathroom. "He's coming along, but still needs to be watched."

And Nathan should have been there to monitor and guide Eddie. It was the first time he'd felt guilty about leaving a project in a supervisor's hands. "I'll check now before we head out."

The colors in the women's bathroom were similar, but lighter. It had a bigger footprint than the men's room, something Abby had insisted on. "Looking good," he said.

Eddie grinned. "I like laying tile."

Nathan stepped closer. "You're doing a good job, too."

The kid nodded. "Thanks, boss."

Boss? Pop was *boss*.

But this crew hadn't seen Pop on-site in months. Nathan was Forester Construction to the employees.

He was Boss, Daddy and...lost without Cheryl.

"Come on, short stuff." He tickled Issy and she giggled. "Let's head upstairs."

She wiggled and he let her down. When she started to run, he warned, "Slowly."

Issy grinned, but slowed to a fast walk. He followed as she clung to the spiral staircase railing. She'd changed so much since she'd arrived.

With everything going on in his life, he'd stopped looking for Heather. He needed to get back to that.

As they rounded the corner, they found Cheryl and Josh standing in front of his apartment. Pain gripped him like the clamps they'd used to build Abby's staircase. Maybe that was why he and Cheryl could never work. They were two objects forced together, that couldn't stick without clamps and glue. Whatever they'd had cementing their relationship had failed.

"Josh!" Issy ran toward him like they'd been apart for years.

Cheryl and Nathan gasped.

Josh held out his arms and Issy gave him a hug.

Cheryl swallowed hard. Was she holding back tears because of Issy speaking or because she was afraid of him?

"What do you want?" His question was harsh. Seeing her and Josh was like jumping into the ocean with open wounds. He needed to heal and it wouldn't happen if she kept showing up.

"We'd like…" She took a deep breath. "We need to talk to you. Please."

He went to brush by them, but stopped. He didn't want to catch her apple scent and remember the other times she'd been close to him. "Door's open."

Josh took Issy's hand and led her into the apartment.

Nathan and Cheryl were alone in the hall. He crossed his arms. What hadn't she said this morning?

"I'm sorry," she whispered.

He stared. Couldn't even respond. Instead, he pointed at the door. "I have to make some calls. Can we get…this done?"

Her shoulders drooped, but she entered the apartment. And her damn apple scent teased him as he followed her into the room.

Josh and Issy sat on the sofa. Cheryl joined the kids and he took the recliner.

"Josh?" Cheryl prompted.

"Mr. Nathan." The kid's hands formed fists in his lap. "I'm…sorry." The words exploded out of his mouth.

Nathan glanced at Cheryl, but she watched her son. "For what?" he asked.

"For throwing the paint." Josh chewed on his lower lip. "For taking the beer."

Nathan huffed out a breath. "Okay."

Josh nodded, starting to get off the sofa.

"Josh." His mother pointed at the cushion.

Josh wiggled back onto the seat. "And for messin' with the medicine."

Nathan exhaled a shaky breath. He'd worried he'd screwed up. Worried he was a bad father. "I didn't give Issy the wrong dose?"

Josh shook his head, squirming. His eyes were as big as a circular saw blade and almost as shiny. Issy was curled in a ball, always aware of the tension in the room.

"Josh would like to make it up to you," Cheryl said.

"How would he do that?" How could a kid make up for destroying what he and Cheryl had almost had?

"Is there anything he can do at the work site?" Cheryl asked.

Pop had always taken Nathan and Daniel to job sites, but Josh wasn't a good candidate. "He doesn't listen."

"I will." Josh looked at his mother then back to Nathan. "I'll listen."

Cheryl mouthed *please*.

What would Pop do? "One hour of cleaning every night for two weeks."

"Two *weeks*?" Josh whined.

Cheryl shot Josh a look. "He'll be there."

Her son nodded, crossing his arms.

"Can the kids go to Issy's room?" Cheryl asked.

Nathan waved and they took off.

Cheryl's brown eyes were as big as her son's. "I'm sorry."

His stomach tightened. "What are you sorry for?"

Cheryl knelt and took his hands.

He wanted to pull away. Wanted to pace. He didn't want her groveling at his feet. "What?"

"I'm sorry. For what I said, what I believed. I was wrong." Her brown eyes shimmered with tears. "Please, forgive me."

"You're sorry."

She nodded, a tear slipping down her cheek.

He couldn't weaken. She'd lashed out at him. Expected the worst of him. He couldn't go through life waiting for her to call him stupid. He didn't need that from the woman he loved. Everything ached, but he pushed the pain back with all his other childhood hurts. Cheryl's reaction proved once again that he wasn't normal.

Standing, he jerked his hands out of hers. "Fine."

She sat back. "Fine?"

He stalked into the kitchen. A beer would hit the

spot right now, but that wasn't him anymore. He didn't know who he was anymore.

But he wasn't a punching bag for Cheryl and her son. "Yes, fine. I accept your apology." He pulled out coffee and filled the machine.

Her sneakers squeaked against the floor. "And what about us?"

He snorted. "You made it clear I wasn't good enough for you or your son."

She laid her head against his back. "I was scared this morning."

He shifted away from her, filling the carafe with water. "We were always short-term," he lied.

Cheryl stared at her feet, her hair falling in front of her face.

He wanted to brush the hair back. Wanted to ease her hurt by kissing her, holding her.

Instead he filled the coffeepot. He needed to protect himself. He needed to be alone with his broken heart.

He'd never be truly alone again. He had Issy. His daughter would be enough. If Heather returned, he would fight for custody.

"Please, Nathan." Cheryl held out her hands. "I don't want to end what we have."

He shook his head. "You did that this morning."

"I was tired and scared. Why can't you understand that?"

"I understand you believed I got drunk around the kids. That I would *throw a beer* at a child." He shook his head. "You believed the worst of me."

She stumbled back a step. Her lips trembled. "But I love you. I'd planned to tell you last night. I...I love you."

Her words tore holes in his heart. "You love me and you still said those things to me? Believed I was that kind of monster?"

"Haven't you ever made a mistake?" She raked her fingers through her hair. "Haven't you ever screwed up?"

"Yeah." Falling in love with her was his biggest mistake.

"Then can't you forgive me?"

"I did."

A choked sob erupted and she slapped a hand across her mouth. "I don't want to lose you."

He gripped the edge of the counter to keep from reaching for her.

"I've lost you, haven't I?" she asked. She must have stepped closer because her voice came from near his shoulder.

"Daddy," a soft voice murmured.

His head jerked up. "What's up, short stuff?"

He scooped his daughter into his arms. Now he couldn't reach for Cheryl. His arms and life were full.

"Paint?" Issy asked, wrapping her arms around his neck.

He hugged her tight. "I can't."

"I promised to take the kids this morning," Cheryl said. "I hope we can still be friends." Her voice cracked on the last word.

He turned back to Cheryl. "You would do that?"

She nodded. Her face was pale and it was hard not to feel sorry for her, but he had to take care of himself and Issy.

If Cheryl took the kids this morning, he could work with Eddie and make phone calls. He could find out if the psychologist would see Issy.

"Fine. I'll take the kids in the afternoon."

But nothing in his life was fine. Not anymore.

NATHAN AND JOSH waited in a separate room at the doctor's office. He inhaled. At least the psychologist had agreed to see Issy.

Maybe this wasn't necessary. She'd called him Daddy. Warmth filled his chest. Daddy.

But there was still the gruesome picture she'd drawn. A little blond figure under a bloody body. *Please find out why Issy's afraid.*

Josh flipped another page in his sketchbook. Nathan caught a glimpse of faces with red spots all over them.

He nodded at the page. "Self-portrait?"

"What's that?" Josh drew a circle with his pencil.

"A picture of yourself."

"I guess." Josh shrugged.

Whatever friendship Nathan and Josh had developed was gone. He didn't have the energy to battle with the kid. Taking care of him didn't mean he had to *care* for him.

Nathan pressed on his chest. There'd been a dull ache there ever since Cheryl had kicked him out of her life. The ache had deepened when she'd begged his forgiveness.

"I can't get the nose," Josh said, pointing at his picture.

Nathan looked at the drawing. "It's Issy."

Josh screwed up his mouth. "I thought you'd like a picture of her."

"I never liked drawing people." But Nathan remembered how. "You've got a nice oval. Now you need to split everything …"

Josh waited.

Instead of trying to find the words, Nathan took a sheet of paper and a pencil. Then he drew an oval and added a line down the middle and one through the center.

"I have to cut everything in two." Josh erased everything but his circle and then drew lines.

"Good." Nathan figured it was easier to draw along with him.

They worked together, adding in eyes and nose, sketching mouths. If Nathan hadn't had so much to worry about, he would have thought they were getting along. But he knew better.

Josh filled in Issy's hair. He stared at his paper. "Are you my mom's boyfriend?"

The ache that had eased while he and Josh sketched was back. "No."

"But—" Josh tapped his pencil on the tabletop.

"But what?"

"You touch her. Hold her hand."

"It won't happen again." Nathan glanced sideways at the kid. "That should make you happy."

"You made my mom cry this morning." Josh's hands clenched.

"Like I said, it won't happen again."

"Mr. Forester?" The receptionist entered their room. "Dr. Rebecca would like you to come in now."

He looked over at Josh.

"Your son will be just fine here," the receptionist added.

"He's not my dad," Josh snapped.

"It's okay, Josh." But the kid's words stung. Lately, every mistake he made with Josh hurt. "Be good."

Josh didn't look up. And probably wouldn't obey. Hopefully there weren't any beer cans lying around.

The receptionist led Nathan to where Dr. Rebecca held open her office door. "Come in."

The psychologist was every child's dream grandmother. Her face was round with deep smile lines and her eyes twinkled.

Issy played with a dollhouse in the corner.

"Did she say anything?" Nathan asked, his voice low.

The doctor shook her head. "No. We did creative communications."

"I just want her life to be normal." Something he'd never had.

The doctor gestured to the two chairs near her desk and they sat. "That's a reasonable hope."

"And…?"

She handed him a picture.

Nathan swallowed. It was similar to the picture Issy had drawn in day care. Red crayon sprayed from a stick man. A smaller stick person with blond hair was smashed under the injured man.

He rubbed the back of his neck. "That's what she drew before. It's awful."

"Since she wouldn't talk, we communicated by pictures. Here's one she drew of herself."

The doctor handed him another piece of paper. This time it was a circle. The face had eyes, yellow hair and a row of x's where the mouth should be.

"I don't understand." Nathan flexed his fingers, trying to keep them from forming fists. "What am I looking at? Her pediatrician said there's nothing physically wrong with her."

"I know." Dr. Rebecca sat back and looked directly at him. "Do you know where her mother is?"

"I can't find her. She said she was going into treatment, but…" He dragged his fingers through his hair. "I don't know where to look."

"Once Isabella drew this picture, I had her draw one with her mother and one with you." She handed him two more pictures.

The first one must be Heather. The blonde woman had something in her hand. Her bright red lips frowned.

"Is this supposed to be Issy?" He pointed to a figure in the corner of the paper. It looked like a ball with arms.

Dr. Rebecca nodded.

The next picture had the blond stick figure on the shoulders of a big stick person. There were smiles on both their faces. He swallowed back the tears that prickled his eyes.

"It's obvious she's not afraid of you." The psychologist tapped first the bigger face and then the little one. "You make her happy."

Nathan nodded, unable to speak.

"I think something traumatic happened and she believes she can't talk about it."

"What can I do?" he choked out. "How can I help her?"

"Do what you're doing. Make her feel safe." She patted his shoulder. "I'd like to see her once a week. I suggested if she couldn't talk, she might sing."

He nodded. "Should I push her?"

"Not push. Encourage." She stood. "I'm afraid I have another appointment."

"Thank you." He picked up the picture of him and Issy. "May I take these?"

"Of course." She patted his arm. "She trusts you. You're doing something right."

He nodded gratefully. "Hey, short stuff."

His daughter looked up, her eyes filled with worry.

"Let's go to grandma's and see if she's made any cookies."

CHAPTER FIFTEEN

"WHY DIDN'T YOU tell us about Issy's drawing before?" Pop asked Nathan.

Issy and Josh were in the tree house with a container of Mom's cookies; no one wanted Pop exposed to their germs any more than necessary. Nathan, Pop and Mom watched them from the shaded patio.

"Because he didn't want you to worry," Mom scolded.

"I'm done with chemo. I just have to have my hip drilled again."

Nathan cringed. He'd been there for Pop's first bone marrow test. Seeing the old man groggy with pain had been awful.

"Why weren't we invited to the party?" Daniel called from the house. He and Bess came through the doorway carrying a twelve-pack of beer.

"It was spontaneous," Mom said. "Can you all stay for dinner?"

"Sure," Nathan said.

"We'd love to." Bess put her arm around Daniel's waist. He brushed a kiss on her nose.

Nathan swallowed. He and Cheryl could have had that closeness. They could have relied on each other. Could have shared the little looks his brother and Bess enjoyed.

"Hey, bro." Daniel offered him a beer.

Nathan shook his head.

"My brother refused a beer?" Daniel slapped his hand on his chest.

"Knock it off." Alcohol had caused enough problems for him.

Bess took a seat next to him and touched his shoulder. "What's wrong?"

No way was he going to talk about him and Cheryl. Instead, he went through what he knew—again—for Daniel and Bess. Let them look at the pictures Issy had drawn. It didn't get easier in the telling.

"How can I help?" Daniel held his gaze.

Nathan stared into brown eyes that were identical to his own. "You'll help?"

"Whatever you need," Daniel vowed.

"Thanks," he choked out. "I have to find Heather and reading…it's too hard."

Daniel nodded. "We'll work together."

Pop cleared his throat. "I've got something to say."

All the adults turned to him.

"Deb, can you get the…" Pop tipped his head to the house.

Mom touched his leg as she stood. "I'd love to."

Nathan couldn't take any more bad news. "What's up?"

"Hold your horses." Pop grinned.

Mom came back with a box and set it next to Pop's lawn chair.

"I'm proud of the way you boys pulled together and kept the business running after I got sick." He turned to Nathan. "You gave up your life in Atlanta."

He turned to Daniel. "You took the reins and didn't let go."

Bess leaned her head against Daniel's shoulder.

"But we're making some changes." Pop pulled open the box flaps. "Starting with a new company name."

"It's always been Forester Construction." Nathan shook his head. The company was an anchor in his life. He didn't want it to change, too.

"Now it's more." Pop handed Daniel and Nathan caps in the company's green color.

"Pop." Daniel read the name on the cap. "This isn't necessary."

"Forester and Sons Construction," Nathan read. For once the words didn't dance. *Sons*.

"The lawyer's making it official, but we're partners." Pop put on a cap. "Well, you each have thirty-three percent of the company. Your mother and I have thirty-four."

Everyone laughed.

Nathan hugged Pop and whispered, "You didn't have to."

Pop patted his back. "I did."

Mom called into the tree. "Kids, can you come here?"

"Don't get too close to Pop," Nathan said as they came down the ladder.

Pop pointed a finger. "I'm feeling good."

"And you're going to stay that way," Nathan replied.

His mother reached into the box and pulled out

miniature caps for Issy and Josh. Nathan's heart squeezed tight.

Nathan adjusted Issy's and pulled her ponytail through the back. "There you go, short stuff."

Josh handed his to Nathan. "Can you help me?"

Surprised, he adjusted the clasp then tapped it on the kid's head. "You can wear that when you help in the evenings, slugger."

Josh grinned. "I will."

"You've got the kid working on-site?" Daniel asked.

"Long story." And Nathan wasn't going to ruin this moment. For the first time in his life he wasn't the family screw-up. The boy who couldn't read belonged.

But the joy was hollow. He wanted to share this triumph with Cheryl.

At least he had Issy. He hugged her tight and she wrapped her arms around his neck. She was his family.

CHERYL RUBBED HER ARMS. The apartment was quiet without Josh, Nathan and Issy. Not that Issy made much noise.

Nathan had sent a text that they were eating at his parents' house. At least that's what she interpreted from the garbled message.

He'd once told her stress magnified his problems. And texting was exhausting, so he usually called. Apparently he didn't want to talk to her.

She stripped off her work clothes, hopped in the shower and scrubbed away the smell of burgers.

She'd made sliders for the wine-tasting. Even

though they'd cooked and served in the courtyard, she still smelled like grilled food. The guests had loved the different patty choices. The food and wine combinations had been her idea, but it was hard to take any pride in that when her world was upside down.

Nathan had forgiven her, but refused to rekindle their relationship. She'd been a fool and lost another man she loved. This time it was her fault.

She rattled around the apartment, picking up toys, stripping beds and doing laundry. Paid a couple of bills and balanced her checkbook. The bathroom needed scrubbing, so she did that. All things she hadn't had time to do while the kids had been sick. She read ahead in her history class and made brownies, adding a mint-chocolate frosting.

It was almost the kids' bedtime. She brewed her tea and sat at the top of the steps, listening to the cicadas' song ebb and flow. Muffled laughter filtered into the courtyard from both Fitzgerald House and Carleton House. A couple held hands on a garden bench. Something she and Nathan could have had, but she'd let slip through her fingers.

A tear snuck down her cheek. She could only blame herself. She leaned against the wooden post. Even after Brad had died, she'd never felt this alone.

A truck rumbled. Nathan.

She met them in the parking area. Nathan climbed out of the driver's seat and gently closed his door. "They both fell asleep." His deep whisper carried across the lot. His eyes held hers until he moved to the back door.

"I'll carry Josh." She started to hurry around to the other side.

"Take Issy." He opened the door. "I've got him."

Cheryl climbed on the running board and unbuckled Issy. The little girl's eyes opened halfway.

"Hi, pumpkin." She wedged her hands behind Issy and lifted her out of the seat. "Let's get you to bed."

Her little arms locked around her neck. "Okay," she sang.

Cheryl hugged her tight, catching Nathan's eye.

He nodded, his smile strained. "That's the tenth word she's sung today."

He hoisted Josh onto his shoulder and grabbed both kids' backpacks.

They moved side by side up the steps. "What did the doctor say?" she asked, breaking the silence.

"I'll…I'll… Maybe…" He shook his head in frustration. "The words are twisting. Let's get the kids to bed and I'll show you."

They went through her apartment. Maybe they should have traded kids and gone their own way, but they'd developed habits. Habits they would have to break.

Nathan carried Josh into his bedroom.

"Do you want him to brush his teeth?" he asked.

"One night won't hurt him," she replied.

Nathan stripped off Josh's shorts and cap and put him in the bottom bunk. "He had his last antihistamine dose at my parents'." He glanced at her. "Daniel made sure each kid got the right amount."

Her face flamed. "I said I was sorry. I was just…"

"I shouldn't have said that." He held up a hand. "You have a right to worry."

But she didn't have the right to call Nathan stupid. That was the worst part of everything she'd done this morning.

"I'll take Issy." He held out his arms. During the transfer, Nathan's hand brushed her skin and tingles skittered through her.

He tucked Issy's head on his shoulder. "If you want to grab the monitor, I'll show you the stuff from the doc."

She tucked Josh in, turned on the monitor and clipped the receiver to her shorts.

Nathan's apartment door was propped open. She could hear him murmuring in Issy's bedroom. She hesitated then headed to the living room. He came in a minute later and collapsed into his recliner.

"Is she asleep?"

He nodded. "I talked to the day care director. They can go back next Monday."

"Good. Good."

He looked up, his gaze icy. "Do you want to keep our old schedule?"

She swallowed. Would she be able to be around Nathan that much? Even exchanging kids required communication and sharing information. She didn't have another support system but could she stand the pain of being near Nathan? "Yes, if…if I haven't ruined everything."

He let his head drop into his hand. "Okay."

The silence between them was as sharp as her chef knife and cut as deep.

She broke the painful quiet. "What happened at the doctor's?"

"The doc wants to see her every week. She thinks Issy believes she shouldn't talk, so she suggested she sing." He grabbed a file and handed it to her without explanation.

The same horrible picture was there, but this time there were three more. A face with *x*'s for a mouth. One with a yellow-haired stick person and a very small figure in the corner. And one with a stick person sitting on top of another. "Is this you?"

He nodded. "And the other is…" He gritted his teeth and shook his head, like he couldn't find the right words. "Issy's mom."

"She drew smiles on your faces."

He nodded.

"You've done a good thing here." She should have seen that earlier.

"She's my daughter." His words were simple.

"You've come a long way from when you wanted me to take care of her." She pushed off the sofa and headed to the door. "You look beat. I'll let you get some sleep."

"Cheryl."

She turned, hoping he would let her crawl into his

lap and hold him. "Yes?" Even she heard eagerness in her voice.

"I'll watch the kids in the morning."

"Oh." She deflated like her first soufflé. "I'll make breakfast."

"We'll eat here."

"Of course. I'll head home." In the hallway between the apartments, she shivered. The summer heat couldn't thaw the ice forming around her heart.

NATHAN SHUT OFF the ball game and tugged over his laptop. He and Daniel had gotten a good start on searching for Heather. Maybe his fingers and brain would let him do a little more.

The screen opened up in Cheryl's email. Just seeing her name hurt. She must not have logged off the last time she'd used his computer. He shouldn't look. This was none of his business. But an email subject line in all caps flashed like neon.

He clicked it open.

The money's not enough. Send more or the video goes out.

Video? The email was sent by J Smith. He ran the mouse over the address and clicked Search Emails. The program popped up four more opened emails.

He started with the earliest one. There was an attachment and he clicked it open.

A woman bobbed on a guy's lap with all the requisite moaning and groaning of low-budget porn. Why was this garbage in Cheryl's email? Then he read the message threatening to turn the video over to the Fitzgeralds if she didn't pay.

Cheryl was being blackmailed? He watched the horrible thing again. It was grainy but Cheryl's face was clear. Except when he saw only her back, it wasn't Cheryl. On one butt cheek, there was the flash of a tattoo. He stopped the video. There. A rose. Cheryl didn't have a rose anywhere.

He ran his hand through his hair. Cheryl must have told this J Smith to jump in a lake—right? This wasn't her. The Fitzgeralds wouldn't believe this crap.

He clicked into her Sent mail, no longer feeling guilty about invading her privacy, and found her note saying she'd sent twenty dollars. Who in their right mind blackmailed someone who barely had anything? "Shit."

He pushed out of the recliner, letting the laptop snap closed. How could she have given in to this? She was smarter than that.

He picked up Issy's monitor, the laptop and headed to Cheryl's apartment.

Nathan paused with his fist in the air, ready to pound on her door. He let his hand slip back to his side and took a deep breath. He couldn't go in guns blazing. One more deep breath and he rapped on her door, straining to hear footsteps.

"Nathan?" she said through the closed door.

"Yeah."

The door popped open. "Is Issy okay?"

He slowed, appreciating that her first thought was his daughter. "She's sleeping."

"So is Josh." She backed into the kitchen, biting her lip. "What's up?"

He set the computer on the table. "I need to understand this."

"I can help you." She leaned over.

He opened the computer to the message she'd sent.

"You looked at my private mail?" Her hand covered her mouth.

"Did you send some asshole money?"

She slumped into a chair, shutting the computer. "Levi."

"Why would you do that?" He stalked to the sink and back.

She exhaled. "Because the kids were sick and I didn't have time to deal with this."

"Because of this crap?" He opened the computer to the video file. Moaning filled the room.

She wrapped her arms around herself. "Turn it off."

He slammed the screen shut. "Do you think anyone who knows you wouldn't guess this was a fake?"

"You know it's not me?"

"Of course I do. The woman has a tattoo on her butt."

"Really?" Her head jerked up.

He nodded. "Why didn't you tell them to go to hell?"

"I didn't get the chance." Her feet rested on the edge of the chair and she wrapped her arms around her legs.

"Come on." He didn't believe her excuses.

"I was ashamed. I worried it would hurt our relationship." She swallowed. "But I destroyed that all by myself."

He knelt next to her chair. "You could have told me."

"I didn't know what to do." Her lips trembled. "And then I missed the deadline."

She'd never trusted him. "We're calling the cops."

Her face went white. "No."

"You can't let this go." He touched her leg. "Did you think once you sent Levi money, his friend wouldn't ask for more? You're smarter than me and I know they won't stop."

"I…" A tear trickled down her cheek.

"Honey, we have to call the cops."

Her voice shook. "I know."

He wanted to take her in his arms and wipe away her tears. That couldn't happen. But he could help her with this problem.

He called the Savannah police department and set up a time the next day to take Cheryl to the station. If it wasn't the kids keeping him from working, it was Cheryl. Then he called Bess and asked her to watch the kids.

"You don't have to go with me," she said after he'd relayed the meeting time.

"We'll go together."

CHERYL EXHALED AS she entered the police station.

Nathan moved to the desk and asked for Detective Gillespie.

After Levi had tried to kidnap Josh, she'd been here. She'd had to admit she'd let Levi steal from her and Josh. She and Josh had lived in a terrible part of town because she'd been afraid Levi would find them.

That time, Gray had solved her housing problem and he and Abby had saved her from Levi. She'd been such a weakling.

It was time to stop relying on other people to fix things for her. She had to stand up for herself.

She glanced at Nathan and straightened her shoulders. He'd barely said a word to her.

Nathan looked over at her. "Are you okay?"

She nodded. She had to be.

"Mrs. Henshaw?" Detective Gillespie walked to where they waited. "Sorry you've had more trouble."

"So am I." She stood. "You can go now, Nathan."

"But…" He held up the computer bag.

"I'll tell the detective what happened." She held out her hand for the bag.

"I want to help." Nathan looked at her, but his eyes were cold.

The detective waited.

"I have to do this myself."

"But you'll need a ride back to Fitzgerald House," Nathan said.

"I'll make sure she's get back," Gillespie said.

She held out her hand and Nathan finally handed her the bag. "Thank you for dropping me off."

Step one in standing on her own two feet.

NATHAN MEASURED AND measured again. Then he checked the specs on the flattop. Damn, everything had better fit. The kitchen equipment arrived in an hour. After Cheryl had sent him away from the police station, he'd spent the morning double-checking all the measurements. His emotions were in a tangle. He felt as if she'd rejected him again.

"This looks great." Daniel strolled into the restaurant.

The tile was laid and grouted. The heated floors worked.

"Gray's on his way." Daniel wiped a hand on the kitchen wall tile. "I'm guessing you didn't lay this on brick."

Nathan shook his head. "We put up drywall."

Daniel prowled around. "I found an interesting support group."

"For me? A single man's guide to child-rearing?"

His brother turned back. "Aren't you and Cheryl helping each other out?"

"Yeah, but she…we're not together anymore."

"What did you do?" Daniel came and stood in front of him.

"Nothing. She thought…" Nathan snorted. He wouldn't air their problems.

"Sorry, bro." Daniel touched his back. "You two looked good together."

"Josh didn't think so." Whoops. No trash-talking Cheryl's son.

Daniel grimaced. "I have noticed that."

Nathan shrugged.

"I found a dyslexia support group." Daniel raised an eyebrow. "They meet every week. The comments on the site sounded inspiring."

Nathan rolled his shoulders. "I've given up on groups."

"I want to help." Daniel moved in front of Nathan, frowning. "I should have done more when we were growing up."

Nathan's heart thumped. "I wouldn't have taken your help. I hated that everything was easy for you."

"I hope we've gotten beyond that." Daniel gave him an awkward one-armed hug.

"Bess really is changing you."

His brother grinned. "I know."

Nathan took a deep breath. "I talked to the Savannah cops about Heather."

He didn't tell his brother that he'd been at the station because Cheryl was reporting a blackmail scheme. That wasn't his story to tell.

"I should have thought of that," Daniel said.

"I need to send the pictures she's drawn." A four-year-old's drawing wouldn't give away an identity, but maybe there was something there they could use. "They'll try to find her."

Gray and Abby came through the door. "Truck's pulling up," Gray said. "Let's get the kitchen set up before Abby rearranges things."

Abby elbowed him. "I heard that."

Gray pulled her to his side and kissed her.

Nathan was going to gag on all the love pheromones flying around.

Cheryl walked in. Her gaze zeroed in on him. Worry creased her forehead and pain filled her eyes.

Daniel looked between her and Nathan and headed to the back door. "Where's the plan?"

Abby held one up. Gray did, too.

"Pinned to the wall." Nathan moved to Cheryl and lowered his voice. "How did it go?"

"They took copies of the emails and that awful video. They're going after the person who sent the video first."

"Good."

Neither of them moved.

"Thank you for making me go to the police," she whispered.

"You're welcome." He stepped away, even though he longed to wrap his arms around her. "Are you here for the kitchen?"

"Abby insisted." She reached for him but stopped when he held up his hand.

He couldn't keep reopening the Cheryl-size hole in his heart. "Let's make sure Abby's got everything."

Nathan, Gray, Daniel and one of the deliverymen

hauled the first box off the truck. Abby and Cheryl cut the cardboard, oohing and aahing over a flattop.

"You can leave the cardboard in the corner," Nathan said. "Josh and I will break it down tonight."

Cheryl nodded, her lip caught between her teeth.

He couldn't do this much longer. With the restaurant close to completion, he would find a permanent home for him and Issy. Then he'd avoid the wrenching pain of seeing Cheryl every day.

CHAPTER SIXTEEN

"MRS. HENSHAW." DETECTIVE GILLESPIE waved her back to an interview room.

"Please, call me Cheryl." She took a seat. "You talk to me almost every day."

Gillespie had kept her updated over the past week. And Nathan had been freezing her out. She shook her head. Pining for a man who couldn't stand to be in the same room with her was fruitless.

"Cheryl, then," Gillespie said.

"What's happening?" she asked.

"We hit a dead end on the IP addresses. They were sent from different coffee shops in Savannah. And, as of this morning, the email account was deleted."

"If the email is gone, maybe I don't need to worry about the video anymore." Hope leaked into her voice.

Gillespie shook his head. "The video is out there somewhere."

"And Levi?"

He grimaced. "There's nothing that ties him to the blackmail demands."

"But I sent him money!"

"A good defense attorney would say that was because you're his sister-in-law. There's nothing in the emails that specifically suggests that he's involved."

"No way." She pushed away from the table and paced. "The video could still go public?"

Detective Gillespie nodded. "I'm sorry."

She stalked back to the table. "I won't let Levi get away with this."

"We don't have evidence connecting him to the blackmail."

"Those pictures are from when Josh and I lived with him. Someone took them when I was sleeping. He's the only one who could have done it." She rubbed the goose bumps on her arms. "Talk to him!"

"I could. But I don't think it will go anywhere unless we find his accomplice. Since the emails didn't come from Coastal State prison, someone in Savannah sent them."

She wouldn't become Levi's victim again. "Then… let me talk to him. He'll brag about what he's done. Can you record our conversation?"

"That might work." Gillespie eyed her. "You've changed."

"I'm tired of being weak. No one is going to rescue me again." Not Josh or the Fitzgeralds or Nathan. "What do I have to do?"

A look of admiration crossed his face. "I need to talk to my captain and make some calls."

"Let me know when I can do this."

THREE HOURS LATER she sat in the Fitzgerald House kitchen. At her request, the Fitzgerald sisters had gathered around the table with her.

"Thank you for meeting with me," Cheryl said.

Abby touched her hand. "Of course."

"Are the kids all right?" Bess asked.

"Yes. Their spots have scabbed over, so they're back in day care."

"Good. Chicken pox is miserable." Dolley pulled a sandwich from the tray in the middle of the table. "What's up?"

Cheryl took a deep breath. "It's Levi."

Abby jerked in her chair. "Is he out of prison?"

"No." She tried to work out how to tell the Fitzgeralds. "He's blackmailing me."

Dolley slapped her hand on the table. "With what?"

"A video. A porn video."

Their mouths dropped open.

"It's not me," she hurried to add. "My face is superimposed on some woman's body."

"Oh, no." Abby took her hand.

Cheryl fought back tears at Abby's kindness. Then she walked the sisters through the emails she'd received.

"That's horrible." Bess rubbed her back. "How can we help?"

"You're all so amazing." Her throat tightened, but she wouldn't cry. "I wanted you to know because they threatened to send you the video."

"Like we would ever believe that of you." Abby squeezed her hand.

"Nathan's the one who spotted a tattoo on the woman's butt. I didn't even notice it."

Abby glanced at Bess. Bess's eyebrows shot up and Dolley laughed aloud.

What had she said? Cheryl replayed her comment about her butt and the tattoo, then blushed.

"Nice to know Nathan's observant," Dolley choked out.

Abby and Bess started to giggle. Cheryl couldn't hold in a snort and finally joined them.

"We should be breaking out the wine," Abby said as their laughter died down.

Bess turned back to Cheryl. "You never said how we can help."

"There's nothing to do right now." She wiped a tear away. How long had it been since she'd laughed this hard? "I plan to confront Levi. Hopefully, he'll confess."

"You go, girl," Dolley said.

"You'd visit the prison?" Abby asked.

Chills crawled down her back. "If I get the okay from the police."

And maybe even if she didn't.

Abby linked their hands. Bess took her other hand. Dolley finished the circle.

"We're here to support you, whatever you need," Abby declared.

Cheryl's chest shook as she exhaled. "Thank you. You're the best."

THE NEXT NIGHT CHERYL, Josh and Issy made dinner. Nathan had asked her to watch Issy for the evening, but he hadn't said where he was going.

Don't let him be on a date.

While keeping her eye on Josh tearing lettuce and Issy mixing biscuit dough, Cheryl tossed chicken in the pan. It sizzled and spit.

Her phone rang. *Gillespie.* She rolled her shoulders and answered.

"We got the okay from my superiors and the prison."

"Really?" She pulled out a kitchen chair, needing to sit.

"When do you want to do this?"

Never. "Are there visiting hours or something?"

"We're cleared to go whenever you're available."

Her stomach flopped. "I'm off Thursday morning."

"I'll pick you up."

"Thank you." She shivered, not wanting to see her brother-in-law again. But she needed to do this for herself and Josh.

At least the Fitzgeralds had her back. A pang shot through her. She might have had the same support from Nathan if she hadn't been such a fool.

After setting a time to meet, she hung up. "Let's finish dinner."

"Who was on the phone?" Josh asked. His face was solemn.

She didn't want Josh to worry. "A friend."

"Mr. Nathan?"

Issy looked up from stirring the dough.

"No."

"Will I meet this *friend*?" Josh asked, almost spitting out the word.

She surely hoped not. "I don't think so."

"You don't have friends," Josh pressed.

"I do." She smiled. "There's the Fitzgeralds, and Gray and Daniel."

"And Mr. Nathan?" Her son tugged on his Forester and Sons cap. It was almost impossible to get him to take the thing off. Her son looked forward to his evening cleanups with Nathan. Amazing.

She flipped the chicken breasts simmering on the stove. "Of course."

"Daddy," Issy said. The little girl glanced up, her eyes wide, as if she were afraid of the word.

"Yes, your daddy." She tried to keep the excitement out of her voice. Each word from Issy was precious.

Cheryl set the lid on the pan, moved over and stroked Issy's back. She handed spoons to the kids. "I think we can make these biscuits now."

She helped them drop the dough on the baking sheet. They were all giggling by the time they were done.

"Mine looks like a dinosaur," Josh said. "Stegosaurus."

"Mine looks like Daddy practicing reading," Issy sang.

That was the most words Cheryl had ever heard Issy say. Well, sing.

"Your dad *practices* reading?" Josh asked.

"Practice makes perfect," Issy sang.

Good for Nathan. Cheryl slid the biscuits into the oven. "Okay, guys, let's clean up this mess."

There was a battle over Josh wearing his cap at the

dinner table and one spilled glass of milk. After dinner, she gave Issy a bath and let Josh manage his own. Then Josh read to Issy until they both nodded off.

Standing next to the bunk beds, Cheryl felt the dull ache in her belly grow. She'd missed having Issy here. Missed Nathan, too. She couldn't wait to tell him how much his daughter had talked.

He and Issy were threaded through the fabric of her and Josh's lives. She'd pulled on the string and everything had unraveled.

Nathan may think he was stupid, but he was so much smarter than she was.

NATHAN ACHED, LIKE a kickboxer had worked out on his head. The dyslexia support group Daniel had found made his brain hurt.

That wasn't all that hurt. He hesitated at Cheryl's door. His heart ached like that same kickboxer had torn a chunk out of that, too.

He knew what was missing. Cheryl. And Josh. Now that he and Cheryl weren't together, he and Josh were getting along. They'd bonded over the kid's punishment. Nathan even looked forward to cleaning up the work site with him each evening.

Forcing his hand up, he knocked.

Soft footsteps and the clack of the locks filled the silence. Cheryl opened the door.

He frowned at her. "You didn't ask who was there."

"I…" Her mouth dropped open. "I knew it was you."

He shook his head, setting off hammers behind his eyes. Big mistake.

"Lord, you look tuckered out," she said. "Are you all right?"

"Long day." He pushed back his hair, winced and stepped inside.

Delicious scents filled the room and his mouth watered. He'd missed dinner. "I'll grab Issy and get out of your hair."

"She fell asleep while Josh read." The lines around her mouth softened. "She can stay the night."

His shoulders slumped. "You didn't have to do that."

"I love Issy and love having her here." She sank against the counter. "She talked a lot tonight."

He smiled. His cheeks hurt like they weren't used to the action. "She did?"

"Well, sang."

"The doc keeps telling her that singing isn't talking." He paced the kitchen. "Smells good in here."

"We made chicken and biscuits." She chewed her lip. "Have you eaten?"

"Didn't have a chance." He stared at her pink lips and couldn't pull his eyes away.

"Sit."

He did. While she got food out of the fridge, he let his head drop into his hands. Exhaustion steamrollered over him.

The microwave dinged and Cheryl set a plate in front of him.

"Thanks." He took a forkful. The taste of the

chicken, mushrooms and herbs made him want to weep in gratitude.

As he shoveled in the deliciousness, Cheryl popped lids on containers, returning them to the fridge. Then she made her evening cup of tea.

"Are you ready for Daniel and Bess's wedding?" she asked.

Nathan had hoped they'd go as a couple. Not now. The food lost its taste. "Gray and I are working on the bachelor party."

Awkward silence filled the kitchen.

"This is great," he finally said around another mouthful.

"The kids liked it." She took a seat across from him. "Any chance you can watch Issy the same time next week?"

"Sure." She stared into her mug as if the answers to all the world's problems were etched in the bottom.

"Maybe for the next month?"

Cheryl finally looked up. "Are you taking a class or something?"

"Something like that." He pinched the bridge of his nose, barely able to think through the jabbing pain. "And maybe Thursday for Daniel's party."

"Of course."

He cut another piece of chicken. "Have you heard any more from the cops?"

"They can't find the person who sent the emails, so they can't tie anything to Levi."

He swore. "There's got to be something they can do."

"Gillespie's working on…something."

"Let me know if I can help," he said. But they weren't together. She hadn't trusted him. He rolled his neck, joints popping.

"You're hurting." Moving behind him, she dug her fingers into his shoulders.

He stiffened. "You don't have to do that."

"You're in pain." She massaged his tense muscles. "Just eat."

Her touch was agony and relief. She manipulated the base of his neck, working her way through his scalp.

Every few minutes he remembered to chew. He couldn't hold his head up. It fell back, resting on her stomach. His eyes closed and he floated on the comfort of her touch.

"This so feels good really." His words were jumbled and not from his dyslexia.

She massaged and kneaded, her fingers stroking the hair off his forehead.

He kept his eyes closed, afraid she'd see his longing.

She stopped, her hands resting on his shoulders. The sound of their breathing and the ticking of the kitchen clock blanketed them. He left his head resting against her.

Too soon, she stepped back. He looked up and wished he hadn't. Her eyes were deep pools of pain.

"Thank you." His voice was rough.

"You're welcome." She moved away, taking his empty dish to the sink.

His chair screeched across the floor. He set a hand

on her back as she loaded his plate in the dishwasher. "Really. Thank you for everything."

"You've done so much for Josh and me." She turned and they were stuck in a cruel mock embrace.

He couldn't stop his impulse. He brushed her hair behind her ear. Her breath whooshed out and he dropped his hand. This wasn't staying away from her.

"I—I'll make the kids breakfast," she stuttered.

"Thanks." He backed toward the door. He'd have to go through this same agony in the morning.

CHERYL'S HAND SHOOK as Detective Gillespie explained the last form she needed to sign.

"Ready?" he asked.

"Ye—" She cleared her throat. "Yes."

"Let's go."

Locks clanged as a guard guided them through the prison. Cameras were everywhere. On each hallway signs warned You Are Being Recorded. Finally they stood in front of a closed door.

"This is where I leave you." Gillespie crouched and looked her in the eyes. "I know Levi frightens you, but he'll be secured."

Secured? "Good."

He touched her shoulder. "Good luck, but you don't need it. You've found your courage."

Had she? She despised the wimp she'd been.

The guard explained, "Henshaw's already in the room."

"Does he know who he's meeting?" Gillespie asked.

"No." The guard tugged on his utility belt. "You just holler when you're ready to leave."

Her stomach wanted to get rid of the bit of breakfast she'd choked down. She was going to be locked in a room with the man who'd burned her son with a cigarette, attacked and stolen from her. The man she'd locked away.

He would not hurt her family again. "Let's do this."

The guard peered through a small side window and unlocked the door. "I'll keep an eye on you."

She squared her shoulders but couldn't keep her hands from quaking. The door slammed shut with a finality that made her jump.

"You?" Levi's gravelly voice sent a shiver down her back.

She took the chair on the opposite side of the table from him. "Me."

Levi had been a high school football player. But he'd gone to fat before Brad had died. Now he'd lost his beer belly and muscles bulged on his arms. A stomach-turning stench of sweat filled the room.

Her hands shook so hard, she folded them in her lap, out of sight.

The chains rattled as he reached for her, but he couldn't touch her. Levi swore and then a sly grin spread across his face. "Surprised to see you with your clothes on."

"You *are* behind that obviously fake video." She couldn't keep the wobble out of her voice.

"I don't know what you're talking about."

"Right." She had to get him to admit his guilt on the record. "The last time my hair was that long was when you were stealing my survivor checks."

"And you got me locked up because of it!" He lunged but his chains held him down. "You owe me!"

She clutched the edge of her chair.

"You aren't smart enough to make that video. Not while you're locked in here."

"I know people, bitch." Levi's teeth snapped together.

"In Savannah?" Who could he know? How could she make him angry enough to tell her? "Have you spent the money I sent you?"

"That piddly little amount? I couldn't even buy a cigarette with that amount. You work for millionaires. I want more or Al sends the video out."

"Al? He's the brains, huh?" *Al who?*

His chains rattled. "*I'm* the brains."

The one thing she could count on was Levi's temper. It amazed her that Brad and Levi were from the same family. "Al might disagree."

"He'll do what his brother George tells him or he'll be in a cell with us!"

Bingo. George must be Levi's cellmate. If this George's brother was the man who'd sent the emails, Gillespie should be able to find him.

She pushed away from the table. "You won't see another dime from me."

"Then we'll send the video to those millionaires

you work for." His chair screeched as he tried to stand. "You'll be out on the street."

"You can't hurt me anymore." She pounded on the door. "I'm done here."

When the door closed behind her, she slumped against the wall.

"Good work." Gillespie gave her a high-five.

Cheryl pulled in a deep breath and stood straight. "You're right."

NATHAN HELD THE shovel while Josh swept garbage into it. Then he dumped the debris in the can. "You're doing a great job, slugger. I think we're done."

Josh ran and set the broom against the wall. "Same time tomorrow?"

"You're done." Nathan ruffled his hair. "No more cleanup."

Josh's jaw dropped. "What?"

"You completed your punishment."

"But I like helping." He pulled his Forester cap off and pushed back his hair. The same action Pop, he and Daniel made.

Nathan tried to swallow, but a dry lump filled his throat. Through this punishment, he and Josh had found their balance. Unfortunately, it was too late to save his and Cheryl's relationship. Once he found a permanent home for him and Issy, he would miss Josh. And Cheryl.

"Can I still help you?" Josh grabbed his hand.

The kid was breaking his heart. "Your mom will have to weigh in on that."

Cheryl wouldn't want Josh hanging around the construction site, around him. "I've got to set up for Daniel's bachelor party."

For once Josh's face didn't light up at his brother's name, but Nathan couldn't find any joy in that.

Why had Cheryl believed Josh's lies? How could she think he would throw a beer at her son? Mix up the doses? How could she call him stupid? Her lack of trust was unforgivable—right?

But his outrage didn't ignite. He was just tired. And he missed Cheryl so damn much.

Nathan guided Josh out the restaurant door. "Your mom wants you back in Fitzgerald House kitchen."

"I wish I could be with you tonight." Josh took his hand again. "Can I?"

"Probably not, slugger." A bachelor party was hardly the place for a six-year-old. There would be drinking. Cheryl wouldn't allow that.

Josh scuffed his shoes as they crossed the courtyard. They walked together into the kitchen holding hands.

Cheryl was piping frosting on small cakes. Issy stood next to her on a stool. His daughter's hair was pulled into a ponytail, just like Cheryl's. She squeezed a plastic bag and drizzled frosting onto a cake set on a tray.

Cheryl looked over at the two of them. Her smile

didn't make it to her eyes. He missed watching her face light up.

"Miss Cheryl," Issy sang. She pointed at her cake.

"Good work, sweetie," Cheryl said.

"It looks delicious." Nathan bounced a kiss off Issy's head. "Be good for Cheryl."

Issy nodded, squirting another layer of frosting on the cake.

Cheryl watched them. Her lip trembled as if she was going to cry.

"Hey." He touched Cheryl's shoulder. "You okay?"

She swallowed, nodding.

Josh stood on his toes to peer at the treats. "Can I have one?"

"After dinner." Cheryl brushed a kiss on her son's head.

Nathan jerked his thumb toward the courtyard. "I need to go."

He headed over to the Carleton House patio. Nigel, the B and B's handyman, wheeled a cart of tables and chairs along the flagstone paths.

"I can take those," Nathan offered.

"Good. I need to bring over a couple of buffet tables." The elderly gentleman headed back to the Fitzgerald carriage house.

Gray emerged from the Carleton carriage house where he and Abby lived and grabbed one end of the cart. "Looks like we'll have a nice night."

Together, they unloaded tables and chairs. And snapped out the tablecloths Abby insisted they use.

Daniel, the guest of honor, arrived with Pop. Within the hour, friends and employees filled the space.

"How's Cheryl holding up?" Gray handed him a beer from the bucket.

Nathan popped the cap off the bottle. Was Gray asking about their breakup? "What do you mean?"

Gray tapped his bottle. "She confronted Levi about the blackmail."

"What?" Nathan almost dropped his beer. "When? Who went with her?"

Gray held up his hand. "That detective who's handling her case. She went to the prison a couple of days ago. She got some names, so they're hoping to find the guy who sent the emails for Levi."

Nathan paced to the fire pit and back. *He* should have gone with her. *He* should have given her support—at least held her hand. Held her.

"You didn't know?" Gray's eyebrows went up. "I thought you and Cheryl…"

"We broke up." Nathan rubbed his forehead. "But I helped her report the blackmail."

"That's good." Gray paused. "It took a lot of guts to confront Levi."

"She's brave and stronger than she thinks." But she was losing weight and didn't have much to spare.

"Maybe the wedding will take her mind off Levi," Gray said.

"Hopefully." But Cheryl's worries weren't all because of Levi. He was part of the problem, too.

"Daniel says you haven't found Issy's mom." Gray tipped back his beer.

Nathan shook his head. "I finally talked to the cops. Issy's mom is a person of interest in a drug distribution ring shooting."

Gray whistled. "Damn. Issy's better off with you."

"I've got a lawyer filing a motion for full custody, but Heather's never been charged with a crime." Nathan took another drink of his beer. "Okay. Time to celebrate my brother's last few days of being single."

Pop fired up the grill and threw on steaks, taking orders for doneness.

Cheryl came through the courtyard pushing a cart with the rest of the food. "How's the beer holding up?" she asked.

"We must be getting old. We're not drinking as quickly as we used to," Nathan said.

She chewed her lip. "I can bring water and soda over."

He couldn't rip his gaze away from her pink mouth. "There's enough, but I'll let you know if we run out."

He helped Cheryl unload potato salad and baked beans onto the buffet table.

"You went to see Levi?" he asked.

Her head snapped up. "Yes."

"I would have gone with you."

Her breath fluttered across his face.

He brushed back a strand of hair that had escaped her ponytail.

"Thank you, but I needed to stand on my own. To let Levi know he couldn't make me a victim again."

"I'm proud of you." Nathan wanted to pull her into a hug, but too much stood between them.

"I should get back." She turned away from him and wiped a nonexistent spot off the table.

"How are the kids?" he asked.

"Marion's watching them until I get back. Then she'll join the Fitzgerald women for their spa evening."

Marion, the head of housekeeping for the B and B, was really good with the kids. "Too bad she can't watch the kids all night so you can have some fun."

Cheryl shook her head. "I'm fine."

"I know they invited you. I should find a sitter." One of the crew members' kids maybe. The Forester construction workers were all at Daniel's party. "Could Amy babysit?"

She looked up. Her coffee-colored eyes filled with sadness. "Amy was invited to Bess's party and she's never had a massage."

He moved in closer. "Have you ever had one?"

"I… No." She twisted her hands in the towel she'd used to wipe the table.

"You take care of everyone but yourself."

"I do that for…" She turned away from him and mumbled something.

Had she said *love*? Now he felt like an ass. "Bring the kids out here. The guys and I won't mind watching them."

"Ooh." Her eyebrows pinched together.

"Please." He caught her hand. "You should do this."

"But everyone's drinking."

"I can have a beer or two and not screw up watching the kids."

"I'll...think about it."

"Do it." He touched her cheek. "You deserve all the fun you can find."

"Okay." She stared at him. "I'll let them know I can go. Thanks."

"Hey, Cheryl," Eddie yelled. "Where's my helper, Josh? He's part of Forester and Sons Construction now."

She smiled. "I'm sending him over if you promise to keep this G-rated."

"Absolutely." Daniel sauntered over. "Bess said you baked a cake."

"I just might have." She nodded. "Something with chocolate and more chocolate?"

"Perfect!" Daniel wrapped an arm around Cheryl. "You're the best."

There was nothing between Daniel and Cheryl, but Nathan wanted to be the only man putting his hands on her.

Cheryl slipped away from his twin. "Enjoy your party. If there are strippers when I come back, I'll tell Bess."

Nathan joined the laughter, but kept his gaze on her as she walked away.

"You sure you two broke up?" Daniel asked. "You're acting more married than Bess and me."

Married? Marriage used to sound so daunting. Just last week, he'd sworn he couldn't be around Cheryl. But when he'd been in pain, she'd taken care of him.

He missed her so much. Maybe he needed to *really* forgive her. But could he trust her?

"I want Cheryl to join the ladies' party." He raised his eyebrows. "If she does, we'll have the kids for a while."

"I never thought I would hear those words come out of your mouth." Daniel slapped his back. "We'll teach them to drink bourbon. Besides, Josh is the ring bearer. He should be here."

"No bourbon." He'd better keep an eye on Daniel, because his brother was over his two-beer limit.

Nathan blinked. For once he was the twin in charge of watching someone's liquor consumption. Weird.

Being a father had changed his life—for the better. He wanted Cheryl and Josh in his and Issy's lives. Could he fix this?

"I'M GLAD YOU'RE joining us," Abby told Cheryl.

Cheryl couldn't help smiling back at her boss. "Thanks. Nathan's taking both kids to Daniel's party. I feel guilty."

Abby crouched next to the table where the kids were eating. "Issy, do you want to join the ladies tonight?"

The girl nodded, her mouth full of pizza.

Abby dusted her hands. "The boys can watch Josh and we'll have fun with Issy."

"Are you sure?" Cheryl asked.

"Yes. Marion's finishing up the wine-tasting and then she'll head up. After you take Daniel's cake over, come along. With school, work and Levi, *you* need a break." Abby gave her a hug. "When the restaurant launches, there will be a job for you."

Cheryl's mouth dropped open. "Really?"

"You've earned it." Abby grinned and headed out of the kitchen. "See you upstairs."

She had the job. Cheryl danced over to the oven and pulled out the last pizzas. She couldn't wait to tell Nathan.

And her smile faded. When would she stop wanting to share her life with him?

Marion came in. "Any more…?" She looked at the counter. "I was going to ask for pizza. You must be a mind reader."

"I know guests love pizza night."

"You really are an important part of the B and B." Marion ran the pizza cutter over the cooling pies. "Abby just told me you're joining the party."

"I'll finish the men's cake then head up." Cheryl pointed at a tray of petits fours. "Those are for the ladies. I thought I would try my hand at them, since we practiced in school." And she'd gotten accolades from her teacher.

"Don't they look gorgeous?" Marion's eyes lit up. "And Daniel's cake is amazing. You made it look like Carleton House. And gave him part of his and Bess's past."

"He's done a lot for Josh and me," Cheryl said.

After piping Congratulations in light blue, one of Bess's wedding colors, Cheryl set the cake on a trolley. "Josh and Issy, come with me."

Josh sighed.

"Don't you want to celebrate Mr. Dan and Miss Bess getting married?"

"Yeah, but…"

She rubbed his hair. "But what?"

"I'd like a dad someday."

Cheryl would never understand the leaps a six-year-old boy's mind could make. What had made him think about this tonight? "You have a dad."

"But I can't see him." He looked at her. "I thought maybe Mr. Nathan…"

She frowned. "You were always mean to him."

Josh shrugged. "I miss him being around all the time."

"You'll get to be with him tonight." Heaven save her from the men in her life and their perverse natures. "You get to have a boy's night with the guys."

"I do?" His eyes lit up.

She tousled Issy's hair. "And we're joining the women."

Issy smiled at her.

Josh helped push the cart. Cheryl carried Issy on her back, trying to make sure her son didn't tip over the cake on the uneven flagstones.

"That looks lovely," one of the guests in the courtyard called. "I don't suppose that's for our thirtieth anniversary."

"I'm sorry." She grinned. "It's for a party."

The woman's husband took her hand. "You got the best anniversary treat. Me."

Cheryl laughed at the couple's joke, but it was bittersweet. She wanted what they had. Thirty years of being with the one she loved.

"Look at that," Daniel called as she and the kids approached the patio steps. "It's Carleton House!"

Carleton House was the project that had brought Bess and Daniel together.

"Let me help." Nathan rushed over. Together they slid the cake onto the buffet table. He stared into her eyes. "It's incredible."

"Do you want me to cut it?" She hated that part of cake making.

"We need pictures first. Liam?" Nathan called.

Liam, Dolley's mentor and boyfriend, brought his camera over. "Let's get the cake designer showing off her creation."

"I don't need to be in the picture." Cheryl waved.

"Yes, you do." Nathan moved her behind the cake. "You created this."

There were too many people staring to keep objecting. But the only ones she cared about were Josh, Nathan and Issy. Seeing their smiles had her grinning back. And Liam's camera clicked.

After checking on their food one last time, she and Issy headed back to Fitzgerald House. "I didn't really want to cut the cake," she whispered to Issy as she carried her up the ballroom's outdoor steps.

"Cake," Issy sang, twisting Cheryl's hair around her finger.

"We have our own special cakes to eat tonight that you helped decorate."

Now if her stomach would just cooperate. Between the kids' chicken pox, losing Nathan, confronting Levi and getting her dream job, her appetite was gone.

"There they are." Dolley opened the terrace doors as they approached.

Women milled around the ballroom, half-filled wineglasses in their hands. Empty prosecco bottles covered the bar.

Debbie Forester saw Issy and waved.

Issy wiggled out of Cheryl's arms. "Nana," she sang.

"Grandbaby doll, how was your day?" Debbie scooped up Issy and twirled her around. The little girl's laugh rang out, making the other women look over and smile. Dolley snapped pictures.

"Not you, too?" Cheryl asked.

Dolley frowned. "What?"

"Your boyfriend took pictures of me and the cake."

A goofy smile covered Dolley's face. "I'm glad he did."

Abby emerged from behind a screen with a green face and wearing a bathrobe. "Oh, good. That cake was amazing. Dolley, you need to put the pictures on the website."

"Will do." Dolley shot a picture of Abby's green face. "There's one for the website."

Debbie gave Cheryl a hug. "It's fun having family at this party."

Hadn't Nathan told his parents they'd broken up?

"My turn." Dolley pulled Issy out of Debbie's arms. "Do you want your face to be green like Abby's?"

Issy looked at Cheryl, her eyes big.

"Go ahead," Debbie said.

Dolley and Issy skipped behind the screens.

Abby walked over with a glass of prosecco. "Mama and Bess are in having massages. Time for you to catch up."

"Oh, I don't need a drink," Cheryl said.

"Not even for Bess's party?" Abby frowned. "After all the work you did for us?"

Maybe one glass wouldn't be so bad. "Okay. But only half a glass. I'm watching Issy. And I should pick up Josh early so the guys can have fun."

"I'll bet the boys *are* having fun," Abby said.

"I know Josh is." She checked her phone just in case.

"No phones." Abby held out her hand.

Cheryl didn't think. She handed over the phone. "What if Nathan calls?"

"He can send someone to get you. Or come himself." Abby shut off Cheryl's phone and tucked it in the pocket of her robe. "Now, let's get you a facial."

Cheryl took a sip of the wine and followed her friend and boss into the back room. Nathan was right. It was time she let herself have fun.

CHAPTER SEVENTEEN

CHERYL SLIPPED ON her sandals, giving her pedicure one more admiring look. The silvery blue matched the dress she planned to wear to the wedding. "Bess, thank you for including Issy and me."

"I'm glad you came." Bess hugged her.

"Here's a sleepy pumpkin." Debbie kissed Issy and handed her to Cheryl. "I can't wait to see her in her flower girl dress."

"Nathan found the perfect dress." Bess brushed back Issy's hair.

"We sure had fun," Cheryl said. "Time to rescue the men from Josh."

"Wait." Abby dug in her pocket. "Your phone."

Everyone followed them onto the terrace.

"See you in the morning." Cheryl turned on her phone. It buzzed with a missed call from Detective Gillespie.

She carried Issy down the steps and sat with her on a garden bench. "I should listen to this message."

"Cheryl. Good news." Excitement filled Gillespie's voice when she played her voice mail. "We found the man who sent the emails. It *was* Levi's cellmate's brother. The guy confessed. He's taking a plea deal and rolled over on his brother and Levi like a goddamn rug. Call if you have questions. Oh—and the video's been secured."

Cheryl clapped a hand over her mouth. "Oh, oh, my."

Issy patted Cheryl's cheek, brushing away a tear. She sang, "Sad, Miss Cheryl?"

"Happy. Very happy." Her legs wobbled as she stood.

Issy held up her arms. Cheryl picked her up and the girl snuggled close.

"Let's go get Josh."

"Joshua," Issy sang.

Lights tucked into Bess's landscape lit the courtyard. Everything seemed brighter, more magical tonight. Levi's blackmail was over. The knots in Cheryl's chest unraveled.

She hurried toward the bachelor party. Chairs surrounded the fire pit. The men had beers in their hands. She stiffened and then relaxed. She'd had two glasses of prosecco, and wasn't turning into a drunk like Mama.

Maybe she'd been wrong. Maybe drinking wouldn't turn Nathan into a cruel man, either.

Josh sat on Nathan's lap, toasting a marshmallow. Cheryl's heart leaped and she squeezed Issy at the sight.

"Don't let it dip too close, slugger." Nathan leaned down to Josh's ear.

Josh tipped his head and grinned. "I like it when they're burned."

Nathan jiggled Josh on his knee. "Isn't this one for me?"

Josh pulled the toasting fork out of the fire. "Only because you're whining."

Everyone laughed.

Cheryl's heart surged. If only.

"Are the ladies done?" Liam's Irish accent lilted across the darkness.

"Issy and I are. The rest are still laughing and eating." She stepped closer to the fire. "It's time for the kids to go to bed."

"Can't I stay?" Josh pleaded.

"Bedtime," she said.

Nathan leaned over and whispered in Josh's ear. A grin broke across her son's face. Cheryl's heart expanded. Nathan hadn't turned away from her son. And somehow they had a new camaraderie.

Her son was blessed with incredible role models. Even if she never found love again, they would always have the Fitzgerald family and maybe the Foresters.

"Time for bed," she called.

Josh sighed, his shoulders rising and falling dramatically enough that she saw it from across the fire. He handed Nathan his toasting fork. "I'll take care of the womenfolk."

Laughter rolled through the group. Josh slapped the high-fives held out for him. Nathan followed in her son's wake.

"I'll help put them to bed." He stepped in front of her, a big, dark shadow. The light from the fire haloed his blond hair.

A few months ago she'd been afraid to be this close to Nathan. Now she yearned to be closer.

"You can stay," Cheryl said.

"I want to be with them, with you."

Cheryl's heart pounded. *With her?* What did he mean?

Nathan knelt. "Come on, slugger."

Josh climbed on his back.

"Daddy," Issy sang.

A grin split his face. He touched Issy's hair.

"She sang a lot tonight," Cheryl whispered.

"That's wonderful." His hand cupped Cheryl's shoulder. "Did you have fun?"

She nodded. "Be surprised when you see Issy's nails."

The little girl had picked the same colors as hers. She bit back a smile. "I could hardly hold her with all the women there. And her grandmama was as proud as a peacock."

"I'm glad."

"Thank you for insisting I go."

Silence settled between them. Before they would have kissed, or wanted to. Now they were just awkwardly quiet.

She wanted this to be real. Wanted them to be a family. She'd been such a fool to mess up what she and Nathan had found.

They worked as a team, putting the kids to bed. She kissed Josh's and Issy's foreheads. "I love you."

"Love you, Miss Cheryl," Issy sang.

"To the moon and back." Josh's voice was sleep-filled.

Nathan kissed his daughter and Issy sang, "To the moon and back, Daddy."

"Can I have a kiss?" Josh called to Nathan.

Nathan jerked around. When he answered, his voice cracked, "You bet, slugger."

Tears slipped down Cheryl's cheeks. She stumbled into the living room and collapsed on the sofa.

"What's wrong?" Nathan took her hand and sat next to her.

It was too hard. She'd lost such a wonderful man. She shook her head.

He touched her chin. "Talk to me."

"You."

Even through her tears, Cheryl could see the confusion in his rich chocolate eyes. "Me?"

"You're…too nice." She wiped at her cheeks. "You're breaking my heart."

He frowned.

"I could have had this—*we* could have had this amazing love, but I messed everything up."

Nathan took a deep breath. His inhale sounded like the slamming of a door.

"I know it's my fault." She turned away.

Nathan caught her shoulders, forcing her to look at him. "Why would you want to be with someone as flawed as me?"

"Flawed? You're good and loving." She grabbed his hand. "Once you put your heart into something, or someone, there's nothing you wouldn't do for them. You would die for Issy."

His gaze locked on hers. He pulled her onto his lap. "For you and Josh, too. I love you, Cheryl."

"What?" Was she hearing things? "After I hurt you?"

Nathan's grin lit up the dim room. "Yes."

His beloved scent of citrus and wood wrapped around her like a blanket. *Please let this be real and not a dream.*

He kissed her eyes. His lips drew patterns across her forehead and down her cheeks. "Don't cry. Not because of me."

She fused their mouths together.

The dance of their tongues was familiar yet different. Everything was more tender, more important.

They loved each other.

Even when the kiss ended, she couldn't stop touching him. She stroked her thumbs across his eyebrows and reacquainted her fingers with the planes of his cheeks and the fullness of his lips.

Laughter from the courtyard intruded on their reunion.

"Daniel's party," she whispered.

His arms tightened around her waist. "I don't want to leave you, but I have to go."

"I know." She swayed, letting the pull of his mouth reel her into his arms. "Come back to me tonight?"

"Yes." He yanked her in for a kiss that had them both breathless. "Yes."

He stood. Her legs wrapped around his hips and held on.

"Maybe I could text…"

She laughed and let her body slide down his. "Go back to your brother's party."

Then *they* would celebrate later.

NATHAN GLANCED AT the light glowing in Cheryl's apartment window—for him.

"What's with the grin?" Daniel asked.

His cheeks were aching a bit. "I'm a lucky son of—"

"Watch how you complete that sentence," Pop called from his chair next to the fire.

"A fabulous father," Nathan added quickly.

"You got that right." Pop pointed his finger. "And I've passed that talent on to you. I'm proud of you, son."

Nathan hadn't though his grin could grow any bigger, but it did.

"You and Cheryl?" Daniel asked.

"Yeah, me and Cheryl." And the kids. Joy warmed him better than the fire.

Gray slapped a hand on Nathan's shoulder. "If you need to get back to Cheryl, I'll close down and make sure everyone gets home safe."

"Tempting." But Nathan was best man. His relationship with his brother was the strongest it had ever been—he wasn't going to blow it now.

"It was a great party." Daniel wrapped an arm around Nathan's and Gray's shoulders. "Thanks, guys. And, Nathan? Tell Cheryl we loved the cake."

"We decimated the cake." Liam joined the group, another piece of cake on his plate. "I'll help clean up."

Nathan had already packed the food. The only things left were the beer and cake, and apparently Liam was working on those leftovers.

"Go," Gray insisted. "We've got this."

"Thank you." Nathan hugged Pop and then his brother. "Congratulations. Bess is lucky to be marrying you."

Daniel sighed. "I'm the lucky one."

Nathan shook his head. He whispered to Gray, "Make sure he takes a cab home."

"Liam and I have this handled." Gray made a shooing motion.

Nathan rushed away. Not even three months ago, he'd been appalled by the idea of staying with one woman. Now? Having Cheryl in his life was like winning the lottery.

He took the steps two at time. Before he made the landing, the door flew open.

Cheryl waited in the doorway, wearing her favorite threadbare T-shirt. She leaped into his arms.

"Kids asleep?" he gasped.

"Yes." She nibbled on his ear. "I just checked on them."

He carried her to the bedroom. The lock clicked into place. Cheryl still clung to him, but chewed her lip. Had she changed her mind? "Is this what you want?"

"Yes." She touched his cheek. "I never dreamed you'd truly forgive me."

"I do. I have." And the weight of his anger faded.

She tugged her T-shirt over her head. "I want you."

He kicked off his shoes and ripped off his shirt. With shaky hands, he shoved down his shorts and briefs.

She led him to her bed. Moonlight softened by sheer white curtains lit their journey back to each other.

The apple scent of her hair had him burying his nose in the silky mass. He kissed her neck, lingering on her collarbone. He turned his attention to her breasts and suckled her puckered nipples.

"Nathan, please."

He laughed, stroking the peaks with his fingertips.

She groaned. "Use your mouth, please."

He gave in to her plea, sucking first one breast and then the next.

Her hips rose and fell. She caught his erection in a grip that shocked a groan from him.

"I've missed you," she whispered. "Missed us."

When he finally joined his body with hers, it was perfect.

"I don't want this to end." He rocked slowly, loving the way she clung to him.

Her eyes were deep, dark pools. She panted with desire. "I can't hold on much longer."

He rocked again and again. And the rocks turned to thrusts.

"Nathan." There was the catch in her voice that signaled her orgasm.

Her muscles clenched around him and she took him

with her. He couldn't stop thrusting, deeper, harder, as he came.

He collapsed in her arms. "Never," he gasped.

"Never," she echoed.

Pulling in a deep breath, he rolled her on top of him. "I-it's...sex has never been this important. I've never made love before."

Her eyes glittered. "It's never been like this for me, either."

He pushed back the hair from her face. "Cheryl, I love you."

"I love you, too." She touched his face. "I'm sorry..."

"No more apologies." He placed a finger on her lips. "I'm sure, over the years, we'll hurt each other again."

"Years?" Wonder filled her face.

He wouldn't do this lying down. "Hang on."

He sat up and tugged Cheryl to face him.

Her eyes were too large. "What?"

"This summer has opened my eyes and my heart." Nathan kissed her hand. "My life is nothing like the way I pictured it. I have a daughter and a woman I love. And Josh. I love him, too."

She swallowed. "I love Issy."

"You make me feel normal. Happy. Like I'm not... broken."

"You aren't!"

"See. That's one of the reasons I love you. You make me whole."

She clutched his hand. "I'm not afraid anymore. You make me strong."

He took a deep breath. "Will you and Josh marry me and Issy?"

"Marry you?" Cheryl squeaked. A smile lit up her face. "Yes. Absolutely yes."

"Yes?" Peace settled over him. Cheryl, Issy and Josh made his life complete.

Gently, he leaned over and kissed the only woman he'd ever loved.

EPILOGUE

NATHAN CROSSED THE Fitzgerald House ballroom toward Cheryl, his fiancée. Not that they'd made any announcements. This was Daniel and Bess's wedding day.

A drunk grabbed Cheryl's arm. *No way.* Nathan hurried to rescue her, but Cheryl slipped out from under the man's arm.

"I'm not interested," she said firmly.

The man blinked. "But you're sssso pretty."

"I've said no." She stood a little taller as Nathan reached her side.

Josh hurried from the opposite end of the ballroom where he'd been sitting with Mom and Pop. "Mom?"

Cheryl held up her hand. "I'm good."

The surprise on Josh's face had to mirror Nathan's. The man backed away. "Sorry."

Cheryl's brown eyes sparkled. "That was…empowering."

Nathan grinned back at her. To Josh, he asked, "Can I talk to you? Man to man?"

Josh frowned. "Now?"

"It won't take long."

"Go on, you two." Cheryl waved Issy over. "Let's dance."

"Yes!" Issy took Cheryl's hands. "'Bye, Daddy."

Words from Issy were such a gift, even if she still

sang them sometimes. But now to business. Nathan smiled at Josh. "Why don't we step out on the terrace?"

Josh skipped ahead, looking natural in his tux. It was hard to believe this was the boy who'd done everything to keep him and Cheryl apart.

"You did a good job with the rings," Nathan said as they sat at a terrace table.

"It was important. Not like scattering rose petals," Josh scoffed.

"You both did a great job." And Isabella had gotten all the oohs and aahs as she'd thrown the petals.

"But *I* had the rings."

"You did." He debated how to ask Josh about marrying his mother. "I was wondering if you want to be in another wedding."

"Would I get to carry the rings?" he asked, raising his eyebrow.

"Sure."

Josh frowned. "Who would it be for?"

"Me. And your mother." He was messing this up. "I want you and your mother and Issy and me to all be a family."

Josh slid back in the chair, his legs sticking straight out. "You'd marry my mom?"

"I love her." He took a deep breath. "And I love you. I'd like to be your dad."

Josh picked at the seam on his pants. "I *had* a dad."

"I know. Maybe I could be… Papa."

"Papa." Josh frowned. "And my dad could still be Dad?"

Nathan nodded, afraid to speak. What if Josh said no?

"What does Issy think? She'd be like my sister, right?"

"We haven't talked to Issy yet." But Issy had been talking more and more. Without singing. It was like she'd been saving up words and they were all tumbling out.

"Would we live in the carriage house?" Josh crossed his arms.

"I think we should look for a house."

"A house?" Josh leaned forward. "Would I get my own bedroom?"

"Yes, and you'd help pick out the house."

Josh looked at him with soulful brown eyes. "I always wanted a dog, but Mom said I couldn't have one until we had a house."

"A dog?"

Josh scooted forward. "Like Carly."

"Carly's more horse than dog. She weighs almost a hundred pounds."

"And she's awesome."

Nathan remembered all the complaints Daniel had made about the puppy. "She used to dig in the garbage."

Josh sighed. "But Mom promised."

"I suppose you want a pool, too." Would his budget survive these kids?

"Really?" Josh's eyes lit up.

"Are we negotiating about a house or are you going to tell me if it's okay for me to marry your mother?"

"That?" Josh grinned. "Mom told me already."

"Then we *are* negotiating." Nathan would agree to most anything to make a family with Cheryl and Josh.

"I think…" Josh chewed his lip, reminding Nathan so much of his mother. "I'll call you Papa."

Nathan swallowed back the lump in his throat. He pulled Josh onto his lap. "I'd like that."

"I love you, Papa."

Nathan hugged his son, hard. "I love you, too."

"Everything okay out here?" Cheryl and Issy came up to the table.

"He asked me if he could marry you and I said it was okay and I'm going to call him Papa and we're going to get a pool and a puppy." Josh took in a deep breath. "And, Issy, I'll be your big brother."

Cheryl blinked. "Wait. Pool and puppy?"

Nathan rubbed the back of his neck. "Our son drives a hard bargain."

"Puppy? Carly?" Issy asked.

"Yeah." Josh held up his hand and Issy gave him a high-five.

Cheryl sank into a chair. "This wasn't supposed to be a negotiation."

"I should have had an attorney with me." He ruffled Josh's hair. "And the kids get to help choose the house."

Cheryl's face lit up. "Of course."

Nathan stood, setting Josh on the terrace floor. "Can you take Issy in and dance with her?"

Josh grimaced. "I guess. Come on, sis."

Nathan pulled Cheryl out of her chair. "Have I told you how beautiful you are?"

Her smile lit up her face. "Too many times to be true."

"You were fearless with that drunk."

"I was, wasn't I?" She grinned.

"So this is what normal feels like." Nathan pulled her close. "A woman by my side, kids to love, a house, a dog and a pool."

Candles shimmered on the tables. Fairy lights twinkled on the patio and the courtyard bushes below. This was the setting Cheryl deserved for a proposal. He took her hand and moved to the balustrade. "I love you."

She sighed. "I love you, too."

He dug in his pocket and pulled out the small box he'd carried all day. "I want to ask you again. Will you marry me and be my family?"

He snapped the lid open. The center diamond was set between two smaller stones.

"It's beautiful." She cupped his face. "I can't wait to marry you."

He slipped the ring on her finger then held it up. "The stones are the kids' birthstones. An emerald for Josh and amethyst for Issy."

"It's perfect." She looked at him, her eyes shining. "And so are you."

"Hardly. I let our son negotiate for a puppy."

"And a pool." Her laugh filled the terrace.

"I don't care." He pulled her in. "Now I get to kiss you."

She threaded her fingers through his hair. "And I get to kiss you."

He dipped her and she laughed.

Should he tell her the jeweler had said they could add more stones to her ring?

Her tongue slid against his.

He would save that news for another day.

* * * * *

Read more in the
FITZGERALD HOUSE *miniseries*
to learn how the Fitzgerald sisters
found their happy endings.

SOUTHERN COMFORTS—
Harlequin Superromance, December 2014
A SAVANNAH CHRISTMAS WISH—
Harlequin Superromance, December 2015
THROUGH A MAGNOLIA FILTER—
Harlequin Superromance, August 2016

And watch for the next book
in the series later in 2017!